Excerpts
From Three Classical
Chinese Novels

Translated by
Yang Xianyi and Gladys Yang

Panda Books

Panda Books
First edition 1981
Reprinted 1984
Copyright 1981 by CHINESE LITERATURE
ISBN 0-8351-1330-2

Published by CHINESE LITERATURE, Beijing (37), China
Distributed by China International Book Trading Corporation
(GUOJI SHUDIAN), P.O. Box 399, Beijing, China
Printed in the People's Republic of China

CONTENTS

Luo Guanzhong

The Battle of the Red Cliff

(An excerpt from *The Three Kingdoms*)

The Three Kingdoms

CHAPTER 43

Zhuge Liang Worsts the Scholars in Argument
Lu Su Rejects the Majority Opinion

HAVING left Liu Bei and Liu Qi, Lu Su and Zhuge Liang went by boat to Chaisang. Once aboard they took counsel together and Lu Su said, "When you see General Sun, don't tell him how powerful Cao Cao's army actually is."

"Don't worry," replied Zhuge Liang. "I know what to say."

When the boat arrived, Lu Su asked Zhuge Liang to wait in the hostel while he went to see Sun Quan.

Sun Quan was conferring in the audience chamber with his civil and military officers. As soon as he heard that Lu Su was back, he called him in and asked: "What did you find out on your trip to Jiangxia?"

"I know the general situation and shall report it to you later," replied Lu Su.

Then Sun Quan showed him a letter from Cao Cao, saying, "This arrived yesterday. I have sent the messenger back, and we are meeting now to decide on a reply."

Lu Su read the letter, the gist of which was as follows:

"At the emperor's command, I have led my army south to punish the guilty. Liu Cong has been captured, his people have surrendered, and I now command a force of a million picked men and a thousand able generals. I hope you will join me, general, in a hunting expedition at Jiangxia to attack Liu Bei, so that we can divide his territory between us and pledge everlasting friendship. Do not hesitate, but give me an early reply!"

"What have you decided?" asked Lu Su as he finished the letter.

"I have not made up my mind yet," answered Sun Quan.

Then Zhang Zhao* said, "Cao Cao has a great army a million strong, and in the emperor's name he is conquering territory on every side. To resist him would be opposing the emperor. And the only natural barrier between us is the Yangzi, but now by conquering Jingzhou he has taken part of the river out of our hands, making it difficult for us to withstand him. In my humble opinion, our safest plan is submission."

All the other advisers chimed in, "Zhang Zhao's proposal accords with the will of Heaven."

Sun Quan thought hard but said nothing. Then Zhang Zhao continued, "Have no doubt about it, my lord. Submission to Cao Cao means peace for the people of Wu, and retaining the six provinces south of the Yangzi."

Sun Quan bowed his head and said nothing. Present-

---

* One of Sun Quan's chief advisers.

ly he went out and Lu Su followed him. Noting this, Sun Quan took his hand and asked, "What do you think?"

"Their advice is the worst possible thing you could do. They may surrender to Cao Cao, but not you."

"Why do you say that?"

"If men like myself went over to Cao Cao, we should be sent home and keep our official posts in the provinces. But in your case, where could you go? At the most you would be made a baron with one carriage and no more, one horse and just a few retainers. That would be the end of your kingship. The others are thinking of themselves. Don't listen to them but make up your mind quickly — this is an important decision."

"They have certainly disappointed me." Sun Quan sighed. "Your view of this is exactly the same as mine. Heaven must have sent you to me! But Cao Cao has just taken over Yuan Shao's army and the troops of Jingzhou too. I fear he may prove too powerful to resist."

Lu Su said, "I have brought Zhuge Jin's brother Zhuge Liang back with me from Jiangxia. You can find out the situation from him."

"What, is the Sleeping Dragon here?" cried Sun Quan.

"Yes, he's resting now in the hostel."

"It's too late to see him today. But tomorrow I shall asssemble all my officials and introduce him to the bravest and the best of our men, after which we can discuss the matter."

With these instructions Lu Su withdrew. The next day he called on Zhuge Liang at the hostel and urged him, "When you see my master today, don't tell him how powerful Cao Cao's army is."

Zhuge Liang replied with a smile, "I shall do as circumstances dictate. I can promise not to let you down."

Then Lu Su took him to Sun Quan's headquarters where they found more than twenty civil and military officers, including Zhang Zhao and Gu Yong, seated in state with high headdresses and broad belts. Zhuge Liang was introduced to them one by one, and after an exchange of greetings he took the guest's seat. Meanwhile his air of refinement and commanding appearance had not been lost on Zhang Zhao and the others, who judged that he must have come to offer advice. Zhang Zhao led the way in trying to bait the visitor. "I am one of the most insignificant scholars of this district," he said. "But is it true, as I have long heard, that while living as a recluse in Longzhong you compared yourself to Guan Zhong and Yue Yi?"*

"In some trifling respects I did," replied Zhuge Liang.

"I heard that Liu Bei called three times at your thatched hut and was as delighted to discover you as a fish getting back to the water, because he aspired to the conquest of Jingzhou and Xiangyang. But today those districts have fallen into Cao Cao's hands. What is the reason for that?"

Zhuge Liang reflected, "This Zhang Zhao is Sun Quan's foremost adviser. Unless I defeat him in argument, what chance have I with his master?" So he answered, "In my opinion, to take the land round the Han

---

* Famous statesmen in the seventh century and fourth century B.C.

River is as simple as turning over your hand.   But my master Liu Bei has too much humanity and sense of justice to want to take the property of a kinsman. That accounts for his letting it go. Liu Cong is a fool who listened to bad advice and surrendered to Cao Cao without consulting others, enabling him to run wild. My master has stationed his troops at Jiangxia and has a good plan which I am not free to divulge."

Zhang Zhao said, "In that case, your deeds hardly match your words.   You compare yourself to Guan Zhong and Yue Yi. But the one was a minister serving Duke Huan of Qi who became chief of all the barons and united the country. The other helped Yan, a weak state, to conquer more than seventy towns in Qi. These two men were truly great statesmen, whereas you in your thatched hut led a frivolous existence, sitting idle all day long clasping your knees.   Now that you have taken service under Liu Bei, you should do good and rid the people of evils, destroying rebels and traitors. In fact, before Liu Bei had you as his adviser, he managed to conquer some territory and take some cities, so that once he had you men expected great things of him — the very children imagined that wings had been given to a tiger, that the Han Dynasty would rise once more and Cao Cao would be destroyed. All the old ministers of Han and the hermits in mountain glades wiped their eyes and waited, believing that the time had come when the clouds would be scattered from the sky enabling the sun and moon to shine forth in splendour, and that you would rescue the people from hardships worse than flood and fire, restoring peace to the empire.   Yet since you joined Liu Bei, his men have been flying before Cao Cao, abandoning their armour and spears.   Failing to serve Liu Biao* well and relieve the people or to support his son and preserve his land, he has lost Xinye, escaped to Fancheng, been defeated at Dangyang and fled to Xiakou, unable to find a refuge anywhere. In short, since you became his adviser, Liu Bei has fared worse than before. Would this have been so with Guan Zhong and Yue Yi? I hope you won't take offence at my blunt, foolish talk."

After hearing him out, Zhuge Liang laughed and said, "A giant roc flies ten thousand *li*, but can the common birds understand his ambition? When a man falls dangerously ill, you must give him gruel first, then some mild restorative. Once his system is well regulated and quiet, you can give him nourishing meat and powerful drugs to cure his illness and preserve his life. If instead of waiting till humours and pulse are in harmony you give him powerful drugs and rich nourishment first, it will be difficult to restore him to health. Liu Bei was defeated at Runan and had to seek protection from Liu Biao. He had then less than a thousand men and none but Guan Yu, Zhang Fei and Zhao Yun as his officers. He was like a man dangerously ill and very weak. Xinye is a small mountainous district, sparsely populated and short of supplies, and Liu Bei simply used it as a temporary refuge, never intending to make it a permanent base. Yet with our scanty equipment, flimsy fortifications, untrained men and supplies sufficient for one day only, we burned Cao Cao's camp at Bowang and flooded his positions at Baihe, frightening his generals Xiahou Dun and Cao Ren into running away. To

* Liu Bei's kinsman, who ruled over Jingzhou. After his death, his son Liu Cong succeeded him, but soon surrendered to Cao Cao.

my mind, not even Guan Zhong or Yue Yi could have employed their troops to any better purpose. As for Liu Cong's surrender, Liu Bei had no knowledge of it and would not take advantage of the general confusion to seize his kinsman's estate. This shows his great humanity and justice. When he withdrew from Dangyang, several hundred thousand civilians, old and young, had flocked to join his just cause, and he would not abandon them; hence his army could only travel ten *li* a day; so he gave up attacking Jiangling and let himself be worsted. This again shows his great humanity and justice. The defeat of a small force by a great multitude is common enough in war. The first emperor of Han was defeated time and again by Xiang Yu, but finally triumphed in the Battle of Gaixia, and this shows Han Xin's brilliant strategy. Han Xin had served his sovereign for a long time without winning many battles for him; for affairs of state require a master plan. It is different in the case of boastful orators who deceive men with empty words: when it comes to talking, no one can surpass them; but in times of crisis when decisions have to be made, not one in a hundred shows any ability. In fact they become the laughing-stock of the whole world!"

Zhang Zhao had not a word to say after this, but another in that assembly demanded loudly, "But what of Cao Cao's power? There he is, encamped with a million men and a thousand generals, rampant as dragons and awe-inspiring as tigers. Already he has swallowed up Jiangxia!"

The speaker was Yu Fan and Zhuge Liang replied, "Cao Cao has merely taken over Yuan Shao's ant-heap and seized Liu Biao's flock of crows. Even if he had several million men, we would not be afraid of them."

Yu Fan gave a scornful laugh. "Your army was defeated at Dangyang and your plans brought to nought at Xiakou, till you had to turn this way and that for help. Yet you still say you are not afraid. But do you think this big talk takes anyone in?"

"Though his cause is just," retorted Zhuge Liang, "Liu Bei has only a few thousand men. How can he resist a cruel horde of a million? He has withdrawn to Xiakou to bide his time. Here in the lower reaches of the Yangzi you have fine troops and ample supplies as well as the strategic advantage of the river; yet you are advising your lord to bend his knees to a rebel, not caring if the whole world laughs at you. I can tell you that Liu Bei is not the man to fear that rebel Cao Cao."

Yu Fan could not answer, but another man sitting there asked, "Are you trying to influence us in the land of Wu with a tongue like that of Su Qin or Zhang Yi?"*

Zhuge Liang saw that this was Bu Zhi, and replied, "You regard Su Qin and Zhang Yi as mere orators, forgetting that they were also men of action. Su Qin was the prime minister of six states, while Zhang Yi was twice prime minister of Qin. They had the ability to restore their states, and were not cowardly bullies who tremble at the sight of a sword. You gentlemen are so intimidated by Cao Cao's crafty and empty threats that you want to surrender. How dare you scoff at Su Qin and Zhang Yi?"

Bu Zhi was silenced but another said, "Tell us your opinion of Cao Cao."

---

* Famous orators in the fourth century B.C.

It was Xue Zong, and Zhuge Liang answered, "That is an uncalled for question — Cao Cao is a traitor to the House of Han."

"You are wrong there," retorted Xue Zong. "The Han Dynasty is approaching the end of its allotted time. Cao Cao has two-thirds of the empire and the people are turning to him. Your master, ignorant of Heaven's will, is still contending with him. When you try to smash a stone with an egg, the result is certain failure."

Zhuge Liang answered sharply, "You talk like a man who bears no allegiance to either father or prince. Loyalty and filial piety are the prime duties of every man in this world. As a subject of Han it is your duty to oppose any man who turns traitor. Cao Cao's forbears lived on government stipends, but instead of showing his gratitude he is trying to usurp the throne. The whole world condemns him yet you claim that destiny is on his side. You are indeed a man who respects neither father nor prince. I shall waste no more words on you. Please say no more!"

While Xue Zong blushed with shame and could not answer, another man joined in, saying, "Though Cao Cao is using the emperor's name to issue orders to the barons, he is none the less descended from the prime minister Cao Shen. Liu Bei claims to be descended from Prince Jing of Zhongshan, yet there is no proof of that. He appears to be a weaver of mats and seller of straw sandals. How can he prove a match for Cao Cao?"

Zhuge Liang saw that it was Lu Ji and said with a laugh, "Aren't you the boy who pocketed an orange when you were sitting among Yuan Shu's guests? Sit still now and listen to me. Since Cao Cao is descended from a former minister, he owes allegiance to the House of Han; yet he is usurping power and humiliating his sovereign. This insolence towards his prince is an affront to his ancestors too; he is not only a rebel against the House of Han but a rebellious son of the Cao family. Liu Bei is a scion of the imperial house, granted a title by the emperor in accordance with his genealogy. How can you speak of lack of proof? Moreover the First Emperor of Han started his career as a station master, yet won the empire in the end. What shame is there, then, in weaving mats or selling sandals? You have the understanding of a child and are not fit to talk with scholars."

Lu Ji was silenced, but another protested, "Zhuge Liang simply distorts the truth without advancing proper arguments. It is no use continuing. But may I ask if he has made a special study of any of the classical canons?"

Zhuge Liang saw that it was Yan Jun. He replied, "All pedants are good for is punctuating texts. How can such men restore states or do great deeds? Yi Yin* of old was a peasant and Jiang Shang** a fisherman, while men like Zhang Liang, Chen Ping, Deng Yu and Geng Yan*** were skilled in the administration of the empire, yet I never heard that they studied the classical canons. They would not fritter away their energies on

---

* Chief adviser of King Tang who founded the Shang Dynasty (1600-1100 B.C.).

** Chief adviser of King Wu who founded the Zhou Dynasty (1100-771 B.C.).

*** Zhang Liang and Chen Ping served under the first emperor of the Han Dynasty (206 B.C.-A.D. 24). Teng Yu and Geng Yan served under Emperor Guangwu who founded the Later Han Dynasty (A.D. 25-220).

pen and inkstone, wasting their time on literary futilities."

Yan Jun bowed his head in dejection and could not answer, but another man spoke up loudly, "You like to boast, sir, but can hardly have any real learning. I feel scholars would laugh at you."

This speaker was Cheng Deshu of Runan, and Zhuge Liang retorted, "There are two types of scholar: the noble and the mean. A true scholar is loyal to his sovereign and loves his country, abiding by the right and hating evil, eager to benefit the men of his time and leave a good name to posterity. A mean scholar on the other hand devotes himself to trivialities. All he can do is flourish a pen, wasting his youth writing poetry and studying the classics till his hair turns white. A thousand words flow from his pen, but there is not one sound principle in his head. Look at Yang Xiong,* so noted for his writing, who stooped to serve Wang Mang** and finally took his own life by throwing himself down from a pavilion. Such a man is a scholar of the mean type. Even if he writes ten thousand words a day, we have no use for him."

Cheng Deshu could not answer. Indeed all the scholars were put out of countenance by Zhuge Liang's eloquent retorts.

Zhang Wen and Luo Tong among the scholars wanted to continue the argument, but just then in came a man who called out sharply, "Zhuge Liang is one of the most gifted men of our time yet you are trying to worst him

---

* A famous Han-dynasty scholar in the first century B.C.

** Usurper of the Han throne.

in argument: this is no way to treat a guest! Cao Cao's powerful army is approaching our land, but instead of thinking how to resist it, you are simply wrangling."

All eyes turned to the newcomer who was Huang Gai of Lingling, the grain officer of Wu. He now addressed himself to Zhuge Liang, saying, "I have heard that although there is profit in talk, it is better to remain silent. Why not keep your valuable advice for our master, instead of debating with this crowd?"

"These gentlemen do not understand practical matters and tried to embarrass me," said Zhuge Liang. "I had to answer them." Then Huang Gai and Lu Su took Zhuge Liang inside. At the middle gate they met Zhuge Jin, and Zhuge Liang greeted him.

"Why didn't you come to see me as soon as you got here, brother?" asked Zhuge Jin.

"I am serving Liu Bei now," answered Zhuge Liang, "and I have to put public affairs before private ones. Till my work is done, I cannot give my attention to personal matters. I hope you will excuse me."

"After you have seen our lord, come and have a chat," said Zhuge Jin, and with that he went off.

"Don't forget what I told you," Lu Su reminded Zhuge Liang, and the latter nodded. When he was conducted into the audience chamber, Sun Quan came down the steps to greet him, showing great respect. After an exchange of courtesies, Zhuge Liang was asked to be seated, while the civil and military officers stood in two rows on either side. Lu Su took his stand beside Zhuge Liang, waiting to see what he would say. While Zhuge Liang presented Liu Bei's greetings, he scrutinized Sun Quan and found him an imposing figure with brilliant eyes and a reddish beard. "This is no common man judging by his looks," he thought. "Such a man may be goaded into action, but not persuaded. When he questions me, I must do my best to arouse him."

After tea had been served, Sun Quan said, "I have heard much about your talents from Lu Su. Now that I have the honour of meeting you, I hope you will give me the benefit of your instructions."

Zhuge Liang replied, "I have neither talents nor knowledge. Your request embarrasses me."

Sun Quan said, "You have recently been at Xinye helping Liu Bei to fight Cao Cao. You must have a good idea of the enemy's strength."

Zhuge Liang answered, "Liu Bei's forces are weak, his officers few, and Xinye is a small town short of grain. How can he stand up to Cao Cao?"

"How big is Cao Cao's army?"

"His cavalry, infantry and naval forces number more than a million in all."

"Is he not claiming more strength than he actually has?"

"Not at all. At Yanzhou he already had two hundred thousand Yellow Turbans; the defeat of Yuan Shao swelled this number by another five or six hundred thousand; he gained nearly four hundred thousand more from the Central Plain, and now has another two or three hundred thousand from Jingzhou. All in all, he commands not less than one and a half million. I said a million in order not to alarm your men here."

Lu Su changed colour at this and looked meaningly at Zhuge Liang, who ignored him.

Then Sun Quan asked, "How many officers has Cao Cao?"

"More than a thousand wise strategists and able commanders."

"Since taking Jingzhou, what other ambitions has he?"

"He is erecting fortresses by the river and preparing warships. Undoubtedly he means to conquer the lower reaches of the Yangzi here."

"If he means to swallow us up, please advise me whether we should fight or not."

"I have my own view of that, but am afraid you would not like to hear it."

"I am eager to hear your valuable opinion."

Zhuge Liang said, "Since the empire fell into turmoil, you have taken the lower reaches of the Yangzi while Liu Bei has gathered troops south of the River Han, and you are contesting for the empire with Cao Cao.   Now Cao Cao has swept aside his chief obstacles and his recent conquest of Jingzhou has impressed the whole realm with might.   Even heroes are powerless to resist him, and that is why Liu Bei has fled here. I hope you will consider your relative strength. If your men of Wu and Yue can fight those of the Central Plain, by all means break with Cao Cao as fast as you can. If not, you had better take the advice of your councillors: lay down your arms and bow like subordinates to Cao Cao." Before Sun Quan could answer Zhuge Liang continued, "If you make a show of submission while secretly withholding allegiance, and cannot reach a decision in this crisis, you will soon be overtaken by calamity."

"If what you say is true," countered Sun Quan, "why hasn't Liu Bei surrendered?"

"Tian Heng* of old was a brave man of Qi who set such store by his integrity that he would not stoop to any shameful action. Now Liu Bei, descended from the imperial house, is a hero known far and wide. If he is unsuccessful it is the will of Heaven, but he will never bow the knee to another."

These words threw Sun Quan into such a passion that he rose abruptly and swept out of the room. His officers sniggered to each other and dispersed.

"Whatever made you talk like that?" cried Lu Su reproachfully. "It's lucky for you that our master is too big-hearted to punish you. Your speech was most insulting to him."

Zhuge Liang threw back his head and laughed. "How touchy he is! I know how to defeat Cao Cao, but not being asked I didn't disclose my plan."

"If you really have a good plan, I shall beg my master to ask you."

"Cao Cao's million are just a swarm of ants in my eyes. The moment I raise my hand they will all be crushed."

Lu Su went to the inner chamber to find his master. Still fuming with rage, Sun Quan glared at Lu Su and said, "Zhuge Liang went too far!"

Lu Su replied, "I reproached him for that too, but he simply laughed and said you were too touchy. He has a plan for overcoming Cao Cao, but does not mean to

---

* When the first emperor of Han united the empire, Tian Heng, king of Qi, held out with five hundred men on an island, refusing to surrender. Forced to leave the island, he killed himself on the road. When news of his death reached his loyal followers, all five hundred killed themselves.

disclose it too readily. Why don't you consult him again?"

Sun Quan's anger vanished at that and he exulted, "So he has a good plan and was deliberately provoking me! My hastiness very nearly cost me dear." He went back to the audience chamber with Lu Su and begged Zhuge Liang to come for another talk. And when he saw Zhuge Liang he apologized, "Forgive me for my discourtesy just now."

Zhuge Liang apologized too, saying, "My words offended you, but pray excuse me."

Then Sun Quan invited Zhuge Liang to an inner room to feast. After they had drunk a few rounds, Sun Quan said, "Cao Cao's chief enemies were Lü Bu, Liu Biao, Yuan Shao, Yuan Shu, Liu Bei and I. Now his first four rivals are gone, leaving only Liu Bei and myself. As ruler of the land of Wu, I cannot submit to another man's control. I have made up my mind to this. Liu Bei is my only possible ally against Cao Cao, but after his recent defeat can he fight again?"

Zhuge Liang said, "In spite of Liu Bei's recent defeat, his general Guan Yu still has ten thousand picked troops while Liu Qi has another ten thousand men of Jiangxia. Cao Cao's army has travelled far and is exhausted; his cavalry pursuing Liu Bei has covered three hundred *li* a day. When an arrow from a powerful crossbow has spent its force, it cannot pierce the flimsiest silk. Besides, the men of the north have no experience of naval warfare, and the men of Jingzhou who went over to Cao Cao were impelled by circumstances, not by their own choice. If you and Liu Bei can work together with one heart, you are certain to overcome Cao Cao. When he is routed he will withdraw to the north, Jingzhou and Wu will remain in a strong position, and the empire will be divided into three. Today must decide your fate. The choice rests with you."

Sun Quan was overjoyed and said, "Your words have shown me my way clearly. My mind is made up. I have no more doubts. This very day we shall discuss mobilizing men for a joint attack on Cao Cao." Having ordered Lu Su to pass on this command, he had Zhuge Liang escorted to the hostel to rest.

When Zhang Zhao heard that Sun Quan was going to war, he told the others, "He's been taken in by Zhuge Liang!" They went hastily to see their master and said, "We hear you are raising an army to fight Cao Cao. Do you think you are stronger than Yuan Shao? In those days Cao Cao's force was small, yet even so he routed Yuan Shao in one action. Now that he is marching south with a million men, how can we take him so lightly? To rush into battle as Zhuge Liang advises is like using firewood to put out a fire."

Sun Quan bowed his head and said nothing, while Gu Yong argued, "Because of his own defeat, Liu Bei wants our army to resist Cao Cao's advance; but why let him make use of us? I beg you, sire, to listen to Zhang Zhao's advice!"

Still Sun Quan was lost in thought and gave no answer. After Zhang Zhao and the others had left, Lu Su went in and said, "Just now your advisers begged you to surrender rather than go to war. They are thinking of their own private interests and their families' safety. I hope you won't take their advice."

As Sun Quan was pondering this, Lu Su continued, "If you hesitate again, these men will lead you astray."

"Leave me for a while," said Sun Quan. "I must give this matter careful thought."

So Lu Su left him. Some of the military officers were in favour of war while all the civil officers wanted peace; hence hot debates ensued. Sun Quan went to his own quarters most ill at ease, unable to make up his mind. When the Dowager Lady of Wu* saw his preoccupation, she asked, "What is worrying you so much that you can neither eat nor sleep?"

Sun Quan answered, "Cao Cao has stationed his troops upsteam and means to advance upon us here. Some of my officers are for surrendering, others for resisting. If we resist, we may be no match for the enemy's hordes. If we surrender, Cao Cao may show no mercy. So I cannot make up my mind."

She replied, "Have you forgotten my sister's last words?"

Then Sun Quan felt like one waking from a dream or recovering from a fit of drunkenness.

> Recalling his mother's dying words,
> He gave Zhou Yu a chance to score a great victory!

Just what those words were, you will hear in the next chapter.

---

* Sun Quan's aunt.

CHAPTER 44

Wily Zhuge Liang Incites Zhou Yu to Action
Sun Quan Decides to Rout Cao Cao

When the Dowager Lady of Wu saw that Sun Quan could not make up his mind, she reminded him of her sister's last words: "Just before his death your brother said: On problems at home consult Zhang Zhao, on problems outside consult Zhou Yu." She urged him to summon Zhou Yu and ask his advice.

Sun Quan, taking heart, ordered a messenger to ask Zhou Yu to return from Lake Boyang where he was training naval forces. But the news of Cao Cao's advance to the Han River Valley had already sent Zhou Yu back at full speed to Chaisang for a council of war. Before the messenger set out he was back. Lu Su as his close friend went to welcome him and explain all that had happened.

"Don't worry," said Zhou Yu. "I know what to do. Just go at once and ask Zhuge Liang to come here." So Lu Su mounted his horse and rode off.

Zhou Yu was resting when it was announced that Zhang Zhao, Gu Yong, Zhang Hong and Bu Zhi had called. He invited them in, and after the usual courtesies Zhang Zhao asked, "Have you heard of the danger we are in, commander?"

"I have heard nothing," was Zhou Yu's reply.

"Cao Cao is encamped with a million men up the River Han. The other day he invited our lord to hunt with him in Jiangxia. Though he may have designs of our territory, he has not disclosed them yet. We have advised our lord to surrender to avert disaster from our land. However, Lu Su has brought Zhuge Liang, adviser to Liu Bei, back from Jiangxia. Thirsting for revenge on Cao Cao, he has goaded our master into preparing for war; yet Lu Su is too ignorant to realize this. The matter is awaiting your decision."

"Is this the view of you all?" inquired Zhou Yu.

Gu Yong and the rest answered, "Yes, we are all agreed."

"I have been considering surrender for some time myself," said Zhou Yu. "I won't keep you now. Tomorrow when I see our lord we shall reach a decision."

Soon after Zhang Zhao and his party left it was announced that Cheng Pu, Huang Gai, Han Dang and some other generals had called. Zhou Yu invited them in and they exchanged greetings.

Cheng Pu asked, "Have you heard, commander, that our land may soon fall into the hands of others?"

"I have heard nothing," said Zhou Yu.

"Since we helped our first lord Sun Jian to found a kingdom, we have fought several hundred battles large and small to win these six provinces. Now our lord, on the advice of his councillors, wants to surrender to Cao Cao. This would be a most shameful and most pitiful course. We would rather die than submit to it! We hope you will persuade our lord to resist, and we shall fight to the death!"

"Is this the view of all of you?" inquired Zhou Yu.

Huang Gai sprang up indignantly and, clapping one hand to his forehead, swore, "I would rather cut off my head than surrender to Cao Cao!"

"We shall never surrender!" cried the others.

"I want to fight it out with Cao Cao too," said Zhou

Yu. "Surrender is out of the question. Please go back now, generals. When I see our lord we shall make a decision."

No sooner had Cheng Pu and his party left than along came some civil officers including Zhuge Jin and Lü Fan. Zhou Yu invited them in and after an exchange of courtesies Zhuge Jin said, "My brother Zhuge Liang has come from the River Han to propose that we ally with Liu Bei and attack Cao Cao together. The civil and military officers are in disagreement over this. Since my brother is the envoy, it is hard for me to say much. We have all been waiting for you to decide the issue."

"What is your estimate of this?" asked Zhou Yu.

"If we submit we shall be safe; if we fight we shall probably perish."

"I know what to do," said Zhou Yu with a laugh. "We must go to our lord tomorrow to settle this."

When Zhuge Jin's group had withdrawn, Lü Meng, Gan Ning and some others were announced. Invited in, they spoke of the same matter. Some were for fighting, others for surrender, and they disputed together.

"We need not discuss this now," said Zhou Yu. "We shall settle this tomorrow with our lord."

When they had left, he laughed scornfully.

That evening Lu Su called again with Zhuge Liang, and Zhou Yu went out of the middle gate to receive them. After they had exchanged courtesies and taken seats, Lu Su said to Zhou Yu, "Cao Cao's hordes are pressing southwards, and our lord cannot decide whether to make peace or fight. He is leaving the decision to you. What is your opinion?"

Zhou Yu answered, "Cao Cao acts in the emperor's name, which makes it hard to oppose him. Moreover he is very powerful, not easy to withstand. To fight means certain defeat; to surrender means safety. My mind is made up. When I have seen our lord we shall send an envoy to Cao Cao to submit."

"But that is wrong!" Lu Su was shocked. "Our kingdom here has lasted for three generations; how can we abandon it suddenly like this? Our former lord Sun Ce said before his death that foreign affairs should be entrusted to you. We were counting on you to preserve our state, relying on as strong a support as Mount Tai. Why are you following the advice of those cowards?"

"Think of all the people in our six provinces," rejoined Zhou Yu. "If they suffer the miseries of war, they are bound to hold me to blame. That is why I have decided to surrender."

"But with your prowess and our strong strategic position, Cao Cao may not succeed," protested Lu Su.

While they argued, Zhuge Liang looked on with folded hands, a scornful smile on his face.

"Why are you smiling like that, sir?" Zhou Yu asked.

"I am smiling at Lu Su for being so impractical."

"Impractical? How?" demanded Lu Su.

Zhuge Liang replied, "Why, this proposal to surrender is very sound."

Zhou Yu cried, "You have a realistic approach. I knew you would agree with me!"

"But how could you say that?" protested Lu Su again to Zhuge Liang.

The latter answered, "Cao Cao is such an able strategist that no one in the world dare oppose him. Lü Bu, Yuan Shao, Yuan Shu and Liu Biao were the only ones to do so; but he destroyed them all, till now he has no opponents. The sole exception is Liu Bei, who is unrealistic enough to contend with him; but Liu Bei is isolated now in Jiangxia, his fate hanging in the balance. If Sun Quan decides to surrender, his wife and children will be safe and he will remain rich and honoured. As for the fate of the country, leave that to Heaven. It need not trouble us."

Lu Su interposed angrily, "You want our master to bend his knees and let that traitor insult him!"

"No, I have a plan," said Zhuge Liang. "We need not carry sheep and loads of wine, nor present territory and seals. We need not even cross the river ourselves. We need only send a single messenger and a small boat to ferry two people across the river. Once Cao Cao has these two people, his legions will strip off their armour, furl their banners and withdraw."

"Who are this pair who can make Cao Cao withdraw?" asked Zhou Yu.

"For us the departure of these two would be like losing one leaf from a great tree or one grain from a granary. But Cao Cao will go away rejoicing if he gets them."

"But who are they?" demanded Zhou Yu again.

"When I was in Longzhong," said Zhuge Liang, "I heard that Cao Cao had built a most magnificent tower at Zhanghe called the Tower of the Bronze Bird, and in it he keeps the most beautiful women he has found. For Cao Cao, you must know, is a lecherous fellow. Someone told him that Lord Qiao of the Lower Yangzi had two daughters, the Elder Qiao and the Younger Qiao, whose beauty makes birds alight and fishes drown, the moon cover her face and flowers blush for shame. In fact Cao Cao has vowed, 'My first desire is to conquer all within the Four Seas and found an empire; my second is to get these two beauties from the Lower Yangzi and keep them in the Tower of the Bronze Bird to amuse me in my old age. Given these, I shall die content.' Now his real aim in leading a million men against this region is to gain possession of these beauties. Then why not seek out Lord Qiao and buy these two daughters of his for a thousand gold pieces? Once we send them to Cao Cao, he will withdraw, satisfied. Fan Li used the same stratagem when he presented Xi Shi* to the king of Wu. Why not do this without delay?"

Zhou Yu asked, "What proof have you that Cao Cao wants these two?"

"His youngest son, Cao Zhi, an able writer, at his request wrote an *Ode to the Tower of the Bronze Bird.* This poem tells how Cao Cao means to be emperor and vows to possess these two beauties."

"Can you remember the poem?" asked Zhou Yu.

"I was so struck by its splendid language that I learned it by heart."

"Please recite it then," said Zhou Yu.

So Zhuge Liang recited:

Attending our sage ruler in search of pleasure,
I ascend the lofty tower to enjoy the view;
We gaze at the vast extent of the royal palace,

---

* In the fifth century B.C. the kingdom of Wu attacked that of Yue, and King Goujian of Yue was captured. Fan Li, a minister of Yue, presented lovely Xi Shi to the king of Wu so that he neglected all affairs of state. Then Yue built up its strength until it was able to get the better of Wu.

Built under the influence of his goodness and
    virtue,
The gates rise high as hills,
The double arches soar to meet the sky;
Magnificent mansions touch the vault of heaven,
And hanging pavilions stretch to the west city;
By the flowing Zhang stands the Tower of the
    Bronze Bird,
Its orchards well-stocked with fruit,
Flanked by two turrets,
The Jade Dragon and the Gold Phoenix;
The daughters of Qiao have been brought from the
    southeast,
And he spends his days and nights in their
    company;
They look down on the splendour of the capital
And up to bright floating clouds;
All talents are gathered here
Fulfilling the lucky omen of the winged bear;*
Warm and soft the breeze in spring,
The tower stands firm beneath the cloudy sky.
Sweet the liquid song of birds;
Both the desires of his house are gained
His benign influence spreads throughout the world.
His capital is solemn and august,
Not even those great conquerors Huan and Wen**
Could rival his sagacious majesty.

---

* In the 12th century B.C. King Wen of Zhou dreamed about
a bear with wings. The next day he met wise Jiang Shang, who
consented to be his adviser and later helped his son King Wu
found the Zhou Dynasty.

** Duke Huan of Qi and Duke Wen of Jin lorded it over the
other states in the seventh century B.C.

His rare benevolence spreads far and wide,
All support his imperial house,
There is peace in the realm;
Great as heaven and earth,
Splendid as sun and moon,
August and noble till eternity,
Our sovereign lives as long as the Eastern
Emperor;*
With dragon pennants he makes his inspections,
In phoenix carriage he travels through the land;
His kindness reaches out to the Four Seas,
Amid abundance all his people prosper;
May this tower stand for ever and ever,
That he may enjoy it till the end of time!

Zhou Yu listened to the end, then leapt to his feet in a tremendous rage. Pointing a finger at the north he swore: "You old scoundrel! This is too much!"

Zhuge Liang promptly rose to remonstrate with him. "In ancient times when the Huns invaded our territory, to make peace the Han emperor gave them princesses in marriage. Why should you grudge two ordinary girls?"

"You don't know, sir," retorted Zhou Yu. "The Elder Qiao is the widow of our late ruler Sun Ce. The Younger Qiao is my wife!"

Zhuge Liang looked horrified. "I didn't know that!" he exclaimed. "I have certainly spoken out of turn. What a blunder! I deserve death!"

"I shall fight that old rebel to the death. I swear it!" cried Zhou Yu.

"Think it over well," advised Zhuge Liang, "or you may be sorry later."

---

* God in ancient Chinese mythology.

"Our last ruler trusted me," declared Zhou Yu. "How can I bow to Cao Cao and surrender? I spoke as I did just now simply to test you. I left Lake Boyang because I meant to march north; and not even a sword or axe on my neck can make me change my mind! I am counting on your help to defeat that rebel."

"If you honour me with your trust, I am glad to offer my humble services. I am at your disposal."

"When we see our lord tomorrow," said Zhou Yu, "we shall make plans to raise troops." Then Zhuge Liang and Lu Su withdrew, took leave of each other and went their separate ways.

The next morning Sun Quan went to his council hall. Ranged on his left were more than thirty civil officers, among them Zhang Zhao and Gu Yong; on his right were more than thirty military officers, among them Cheng Pu and Huang Gai. In ceremonial dress, with swords and pendants, they attended in due order. Presently Zhou Yu came in. When he had paid his respects and been greeted in turn, he said, "I hear that Cao Cao has stationed troops by the River Han and sent us a dispatch. What is your respected opinion, my lord?"

Sun Quan showed him Cao Cao's note. After reading it Zhou Yu said with a laugh, "The old rebel must think our men are no match for him that he dare insult us like this!"

"What do you think?" asked Sun Quan.

"Have you discussed this matter with your officials?"

"We have been discussing it for several days. Some advise me to surrender, others to fight. Unable to make up my mind, I want you to decide the question."

"Who advised you to surrender?" asked Zhou Yu.

"Zhang Zhao and all his party."

Zhou Yu turned to Zhang Zhao and asked to know his reasons.

Zhang Zhao said, "Cao Cao has the emperor under his thumb as he conquers territory on every side, and he does everything in the name of the government. His recent conquest of Jingzhou has made him even stronger. The Yangzi is our sole defence against him, but now he has thousands of warships and is advancing upon us by land and by water. How can we withstand him? We had better submit and devise some other plan later."

Zhou Yu said, "This is the argument of a pedant. Three generations have passed since we founded our state. Are we to throw it away so lightly?"

"In that case, what should we do?" asked Sun Quan.

Zhou Yu said, "Cao Cao calls himself the prime minister of Han, but is in fact a traitor. With your peerless courage and military genius, the region of the Lower Yangzi inherited from your father and brother, and your brave troops and ample supplies, you should advance boldly to rid the empire of evil men. How can you yield to a traitor? Moreover in his present campaign Cao Cao is breaking all the rules of war. The north is unsubdued, while Ma Teng and Han Sui are stirring up trouble in his rear, yet he persists in this southern expedition. That is his first mistake. His northern troops are unused to fighting on the water, but he is giving up his cavalry and trusting to boats to conquer us. That is his second mistake. This is the coldest time of winter and his horses lack fodder. That is his third mistake. He has brought his men from the Central Plain all this way to our rivers and lakes, and being unaccustomed to the climate many of them have fallen ill. That is his fourth mistake. Because he has made all these mistakes, even though his force is great he will be defeated. This is our chance to capture Cao Cao. Give me a few thousand picked troops and I shall advance to Xiakou and defeat him for you!"

Greatly relieved, Sun Quan leapt up and said, "Yes, that old rebel has been plotting for years to overthrow the House of Han and make himself emperor; but he was afraid of Yuan Shu, Yuan Shao, Lü Bu, Liu Biao and myself. Now the others have perished; I am his sole rival. One of us must give way to the other. You say we should fight him and that is my idea exactly. Heaven has sent you to help me!"

Zhou Yu said, "I shall gladly fight to the death for you. But you, on your part, must not hesitate!"

Sun Quan drew his sword and hacked off a corner of the table, exclaiming, "If any man dare to urge surrender to Cao Cao, he will meet the same fate as this table!" Thereupon he presented the sword to Zhou Yu and appointed him High Marshal, with Cheng Pu as his second in command and Lu Su as aide-de-camp. He authorized Zhou Yu to kill with this sword any officer who refused to obey his orders.

Zhou Yu took the sword and turned to address the assembly. "Our lord has charged me to lead our army against Cao Cao. You will all report tomorrow at my headquarters by the river to receive orders. Anyone who disobeys will be punished according to the Seven Prohibitions and the Fifty-four Penalties." With that he took his leave of Sun Quan and withdrew. The other officers left without a word.

Upon his return Zhou Yu asked Zhuge Liang over to

consult with him. "Today we reached a decision in the council hall," he said. "Now I want your advice on how best to defeat Cao Cao."

"General Sun is still rather uneasy," replied Zhuge Liang. "You cannot consider it as settled yet."

"Why do you say that?"

"He is fearful of Cao Cao's numbers and does not believe our small force can defeat such a host. We shall only succeed if you can allay his doubts by explaining away those numbers."

"An excellent idea," replied Zhou Yu, and went back to see Sun Quan.

"It must be some matter of importance that brings you here at night," said Sun Quan.

"Tomorrow we start mobilizing our forces," replied Zhou Yu. "Have you any doubts left, my lord?"

"Only about Cao Cao's numbers," Sun Quan told him. "Our force is too small to resist such a multitude. That is my only worry."

Zhou Yu said with a laugh, "That is why I have come to explain the situation to you. Cao Cao's letter speaks of a million troops on land and water, and that has made you worried and uneasy; but you have not examined the real facts of the matter. The truth is that he has no more than a hundred and fifty or sixty thousand from the Central Plain, and these men are exhausted. He has another seventy or eighty thousand of Yuan Shao's men; but most of them are half-hearted and full of doubts. When to some exhausted troops you add some half-hearted men, their number may seem large but they are nothing to fear. With fifty thousand men I can defeat them. So have no further anxiety, my lord."

Sun Quan slapped Zhou Yu on the back and said, "You have set my mind at rest. Zhang Zhao is a fool who has let me down completely, but you and Lu Su see eye to eye with me. You can go into action at once with Lu Su and Cheng Pu — pick your troops and set off. I shall send you reinforcements and further supplies. If your vanguard action is unsuccessful, come back here and I shall settle with Cao Cao myself. You have nothing to worry about."

Having thanked Sun Quan and withdrawn, Zhou Yu reflected, "So Zhuge Liang guessed what was on my master's mind. He is a better tactician than I am. As time goes on he will become a serious rival. I had better kill him." That same night he had Lu Su brought to his headquarters and told him that he wanted Zhuge Liang put out of the way.

Lu Su objected, "We have not yet defeated Cao Cao. By killing an able man we should be depriving ourselves of useful help."

"If he helps Liu Bei, he will prove a threat to us."

"Zhuge Jin is his brother. Why not ask him to persuade Zhuge Liang to come and serve our state?" To this Zhou Yu agreed.

The next morning Zhou Yu went to his headquarters and took his seat in the council tent. Guards armed with swords and axes stood on both sides, while the civil and military officers were summoned to receive orders. Only Cheng Pu, who was older than Zhou Yu and had been displeased when the latter was made the commander, absented himself now on the pretext of illness, sending his eldest son Cheng Zi in his place.

Zhou Yu addressed his officers as follows: "The law

is no respecter of persons, and you gentlemen must carry out your tasks well. Now Cao Cao is a worse despot than Dong Zhou,* for he is holding the emperor prisoner in Xuchang and has advanced with his cruel hordes to our borders. I am under orders to resist him, and you must press forward with all your might. Our army must not injure the people anywhere. Good work will be rewarded and crimes punished impartially."

Having issued this order, he put Han Dang and Huang Gai in charge of the vanguard. They were to set out at once with their warships and wait at Sanjiangkou for further orders. Jiang Qin and Zhou Dai were to lead a second force, Ling Tong and Pan Zhang a third, Taishi Ci and Lü Meng a fourth, and Lu Xun and Dong Xi a fifth, while Lü Fan and Zhu Zhi were appointed inspectors. These six contingents were to set off by land and water to reach their destination by an appointed time.

The officers went off to prepare ships and arms, while Cheng Zi returned and told his father what dispositions Zhou Yu had made. Cheng Pu was greatly impressed. "I used to despise him as a weakling who would never make a general," he said. "But it seems he is a commander of the first order. I must support him!" He went to headquarters to apologize, and Zhou Yu treated him with marked respect.

The next morning Zhou Yu sent for Zhuge Jin and told him, "Your brother Zhuge Liang is a fit councillor for a king. Why should he stoop to serve a man like Liu Bei? Now that, as luck would have it, he has come

---

* A usurper of the Han throne before Cao Cao came to power.

to our land, I want you to use your eloquence to prevail on him to leave Liu Bei and join us. Then our lord will have a good adviser, and you will be able to see your brother more often. Wouldn't this be an excellent thing? Do see to this for us!"

"I am ashamed to have been of so little use since coming to this land," replied Zhuge Jin. "I shall certainly do my best to obey your orders."

He mounted his horse and rode straight to the hostel, where Zhuge Liang welcomed him in and bowed to him. Then they talked of the past and Zhuge Jin asked with tears, "Do you remember the story of Bo Yi and Shu Qi?"*

"Zhou Yu must have sent him to win me over," thought Zhuge Liang. He answered, "Yes, they were sages of ancient times."

"Though starving to death at the foot of Shouyang Mountain, those two brothers stayed together. We were born of one mother and suckled at the same breast, yet now we are parted, serving different lords. Aren't you ashamed when you think of Bo Yi and Shu Qi?"

"You are speaking of human feelings, but I am standing by my principles too. Both of us are subjects of Han, and Liu Bei belongs to the imperial house. If you will leave the land of Wu and serve Liu Bei with me, you will be doing your duty as a subject and we

---

* Sons of the Lord of Guzhu, a baron of the Shang Dynasty in the 12th century B.C. Shu Qi was appointed his heir, but after their father's death he ceded the title to his brother. The latter declined it and left home, to be joined by Shu Qi. When the Zhous overthrew the Shangs, the two brothers, loyal to the old dynasty, fled to Shouyang Mountain, where they starved to death rather than eat the grain of Zhou as subjects of the conquerors.

two brothers shall be able to stay together. This would satisfy human feelings and principles too. What do you say to that?"

Zhuge Jin reflected, "I came to win him over, but now I am the one being persuaded!" Since he had no fitting reply to make, he rose and took his leave. Returning to Zhou Yu, he told him what had happened.

Zhou Yu asked, "What do you think, then?"

"I have been too well treated by our lord to turn away from him," replied Zhuge Jin.

"Since you mean to serve our master loyally, let us say no more about it. I have my plan to subdue your brother."

> A wise man should ally with other wise men;
> Yet men of genius can seldom endure each other.

But to know how Zhou Yu tried to get the better of Zhuge Liang, you must read the next chapter.

CHAPTER 45

Cao Cao Loses Troops at Sanjiangkou
Jiang Gan Is Trapped in a Gathering of Heroes

After hearing Zhuge Jin's report, Zhou Yu hated Zhuge Liang even more. He was determined to kill him. The next day, having mustered his troops, he went to take his leave of Sun Quan, who told him to go on ahead and promised to follow later with reinforcements.

Then Zhou Yu set off at the head of his troops with Cheng Pu and Lu Su. Zhuge Liang, asked to accompany them, consented readily. They embarked, hoisted sail and set off towards Xiakou. Some fifty *li* or more from Sanjiangkou they anchored and encamped along the shore by the western hill. Zhou Yu had his tent in the middle with troops stationed round him, while Zhuge Liang took up his quarters in a small ship.

As soon as Zhou Yu's dispositions were made, he invited Zhuge Liang to his tent for a discussion. After an exchange of courtesies, Zhou Yu said, "Although Cao Cao had less men than Yuan Shao, he was able to defeat him by taking Xu You's advice and cutting off the enemy's grain supply at Wuchao. Now Cao Cao has 830,000 men to our fifty or sixty thousand. How can we worst him? We shall have to cut off his supplies first too. I have discovered that the grain and forage for his army are stored on Mount Jutie. You have spent so long in this part of the country that you must know the terrain well. I would like you to go there with Guan Yu, Zhang Fei and Zhao Yun. I shall assist you with a thousand men. I wish you to set out immediately. Since we both want to serve our masters well, please do not refuse."

Zhuge Liang thought, "After failing to win me over, he means to kill me. If I refuse I shall be a laughing-stock. I had better agree and find some other way out." To Zhou Yu's delight, he accepted readily.

When Zhuge Liang had left, Lu Su asked Zhou Yu in private, "Why are you sending him to cut the grain supply?"

"I want to kill him without laying myself open to scorn," replied Zhou Yu. "I hope Cao Cao will do the job for me, to spare me trouble in future."

Then Lu Su went to Zhuge Liang to see whether he suspected anything. He found him quite unconcerned, preparing his troops to set off. This was too much for Lu Su, who dropped him a hint, saying, "Do you expect to succeed in this mission, sir?"

Zhuge Liang replied with a laugh, "I am adept at all kinds of fighting, aboard ship, on foot, on horseback or in chariots. Of course I shall succeed. I am not like you and Zhou Yu, skilled in one kind of fighting only." When Lu Su asked what he meant by this, he said, "I have heard urchins in your country chanting:

> For an ambush or holding a pass, Lu Su is best;
> For river fighting, Zhou Yu outdoes the rest.

All you can do is lay ambushes and hold passes, while Zhou Yu can fight on water but not on land."

Lu Su reported this to Zhou Yu, who flared up and exclaimed, "What makes him think I can't fight on land? He needn't go then! I shall take ten thousand horsemen myself and cut off Cao Cao's supplies."

Lu Su told this to Zhuge Liang, who said with a laugh, "He asked me to cut their supply route in the hope that Cao Cao would kill me. That was why I provoked him with that remark which was more than he could stomach. But this is a time when every man counts. The Marquis of Wu must work in harmony with my master Liu Bei if we are to succeed. If each tries to harm the other, our whole scheme will fail. Cao Cao is exceedingly crafty and has more than once cut off his rivals' supplies. He is bound to have stationed strong forces to guard his own. If Zhou Yu attempts this, he will only be captured. What we should do is stick to fighting on water till we have exhausted those northern troops, then find some good means to defeat them. Do try to persuade Zhou Yu of the wisdom of this."

Lu Su went that same night to repeat this to Zhou Yu. The commander shook his head and stamped his foot. "That man is ten times as clever as I!" he exclaimed. "If I don't get rid of him now he will ruin our country!"

"This is a time when every man counts," said Lu Su. "You must put our country's welfare first. You can deal with him once we have defeated Cao Cao."

To this Zhou Yu agreed.

Meanwhile Liu Bei had ordered Liu Qi to hold Jiangxia while he led his troops to Xiakou. When he saw far off on the south bank a multitude of flags and a forest of lances, he knew that the armies of Wu had joined in the fight. So he moved all his troops from Jiangxia to Fankou. There, mustering his men, he said, "We have no news of Zhuge Liang since he went to the land of Wu. Who will go and find out for me how he is getting on?"

Mi Zhu volunteered to go, and Liu Bei prepared gifts as well as sheep and wine, sending him to Wu ostensibly to feast the troops, but in fact to find out news.

So Mi Zhu went downstream in a small boat till he came to Zhou Yu's camp. The soldiers reported his arrival to their commander, who invited him in. Mi Zhu bowed, presented Liu Bei's greetings and handed over the wine and other gifts. Zhou Yu, having accepted these, gave a feast to entertain him.

"Zhuge Liang has been here a long time," said Mi Zhu. "I should like to take him back with me."

Zhou Yu said, "He is advising me on the best way to defeat Cao Cao. How can he leave now? I would like to see Liu Bei as well to discuss our plans, but an army commander cannot leave his post. If your master would do me the honour of coming here, I should be delighted."

Mi Zhu agreed and took his leave.

Once he had gone Lu Su asked Zhou Yu, "What plans do you want to discuss with Liu Bei?"

"For boldness and daring Liu Bei stands alone," said Zhou Yu. "He must be removed. I am taking this chance to lure him here and kill him, to rid our country of a future danger."

Lu Su tried to dissuade him, but Zhou Yu turned a deaf ear. In fact he issued secret orders for fifty men armed with swords and hatchets to conceal themselves behind the curtain when Liu Bei came. The drop of a cup would be the signal to kill him.

Upon his return Mi Zhu passed on Zhou Yu's invitation to Liu Bei, who ordered a fast boat to be prepared and was eager to set off without delay. Guan Yu advised against this, saying, "Zhou Yu is very crafty, and there is no word from Zhuge Liang. I suspect a trick. Don't undertake this so lightly."

But Liu Bei argued, "We have allied with Wu to defeat Cao Cao. To refuse Zhou Yu's invitation would be behaviour unworthy of an ally. We can never succeed if we distrust each other."

"If you insist on going, brother, I'll go with you," said Guan Yu.

"And so will I!" cried Zhang Fei.

Liu Bei said, "Guan Yu alone will be enough. Zhang Fei and Zhao Yun can defend our camp while Jian Yong holds Exian. I shall not be long."

Having given these orders, he embarked with Guan Yu on a small ship with a score or so of men. The oarsmen rowed swiftly down the river. The war vessels of Wu and the flags and armed men deployed in good order on both sides rejoiced Liu Bei's heart. Soldiers reported his arrival to Zhou Yu, who asked, "How many ships has he brought with him?"

They replied, "Only one, with about twenty men as escort."

Zhou Yu laughed. "Then his fate is sealed!"

He ordered his armed men to hide themselves while he went out to welcome the visitors. Liu Bei came with Guan Yu and his men to the headquarters. After an exchange of greetings, Zhou Yu asked Liu Bei to take the seat of honour. But the latter protested, "You, general, are famed throughout the world, while I am a man of no ability. How can I accept such an honour?" He simply took the seat of a guest and Zhou Yu entertained him to a feast.

Now Zhuge Liang, chancing to go to the river shore, was horrified to hear of his mater's arrival. Hurrying to the headquarters to have a look, he saw Zhou Yu with murder on his face and the armed men massed behind the curtains. In great dismay he asked himself, "What's to be done?" But when he looked at Liu Bei, his master was chatting and laughing without constraint. Moreover standing behind him with his hand on his sword was Guan Yu. Zhuge Liang heaved a sigh of relief. "Then there is no danger!" So instead of entering he returned to the river bank to await Liu Bei.

When host and guest had drunk several cups together, as Zhou Yu rose to offer a toast his eye fell on Guan Yu with his drawn sword. He hastily asked who this was.

Liu Bei replied, "My sworn brother, Guan Yu."

Startled, Zhou Yu asked, "The man who killed both Yan Liang and Wen Chou?"

"The very same," said Liu Bei.

Zhou Yu broke into a cold sweat and filled a cup for Guan Yu. Presently Lu Su came in and Liu Bei asked, "Where is Zhuge Liang? May I trouble you to fetch him?"

"Wait till we have defeated Cao Cao," said Zhou Yu. And Liu Bei did not dare to insist. Guan Yu gave him a meaning look, and taking the hint he rose to his feet, saying, "I must leave you now. When the enemy is routed and our task done, I shall come to offer my congratulations."

Zhou Yu did not press him to stay, but saw him out of the camp.

When Liu Bei, Guan Yu and their men reached the river, they found Zhuge Liang in their boat. Liu Bei was exceedingly pleased, but Zhuge Liang said, "Do you realize the danger you were in today?"

"Why, no," replied Liu Bei.

"If not for Guan Yu, Zhou Yu would have murdered you."

Then Liu Bei, sensing the truth of this, asked Zhuge Liang to go back with them to Fankou. But he said, "Although I am in the tiger's mouth, I feel as secure as Mount Tai. Get ready your ships and men, and on the twentieth of the eleventh month send Zhao Yun with a boat to the south bank to meet me. Don't let there be any blunder!"

When Liu Bei asked for some explanation, Zhuge Liang would only say, "When the southeast wind springs up, I shall return."

Liu Bei would have questioned him further, but Zhuge Liang urged him to set sail at once. So Liu Bei, Guan Yu and their men embarked again. They had not gone far when fifty or sixty vessels came downstream to meet them. In the prow of the first stood a general holding a lance. It was Zhang Fei, who had come to their assistance, fearing Liu Bei might be in danger and Guan Yu alone unable to rescue him. They all returned to their headquarters together.

Zhou Yu went back to his camp having seen Liu Bei off, and Lu Su went in to ask him, "After luring Liu Bei here, why didn't you kill him?"

"Because of Guan Yu, a tiger among generals, who never left Liu Bei's side. If I had made any move, he would have killed me."

Lu Su was most impressed. Just then the arrival was announced of a messenger from Cao Cao with a letter. Zhou Yu ordered him to be brought in and took the letter. But the superscription, "To Marshal Zhou from the Prime Minister of Han," threw him into a rage. He tore up the letter without reading the contents, scattered the shreds on the ground and ordered the messenger to be put to death.

Lu Su remonstrated, "When two states are at war, they do not kill each other's envoys."

Zhou Yu retorted, "I do it to show our might."

So the man was decapitated and his head sent back.

Then Zhou Yu ordered Gan Ning to lead out the vanguard, Han Dang the left wing and Jiang Qin the right wing, while he followed with the main force. The next day they ate before dawn at the fourth watch, and at the fifth watch set sail with a great sounding of drums.

When Cao Cao learned what Zhou Yu had done, his anger knew no bounds. He made Cai Mao, Zhang Yun and the other Jingzhou officers who had come over his vanguard, while he himself headed the main expeditionary force, and they sailed as fast as they could to Sanjiangkou. There they were intercepted by the ships of Wu. The officer in charge of the fleet cried out from the foremost vessel, "I am General Gan Ning. I challenge you to battle!"

Cai Mao sent his younger brother Cai Xun against him. But as his ship approached, Gan Ning loosed an arrow at him and Cai Xun fell. Then Gan Ning ordered his fleet to attack in force, and thousands of bowmen discharged a hail of arrows. Cao Cao's vessels, compelled to give way, were attacked on the right by Jiang

Qin, on the left by Han Dang. Most of his men, being northerners, were not used to fighting on water: they could hardly keep their footing on a moving boat. When Gan Ning attacked with both wings and Zhou Yu sent more ships to join the fray, Cao Cao's forces suffered heavy casualties. The battle lasted till the afternoon.

Then, although Zhou Yu had the upper hand, since he was greatly outnumbered he had gongs sounded to call off his fleet.

Cao Cao's forces withdrew, defeated. Back in his camp, having made fresh dispositions, he sent for Cai Mao and Zhang Yun and reproached them, "The men of Wu are few yet they worsted us. You did not do your best."

Cai Mao replied, "The Jingzhou marines have not had exercises for a long time while the troops from the north have done hardly any fighting on water. That is why we were defeated. We must set up a naval camp, train the men from the north inside and those from Jingzhou outside, drilling them every day till they are adept. Then they will be able to fight."

"As naval commanders, that is up to you," retorted Cao Cao. "What is the use of telling me this?"

So Zhang Yun and Cai Mao set about training marines. They established twenty-four "Water Gates" with large vessels outside as a rampart, while the smaller ships moved about freely inside. At night when lanterns and torches were lit, both sky and water glowed red. On land their fires stretched in unbroken line for more than three hundred *li*.

Zhou Yu went back in triumph to his camp, feasted his troops and sent word of his victory to the Marquis of Wu. But that night, when he climbed to the top of a hill, saw all the fires on the west lighting up the sky and was told that those were the fires of the northern forces, his heart sank within him. The next day, deciding to reconnoitre the enemy's camp, he had a galley made ready with drummers and musicians as well as brave officers armed with powerful bows. They set sail upstream. Approaching the enemy camp, Zhou Yu gave orders to anchor and had music played while he scanned Cao Cao's fleet.

He exclaimed in dismay, "They certainly know what they are about! Who are their commanders?"

He was told, "Cai Mao and Zhang Yun."

Zhou Yu reflected, "Those two have spent a long time in our country and are thoroughly experienced in naval warfare. I must find some way of getting rid of them before I can beat Cao Cao."

Meanwhile sentinels had hastened to report to Cao Cao that Zhou Yu was spying on their camp. Cao Cao ordered out some ships to capture him. When Zhou Yu saw the signal flags moving, he promptly gave the order to weigh anchor, the oarsmen on both sides pulled steadily together and the galley shot swiftly downstream. By the time Cao Cao's ships came out after them, they were a good ten *li* away. The pursuers had to go back and report their failure.

Cao Cao told his officers, "Yesterday's defeat has made our men lose heart. Now the enemy has spied on our camp. How are we to beat them?"

At once a man stepped forward and said, "I used to be Zhou Yu's fellow student and good friend. I have sufficient powers of persuasion to win him over."

Overjoyed, Cao Cao saw that the speaker was Jiang Gan of Jiujiang, one of the secretaries.

"Do you know Zhou Yu well?" he asked.

"Rest assured, my lord," replied Jiang Gan. "If I go to the south bank, I shall succeed!"

"What do you need to take with you?"

"Just a servant-boy and two men to row my boat."

Cao Cao was pleased and called for wine to see Jiang Gan on his way.

In a plain cloth cap and gown, Jiang Gan went by a small boat straight to Zhou Yu's camp, where he told them to announce, "Your master's old friend Jiang Gan has come to call."

Zhou Yu was in his tent at a council when he heard of Jiang Gan's arrival. He laughed and told his officers, "Their orator has come!" Then he whispered into their ears, and they hurried off to carry out their instructions.

Having changed his clothes, Zhou Yu went out accompanied by several hundred men all in bright silk and coloured caps. Jiang Gan stepped up proudly with his servant-boy in blue. After Zhou Yu had welcomed him, Jiang Gan asked, "Have you been well since we last met?"

Zhou Yu said, "You must have had a hard time crossing rivers and lakes as an emissary for Cao Cao!"

Taken aback, Jiang Gan replied, "I haven't seen you for so long that I came to talk over old times with you. What makes you suspect that I am an emissary of Cao Cao?"

Zhou Yu laughed. "Though I lack the intelligence of

the old musician Shi Kuang,* I can understand the idea behind the music."

"If that is the way you welcome old friends, I had better take my leave."

With a smile Zhou Yu took him by the arm. "I was afraid you were here to speak for Cao Cao. If you have no such intention, don't go just yet."

Together they entered his tent. When they had exchanged courtesies and taken their seats, Zhou Yu sent for all his brave officers. Two groups of men filed in: civil and military officials in rich silk robes, and army commanders in their silver armour. Zhou Yu introduced them and they took seats on both sides. A great feast was served, martial music was played, and a series of toasts was offered.

"This is my old classmate and pledged friend," Zhou Yu told his officers. "Though he comes from the north bank, he is not here to speak for Cao Cao. You have no call to suspect him." He took off his sword and handed it to Taishi Ci saying, "Wear this and act as master of ceremonies. We shall speak of nothing today but our old friendship. If any man mentions Cao Cao or our present campaign — off with the fellow's head!"

Taishi Ci assented and sat down with the sword. Jiang Gan was almost too terrified to speak.

Zhou Yu said, "Since I assumed command, I have not drunk a drop of wine. Today as my old friend is here and our hearts are free from suspicion, I shall drink as I please." With a hearty laugh, he drank deep. The goblets passed quickly round. When the drinking

---

* A musician of the sixth century B.C. who could predict good fortune or bad from a tune.

was at its height, Zhou Yu took Jiang Gan's hand and led him out of the tent. Soldiers were standing outside, fully armed with spears and halberds.

"Don't you think my men are a brave sight?" asked Zhou Yu.

"As stout as bears or tigers," replied Jiang Gan.

Zhou Yu led him to the back of the tent, where grain and forage were piled up mountain-high. "Wouldn't you say I have plenty of grain and forage?"

"Brave troops and ample supplies — just as I'd heard," said Jiang Gan.

Pretending to be drunk, Zhou Yu burst out laughing. "When you and I were students together, little did we think a day like this would come!"

"This is no more than your great talents deserve."

Still clasping Jiang Gan's hand, Zhou Yu went on, "When a true man finds a master who knows his worth, he is bound by a subject's loyalty to his sovereign and the close ties of kinsmen. His advice is carried out, his plans are followed, he shares good times and bad alike with his lord. Not even orators like Su Qin, Zhang Yi, Lu Jia and Li Yiji* with their floods of eloquence and tongues sharp as daggers could shake my allegiance now!" He bellowed with laughter again, while Jiang Gan turned pale. Then Zhou Yu took him back to drink with the others, and pointing to them said, "These are the best and bravest of the Yangzi Valley. We can call this a gathering of heroes!" They drank till evening when the candles were lit. Then Zhou Yu rose to perform a sword dance and sang this song:

---

* Lu Jia and Li Yiji were famous orators at the beginning of the Han Dynasty.

A man should live to make a name,
For life's well spent achieving fame;
Let me get drunk now fame's in sight,
And tipsy sing with all my might!

They all laughed and applauded this song. Then since it was late, Jiang Gan asked permission to retire because he could drink no more. The host ordered the table to be cleared and the others left.

"It's a long time since we shared a couch," said Zhou Yu. "But we shall sleep together tonight." Looking absolutely drunk, he dragged Jiang Gan into his tent and they lay down together. Zhou Yu flung himself down fully dressed, vomiting and fouling the bed. Jiang Gan, however, could not sleep. His head on the pillow he heard the army drum sound the second watch, and sitting up found the lamp was still alight. He looked at Zhou Yu who was snoring thunderously. On the table in the tent lay a pile of papers. He got up stealthily to have a look, and found they were letters, one bearing the signatures of Cai Mao and Zhang Yun. Utterly amazed, he read it. The contents were briefly as follows: " . . . We surrendered to Cao Cao not in any hope of reward but because we were driven to it by circumstances. We have fooled the northern armies and trapped them in this naval camp. When our chance comes we shall present you with Cao Cao's head. You may expect a further message soon. Rest assured that you can trust your humble servants. . . ."

"So Cai Mao and Zhang Yun are in league with the army of Wu," reflected Jiang Gan. He hid this letter in his clothes and was about to look through the others when Zhou Yu turned over. At once he put out the light and returned to bed. Zhou was muttering in his sleep, "Jiang Gan, in a few days I'll show you Cao Cao's head...." Jiang Gan forced himself to reply, and Zhou Yu went on, "Wait friend, and you'll see Cao Cao's head!..." But when questioned further he was sound asleep. Jiang Gan lay there wide awake till nearly the fourth watch, when someone came in and called, "Are you awake, commander?"

As if suddenly awakened, Zhou Yu asked, "Who is this on my bed?"

"You invited Jiang Gan to sleep with you," was the reply. "Had you forgotten?"

"This is the first time in my life that I've been drunk," declared Zhou Yu penitently. "I had too much wine yesterday and it made me careless. I hope I didn't give away any secrets."

The other said, "Someone is here from the north bank."

"Hush!" said Zhou Yu. "Keep your voice down." He called Jiang Gan, who pretended to be asleep. Zhou Yu went outside and Jiang Gan strained his ears to overhear their conversation.

The other said, "Commanders Zhang and Cai say they haven't yet had a chance to kill him." Then his voice dropped till it became inaudible. Presently Zhou Yu came back and called Jiang Gan's name again, but the latter made no reply, pretending to be asleep, his head under the bedding. Then Zhou Yu undressed and went to bed again.

Jiang Gan thought, "Zhou Yu is no fool. When he finds the letter gone in the morning he will kill me." So at the fifth watch he rose and called Zhou Yu, but his host seemed fast asleep. Then Jiang Gan dressed and crept quietly out of the tent calling his servant-boy, he left the headquarters.

"Where are you going, sir?" the soldiers asked him.

"I don't want to be in the way, so I'm leaving now."

And the soldiers did not stop him.

Boarding his boat, Jiang Gan returned with all speed to Cao Cao.

"How did it go?" he was asked.

"Zhou Yu is too high-minded to be prevailed upon."

"Another failure for him to laugh at!" Cao Cao was angry.

"Well, even if I failed to persuade him, I have found out something. Please send these others away and I will tell you." With that Jiang Gan produced the letter and told Cao Cao all that had passed.

"The scoundrels! How dare they!" bellowed Cao Cao, and sent immediately for Cai Mao and Zhang Yun. "I want you to start an offensive!" he ordered them.

Cai Mao answered, "Our forces are not yet properly trained. To attack now would be rash."

"They won't be trained, I suppose, until you have presented my head to Zhou Yu!" roared Cao Cao.

Both officers were completely at a loss and did not know what to say. Cao Cao ordered his guards to drag them out and kill them. In a short time their severed heads were brought to his tent, and only then did he realize that he had fallen into the enemy's trap. When the other officers came to ask the reason for this execution, though Cao Cao knew that he had been deceived he would not admit his mistake.

"They were lax in discipline," he said, "so I had them executed."

The others were aghast but could do nothing. Then Cao Cao appointed Mao Jie and Yu Jin as his new naval commanders.

When spies passed this news to the south bank, Zhou Yu exclaimed in delight, "These two were my only cause for anxiety. Now they have gone, I have nothing to worry about."

Lu Su said, "If you keep this up, without any doubt Cao Cao will be defeated!"

"I don't think any of the others saw my game except Zhuge Liang," said Zhou Yu. "He is wiser than I and this trick can hardly have escaped him. Go and sound him out, will you, and let me know whether he saw through it or not."

> He used his success in sowing strife
> To test the man with the discerning eye.

But to know whether Lu Su carried out instructions or not, you must wait for the next chapter.

CHAPTER 46

By a Ruse Zhuge Liang Borrows Arrows
Huang Gai Proposes a Stratagem and Is Beaten

Lu Su went as instructed to Zhuge Liang's boat. He was asked into the cabin and both men sat down.

"The fighting has kept us so busy these last few days that I haven't come to hear your instruction," said Lu Su.

Zhuge Liang replied, "It was most remiss of me not to have gone to congratulate your commander."

"Congratulate him for what?"

"The matter Zhou Yu has sent you to find out whether I knew about or not. That calls for congratulations."

Lu Su turned pale and asked, "But how did you know?"

"The trick was only good enough to fool Jiang Gan. Though Cao Cao was taken in at the time, he must have realized his mistake at once; only of course he won't admit it. Now that Cai Mao and Zhang Yun are dead, your troubles are over. This certainly is a case for congratulation. I hear that Cao Cao has appointed Mao Jie and Yu Jin as his new admirals— his fleet is as good as doomed."

Flabbergasted, Lu Su made small talk for a while before taking his leave.

"Please don't tell Zhou Yu that I knew this," said Zhuge Liang. "He would be jealous and find some excuse to kill me."

Although Lu Su agreed, he went straight to Zhou Yu and reported all that had happened.

Staggered, Zhou Yu exclaimed, "Shall this man live? I am determined to get rid of him!"

"If you kill Zhuge Liang, Cao Cao will laugh."

"I shall find some plausible pretext so that he can't complain of any injustice."

"How will you do that?"

"Don't ask me. Just wait and see."

The next day Zhou Yu assembled his officers and summoned Zhuge Liang to a council. The latter went there cheerfully, and after they had taken seats Zhou Yu asked, "What arms are most important in naval fighting? We shall be engaging the forces of Cao Cao soon."

"On the river, arrows are best," said Zhuge Liang.

"I agree with you. But we are rather short of arrows. Would you undertake to supply a hundred thousand for our next fight? Since this is for the common good, I am sure you won't refuse!"

"I shall certainly do my best to carry out your orders," said Zhuge Liang. "May I ask when you want the arrows?"

"Could you have them ready in ten days?"

"The enemy may be here any time. Ten days would be too late."

"In that case how long do you think you will need?"

"In three days I can give you a hundred thousand arrows."

"We don't appreciate jokes in the army!" said Zhou Yu.

"How dare I joke with you, commander?" protested Zhuge Liang. "Give me a written order. If I haven't done the job in three days, I am willing to accept any punishment."

In high good humour Zhou Yu ordered his adjutant to draw up an order forthwith. Then he drank to Zhuge Liang's success and said, "When this task is completed, you will be rewarded."

"It is too late to start today. I will start tomorrow," said Zhuge Liang. "Three days from tomorrow you can send five hundred men to the river bank to fetch the arrows." After drinking a few more cups he took his leave.

"Do you think he is up to some trick?" asked Lu Su.

"I think he has signed his own death warrant," said Zhou Yu. "I didn't push him into this. He asked for that formal order before the whole council. Even if he sprouts wings he can hardly escape this time. I shall just tell the workmen to hold things up and not supply him with the material he needs, so that of course he can't produce the arrows. Then, when I condemn him, no one can protest. Go and see what he's doing now and keep me informed."

So off went Lu Su to see Zhuge Liang, who said, "I asked you not to let Zhou Yu know or he would kill me. But you couldn't hold your tongue, and now I'm in trouble. How am I to make a hundred thousand arrows in three days? You must come to my rescue."

"You brought this on yourself," replied Lu Su. "How can I help you?"

"I want the loan of twenty boats, each manned by thirty men. All the boats should have black cloth curtains and a thousand bundles of straw lashed to both sides. I shall make good use of them. On the third day I promise to deliver the arrows. But on no account tell Zhou Yu, or my plan will fall through."

Although Lu Su was puzzled, when he went back to

Zhou Yu he did not mention the boats. He said only that Zhuge Liang had not asked for bamboo, feathers, glue or varnish, but had some other way of producing arrows.

Zhou Yu was puzzled too but simply said, "Well, we'll see what he has to say in three days' time."

Lu Su quietly prepared twenty fast ships each manned by more than thirty men, as well as the curtains and straw. The first and second days, Zhuge Liang made no move. Before dawn on the third day at about the fourth watch, he secretly invited Lu Su to his boat. When asked the reason he said, "I want you to come with me to fetch those arrows."

"Where from?"

"Don't ask that. You will see."

Then Zhuge Liang had the twenty ships fastened together with a long rope and made them row towards the north bank. The night was foggy and mist lay so thick on the river that men face to face could hardly see each other. He urged the ships forward till by the fifth watch they were close to Cao Cao's camp. Then they were ordered to form a line with their prows to the west, while the crews beat drums and raised a mighty clamour.

Lu Su was alarmed and asked, "What if the enemy attacks?"

Zhuge Liang said with a laugh, "I doubt if Cao Cao will come out in this heavy fog. Let us pass the time pleasantly drinking and go back when the fog lifts."

When Cao Cao's troops heard the clamour and beating of drums, Mao Jie and Yu Jin hurried to report to their chief. His orders were, "If their fleet has arrived in a heavy fog like this, they must be up to some trick.

Don't do anything rash. Get the bowmen in your fleet to shoot at them." He also sent orders to Zhang Liao and Xu Huang to take three thousand archers from their army to the bank at once to help the marines. By the time this order was delivered, the admirals had already ordered bowmen to let fly their arrows to prevent the men of Wu from attacking their camp. Soon a host of army archers also arrived, and all shot together at the river. Arrows fell like rain. Then Zhuge Liang made his crews turn so that their prows pointed east and go closer to the camp so that more arrows might hit them, while they went on sounding drums and raising a din. When the sun rose and the mist began to scatter, he gave orders for a speedy return. By then the straw on all the boats was bristling with arrows, and Zhuge Liang ordered the crews to shout, "Thank you, Cao Cao, for your arrows!" By the time this was reported to Cao Cao, the swift light boats were more than twenty *li* downstream, and it was impossible to overtake them. Cao Cao was sorry, but there was no help for it.

As they were returning, Zhuge Liang told Lu Su, "There must be five to six thousand arrows now in each boat. So with no effort at all we have got more than a hundred thousand. They will come in handy tomorrow to shoot at Cao Cao."

"You are quite miraculous," exclaimed Lu Su. "How did you know there would be such a fog today?"

"A general is mediocre unless he knows the laws of heaven and earth, the changes of nature and the complexities of army formations. I calculated three days ago that there would be a heavy fog today. That's why I dared set the limit at three days. Zhou Yu offered me ten days but withheld workmen and materials, obviously meaning to fasten the blame on me in order to have me killed. But my fate is governed by Heaven — how can he harm me?"

Lu Su could not but agree. When the boats reached the shore, five hundred of Zhou Yu's men were waiting there. Zhuge Liang told them to take the arrows from the boats, and they carried more than a hundred thousand to Zhou Yu's headquarters. When Lu Su went to Zhou Yu's camp and told him how Zhuge Liang had come by these arrows, the commander was amazed. He said with a sigh, "Zhuge Liang's powers of calculation are more than human! I am no match for him."

Presently Zhuge Liang came to the camp and Zhou Yu went out to meet and congratulate him. "Your miraculous calculations are most admirable," he said.

"That was just a trick," said Zhuge Liang, "nothing remarkable."

Zhou Yu asked him into his tent for a drink and said, "My lord sent a messenger yesterday urging me to launch an attack, but I have no good plan of action. May I have the benefit of your advice?"

Zhuge Liang declined, saying, "I am a man of no talent. How can I suggest any good plan?"

Zhou Yu said, "The other day I saw Cao Cao's naval camp. It seemed very well organized and most impressive. We cannot hope to take it by the usual methods. I have thought of a plan, but am not sure whether it will answer. I hope you will decide for me."

"Don't say what it is, commander," said Zhuge Liang. "Let each of us write it in the palm of his hand and see whether our views coincide."

Zhou Yu agreed and called for a pen and inkstone. When he had written, he passed the pen to Zhuge Liang, who wrote something in his turn. Then they moved their seats closer to look at each other's palm, and both burst into laughter. For both had written exactly the same word, "fire".

"Since we agree on this, let us count it as settled," said Zhou Yu. "Don't let anyone into the secret."

"Certainly not. This is for our common interest. As I see it, although Cao Cao has been tricked by us twice, he will not be expecting this. You can go ahead confidently."

After drinking together they parted, and no other officer knew of their plan.

Meanwhile Cao Cao was thoroughly annoyed at having lost a hundred and fifty thousand arrows to no purpose. Then Xun You put forward a plan.

"Sun Quan has two good strategists, Zhou Yu and Zhuge Liang; so we cannot easily get the better of them. Let us send over men who will pretend to surrender but actually serve as spies in the enemy camp and pass information to us. This is the way to defeat them."

"Just what I was thinking," said Cao Cao. "Who is there in our army who can go?"

"Cai Mao was killed but his kinsmen are still in the army. His cousins Cai Zhong and Cai He are both lieutenants. You can win them over by showing them special favour, then send them over to Wu. The enemy will not suspect them for a moment."

Cao Cao agreed and that same night sent secretly for these men. "I want you to take a few men and pretend to surrender to Zhou Yu," he told them. "If you hear any news, send us a secret message. Once the war is won, I shall reward you well. But mind you do not betray us!"

They replied, "Our wives and children are in Jingzhou. How dare we think of treason? Rest assured, Your Lordship. The heads of Zhou Yu and Zhuge Liang will soon be lying at your feet!"

Cao Cao gave them rich gifts, and the next day they set off with five hundred men in several boats, sailing to the south bank with a favourable wind.

Zhou Yu was preparing his attack when some boats from the north were reported to have arrived with Cai Mao's cousins, deserters from the other side. Zhou Yu had them brought before him. They bowed and said, weeping, "Our cousin was innocent, yet that scoundrel Cao Cao killed him! To avenge him we have come to surrender to you. Let us stay and put us in your vanguard!"

Zhou Yu showed great pleasure and gave them handsome gifts, then ordered them to join Gan Ning in the vanguard. They bowed and thanked him, believing they had taken him in.

But Zhou Yu secretly sent for Gan Ning to warn him, "These men have come without their families. They cannot really be deserters, but spies sent by Cao Cao. I mean to turn the tables on them and let them pass on information for me. So treat them well, but be on your guard. The day that we go into action, we shall sacrifice them to our flag. Be very careful and see you make no mistake!"

When Gan Ning had gone, Lu Su came in. "I suspect that Cai Zhong and Cai He are here under false pretences," he said. "Don't let them stay."

Zhou Yu retorted, "They are here to avenge the

death of their cousin. Where is the pretence? If you are so suspicious, no one will come over to our side."

Lu Su withdrew, silenced, to tell this to Zhuge Liang, who simply smiled.

"Why do you smile?" asked Lu Su.

"Because you don't understand Zhou Yu's ruse. The river is too wide for spies to come and go easily. So Cao Cao has sent these two self-styled deserters to spy on us. Your commander is using their own trick against them, to pass on false information. All's fair in war, and he has done the right thing."

Then Lu Su understood.

That night as Zhou Yu sat in his tent, Huang Gai slipped in to see him.

"Coming at this hour," said Zhou Yu, "you must have some good proposal to make."

"The enemy outnumbers us and a long stay here is not to our advantage. Why don't we burn them out?"

"Who suggested this plan to you?" demanded Zhou Yu.

"No one. It is my own idea."

"This is exactly what I have in mind. That is why I have kept that pair to pass on false information. The only trouble is that I have no one here to pretend to desert to the enemy."

"Let me do that," offered Huang Gai.

"Unless you bear marks of ill treatment, they will not trust you."

"The Sun family have shown me such favour that I would dash my brains out for them without regret!"

Zhou Yu bowed his thanks, saying, "If you will really put up with bodily injuries to gain our end, our country will be in your debt."

Again Huang Gai assured him, "Kill me, I do not mind." With that he left.

The next day Zhou Yu sounded drums to summon all his officers to his tent. Zhuge Liang was present too.

Zhou Yu said, "Cao Cao is here with a million men, his camp extends for more than three hundred *li*. We cannot defeat him in a single encounter. Each of you must prepare grain and forage to hold out for three months."

He had barely finished speaking when Huang Gai stepped forward and said, "Three months? Supplies for thirty would be no use. If we can defeat them this month, well and good. If not, we may as well take Zhang Zhao's advice: throw down our arms, and surrender!"

"My orders are to defeat Cao Cao!" cried Zhou Yu in a fury. "I have promised my lord to kill all who dare speak of surrender. Here we are grappling with the enemy, yet you talk of surrender to lower my men's morale. I'll have your head for this — that will show the others!"

He ordered his men to drag Huang Gai out and kill him.

But now it was Huang Gai's turn to rage. "Since I joined our lord Sun Jian, I have fought in the southeast for three of their house! You are nothing but an upstart."

Zhou Yu in a passion ordered his instant death. But Gan Ning interceded for him saying, "Huang Gai is a senior officer of Wu. I beg you to pardon him!"

"How dare you plead for him?" shouted Zhou Yu.

"Are you undermining discipline too?" He ordered his men to drive Gan Ning out with clubs. The other officials fell on their knees, entreating, "Huang Gai does indeed deserve death, but his loss would weaken our army! Pardon him this time, but mark his fault against him. You can put him to death after we have defeated Cao Cao."

They had to plead hard and long before Zhou Yu relented sufficiently to say, "If not for you I should have had his head! Very well, I will not kill him." He ordered his guards to give Huang Gai a hundred blows instead. When they urged him again to be merciful, Zhou Yu toppled over the table in his fury, ordered them out and insisted on the punishment. So Huang Gai was stripped, thrown to the ground and given fifty strokes. Once more the officers begged for a remission. Zhou Yu leaped from his seat and pointing his finger at Huang Gai cried, "Insolent wretch! I shall spare you the other fifty now. But next time you dare flout me your punishment will be doubled!" Swearing angrily under his breath he withdrew, while the others helped Huang Gai up. Bleeding and torn from his cruel beating, he was carried back to his tent. Several times he fainted away. All who saw him shed tears.

Lu Su was one of those who went to see him. Then he called on Zhuge Liang in his boat and said, "When Zhou Yu was so angry today and punished Huang Gai, those of us under his command dared not plead too hard for fear of offending him. But why did you, a guest, fold your arms and watch without uttering a word?"

Zhuge Liang smiled and said, "Don't try to fool me!"

"However can you say that?" protested Lu Su. "Since

we crossed the river together I have never once fooled you."

"Surely you know that cruel beating was a ruse on Zhou Yu's part. How could I intercede?"

As light dawned on Lu Su, Zhuge Liang went on, "Without marks of suffering, how could he take Cao Cao in? Now Huang Gai will be sent there as a deserter, while Cai Zhong and Cai He report what happened today. When you see Zhou Yu, though, don't tell him I saw through his ruse. Say I was just as shocked as all the others."

Lu Su returned to Zhou Yu, who saw him in private.

"Why did you have Huang Gai so cruelly beaten?" asked Lu Su.

"Do the officers resent it?"

"Most of them are very upset."

"What did Zhuge Liang make of it?"

"He blames you for being so heartless."

At that Zhou Yu laughed and exulted, "This time I fooled him!"

"What do you mean?" asked Lu Su.

"That beating Huang Gai got was part of a ruse. I am sending him as a deserter to Cao Cao, but I had to maltreat him first to fool them. Soon I shall go into action and burn their fleet. This is the way to beat Cao Cao."

Lu Su marvelled inwardly at Zhuge Liang's perception, but this time he said nothing.

Meanwhile Huang Gai was lying in his tent, and when brother officers came to condole with him, he said nothing but only sighed. However, when his aide-de-camp Kan Ze called, Huang Gai asked him into his sleeping quarters and sent away the attendants.

"Has Zhou Yu something against you?" asked Kan Ze.

"Nothing," replied Huang Gai.

"In that case, was your punishment just a ruse?"

"How did you guess?"

"I was pretty sure of it from his behaviour."

"I have been most generously treated by the house of Sun, all three of them,' said Huang Gai. "My only way to show my gratitude was by proposing this plan to defeat Cao Cao. I am suffering for it, but I have no regrets. Of all the men in the army, you are the only one I can confide in. Because you are loyal and just I dare tell you this."

"I take it you want me to deliver a letter to Cao Cao offering to go over?"

"Exactly. Will you do it?"

Kan Ze accepted the mission willingly.

> A brave general risks his life to repay his lord,
> A wise adviser shares his resolve to save their land.

To learn what else Kan Ze said you must read the next chapter.

CHAPTER 47

Kan Ze Presents a False Offer of Surrender
Pang Tong Proposes Chaining the Ships Together

This Kan Ze was a native of Shanyin in the province of Guiji. Son of a humble family, he was so eager to study that even when working as a hired hand he used to borrow books, and what he had once read he never forgot. He was an eloquent and fearless youth. After Sun Quan appointed him an adviser, he and Huang Gai became good friends, and it was his courage and persuasiveness that had made Huang Gai choose him to undertake this mission.

Kan Ze accepted readily, saying, "If a man can achieve no great deed in this world, he will perish like the grass and trees. Since you are sacrificing yourself for our lord, who am I to worry about my worthless life?"

Huang Gai struggled up from his bed to bow his thanks.

"There is no time to waste," said Kan Ze. "I must go at once."

"Good," said Huang Gai. "I have written the letter already."

Kan Ze took the letter and that same night, disguised as a fisherman, he went by a small boat to the north bank. It was frosty and the sky was full of stars. About midnight he reached Cao Cao's camp, where scouts seized him and reported at once to their chief.

"Is he a spy?" asked Cao Cao.

The men answered, "He looks like a fisherman but says he is Kan Ze, one of Sun Quan's advisers, come on secret business."

Cao Cao ordered him to be brought in, and Kan Ze was led into the brightly lighted tent where Cao Cao was sitting gravely at his desk.

"What business brings an adviser from Wu here?" asked Cao Cao.

Kan Ze answered, "People say that you welcome able men, but your question hardly bears that out. I think Huang Gai has made a mistake."

"Our two states may join battle at any time now, yet you come here in secret — why shouldn't I question you?"

"Huang Gai is a senior general of Wu who has served three successive rulers," said Kan Ze. "Now in front of all the other officers, Zhou Yu has had him cruelly and wantonly beaten. In his fury he wants to desert to you and take revenge. He discussed it with me, and since he and I are like brothers I came straight here in secret to deliver his letter. I hope you will accept him."

"Where is his letter?"

Kan Ze produced it and presented it.

Cao Cao opened it beneath the lamp and read:

> My debt of gratitude to my liege lord constrains loyalty to him, yet now we are pitting the troops of our six southern provinces against the million and more of the central plain. We are outmatched, as all can see. Every one of our officers, wise or foolish, knows this. Only that upstart Zhou Yu is such an opinionated and conceited fool that he wants to smash a stone with an egg. Like a tyrant he has punished me for no fault of my own, with no regard for my fine record. His unwarranted insult to me, a senior officer, is more than I can

stomach. I hear that you, Prime Minister, keep faith and treat gentlemen with due consideration. Then let me surrender with my troops and wipe out my shame by bold deeds. I shall bring my own ships, grain, forage and equipment. With tears of blood I make this request and beg you not to doubt me!

Cao Cao turned the letter this way and that and read it again and again. Then he banged the desk abruptly and glaring angrily at Kan Ze exclaimed, "Huang Gai is trying to trick me with this talk of ill-treatment. His offer to surrender is a plot, not to say an insult to my intelligence!" He ordered his men to drag Kan Ze out and kill him. The prisoner did not change countenance, however, but merely threw back his head and laughed aloud. Cao Cao called him back and bellowed, "I have seen through your trick. What is there for you to laugh at?"

"I wasn't laughing at you but at Huang Gai for sizing you up wrongly."

"What do you mean?"

"If you want to kill me, go ahead. Why waste time talking?"

"I have read all the books on the art of war and know all the tricks there are. This dodge of yours might fool others, but not me!"

"What is there in the letter that doesn't ring true?"

"I'll point out the holes in it so that you can't blame me for killing you. If he'd really meant to surrender, he would have named a time. What have you to say to that?"

Kan Ze laughed. "And you boast of your knowledge

of strategy! You had better withdraw at once with all your troops. If you fight, Zhou Yu will certainly capture you. How ignorant you are! To think I should die at the hands of such a man!"

"I ignorant? Why?" demanded Cao Cao.

"You are ignorant of strategy and you have no common sense. Isn't that enough?"

"Tell me, then, in what I am wrong?"

"Why should I, when you are so rude to able men? Just go ahead and kill me."

"If you can convince me, I'll treat you differently."

"How can a man make an appointment when he wants to do something behind his master's back? If we fixed a time but could not get away, and you sent men to meet us, the secret would be out. We must seize our chance when it comes. It's impossible to set a time beforehand. No, you have no common sense: all you can do is kill good men unjustly. This shows how ignorant you are."

At this Cao Cao's attitude changed. Leaving his seat he apologized to Kan Ze, saying, "I did not see clearly. Forgive me for offending you."

"Both Huang Gai and I were as eager to come over as children to see their parents. How could this be a trick?"

Delighted, Cao Cao said, "If the two of you will do me this great service, you shall have richer rewards than all the others."

"We are not coming over for the sake of rewards. We believe this to be the will of Heaven and of men."

Then Kan Ze was offered wine. And while they were drinking a man came in to whisper something to Cao Cao, who said, "Show me the letter!"

The man did so and the contents evidently pleased him.

Kan Ze thought, "It must be from Cai Zhong and Cai He reporting the punishment of Huang Gai. So Cao Cao is pleased and convinced that our offer is genuine."

Then Cao Cao said to him, "I'll trouble you to go back, sir, to arrange matters with Huang Gai. As soon as you send word, I will have a force waiting."

"But I have already left. I can't go back. Please send someone else you can trust, Prime Minister."

"If I send someone else, the secret may come out."

After repeated refusals, Kan Ze said, "Well, if I must go, there is no time to waste. I must be off at once."

Cao Cao offered him money and silk, but he declined them. Leaving the tent he rowed his small boat back to tell Huang Gai all that had happened.

"If not for your ready tongue," his friend remarked, "my beating would have been wasted."

"I'll go now to find out what Cai Zhong and Cai He are doing," said Kan Ze.

When Huang Gai agreed, he went to Gan Ning's headquarters, and the general invited him in.

"My heart bled for you yesterday," said Kan Ze, "when you tried to help Huang Gai and Zhou Yu insulted you."

Gan Ning smiled and made no comment. As they were talking the two spies came in and Kan Ze gave Gan Ning a meaning look. Taking his cue, Gan Ning gnashed his teeth and banged the table, shouting, "Zhou Yu thinks so highly of himself that the rest of us count for nothing! After what he did to me, how can I face my colleagues?"

Kan Ze made as if to whisper something to him, and Gan Ning bowed his head in silence, sighing.

When the two spies saw that they seemed ripe for desertion, they tried to provoke them by asking, "Why are you so indignant and upset?"

"How can you understand the conflict in my heart?" replied Kan Ze.

Cai He said, "I suspect that you want to leave Wu and go over to Cao Cao."

At that Kan Ze turned pale, while Gan Ning sprang up and drew his sword, exclaiming, "They have guessed! We must kill them to silence them."

In panic, the spies protested, "Don't worry, gentlemen! We'll let you into our secret."

"Quick, then!" said Gan Ning.

"Cao Cao sent us; we are not deserters," said Cai He. "If you want to go over to his side, we can introduce you."

"Is this the truth?" demanded Gan Ning.

With one voice they swore that it was.

Gan Ning put on a pleased look then and cried, "Why, this is a heaven-sent opportunity!"

The Cai brothers said, "We have already let the Prime Minister know how you and Huang Gai were insulted."

Kan Ze told them, "I have taken him a letter from Huang Gai and come back to persuade Gan Ning to join us."

Gan Ning said, "When an honest man encounters a wise lord, he should serve him with all his heart."

Then the four drank wine together and opened their

hearts to each other. The spies wrote a letter on the spot to their master, telling him that Gan Ning would help them from within the enemy ranks. Kan Ze also wrote and sent his letter secretly to Cao Cao, confirming that Huang Gai meant to go over and was merely biding his time. When a boat with a green flag was sighted, that would be his.

Not even these letters however, could dispel all Cao Cao's doubts. He summoned his advisers and told them, "Gan Ning down river has been insulted by Zhou Yu and wants to help us from their camp. Huang Gai has been punished and sent Kan Ze to offer to come over. But I don't trust either of them completely. Who will go to Zhou Yu's headquarters to find out the truth?"

Jiang Gan stepped forward and said, "Last time, to my great shame, I failed in my mission. Now let me risk my life again, and I promise to find out the truth for you."

Very pleased, Cao Cao told him to set off at once.

Jiang Gan rowed a small boat to the southern camp, and asked someone to announce him. Zhou Yu was delighted at his return, and said, "With him here, my success is sure!" He asked Lu Su to get Pang Tong to do something for him.

Now this Pang Tong of Xiangyang had come to the Lower Yangzi to escape from the wars. Lu Su had recommended him to Zhou Yu, but before he presented himself Zhou Yu had sent to ask him, "By what means can we defeat Cao Cao?"

And Pang Tong had told Lu Su, "You must use fire against him. But when one boat on the river catches fire, the others will drift away. I suggest that you propose chaining their ships together. This is the one way to succeed."

Lu Su relayed this to Zhou Yu, who agreed heartily and said, "Pang Tong is the only one who can help me achieve this."

Lu Su said, "Cao Cao is too crafty. How can he go?"

Zhou Yu was casting about for some solution at the time of Jiang Gan's arrival. Now, very pleased, he sent Pang Tong his instructions, then sat waiting in his tent for Jiang Gan.

The fact that Zhou Yu did not come out to meet him made Jiang Gan rather apprehensive, and he moored his boat in a quiet spot before going to his old friend's headquarters. When the two men met, Zhou Yu said with a look of displeasure, "What did you mean by treating me so badly?"

"I don't understand." Jiang Gan laughed. "For the sake of our old friendship I came to have a heart-to-heart talk with you."

"You will never persuade me to betray my master till the ocean dries up and boulders rot," said Zhou Yu. "Last time, because of our friendship, I entertained you to a good drinking bout and shared my bed with you. Yet you stole one of my private letters and left without saying goodbye. You betrayed me to Cao Cao, who killed Cai Mao and Zhang Yun so that my plan miscarried. What mischief are you up to now? If not for old times' sake, I would cut you in two! I can't send you back, because in a few days' time we are going to attack. If we let you stay here, you might find out some secrets." He ordered his men, "Take him to the monastery in the Western Hills. Let him go after Cao Cao is beaten."

Before Jiang Kan could speak, Zhou Yu had withdrawn. Guards brought a horse for the visitor and he was conducted to a small monastery at the back of the hills, where two soldiers were left to see to his needs.

Jiang Gan was too perturbed to eat or sleep. That night the stars were bright, and walking alone to the back of the monastery he heard someone reading aloud. Approaching the sound, he found a straw hut by the cliff with a light inside. Going closer and peering in, he saw a man with a sword reading an old military treatise under the lamp.

"This must be an unusual man!" thought he and knocked. The door was opened by the reader, who had a distinguished appearance. When asked his name he replied that he was Pang Tong.

"Surely not Master Phoenix Fledgling?" exclaimed Jiang Gan.

"Yes, I am he."

"I have long heard of your fame." Jiang Gan was delighted. "But what are you doing in this lonely spot?"

"Zhou Yu is so conceited and overbearing that I am living here in retirement. And may I know your name, sir?"

When Jiang Gan had told him, Pang Tong invited him in and they sat down to talk.

Jiang Gan said, "With your gifts, you would be welcome anywhere. If you would care to go to Cao Cao, I can introduce you."

Pang Tong said, "I have been wanting for some time to leave. If you will present me, let us go at once. If I stay here much longer, Zhou Yu will do me some injury."

So they left the hill in the dark, found Jiang Gan's

boat by the bank, and rowed as fast as they could to the north camp.

Upon reaching Cao Cao's stronghold, Jiang Gan went in first to make his report. When he knew that the celebrated Phoenix Fledgling was there Cao Cao went out of his tent to invite him in, and after they had taken seats Cao Cao said, "That young fellow Zhou Yu has too high an opinion of himself; he is a bully who ignores good advice. Your name has long been known to me, and now that you have honoured me with your presence I hope you will give us the benefit of your advice."

Pang Tong said, "I have heard much of your skill in strategy. May I have a look at your forces?"

Cao Cao called for horses and invited the guest to inspect his land units first. They rode up to high ground for a better view, and Pang Tong said, "Your army is encamped by hills and a forest, the front connected with the rear, with openings through which the men can move forward or back. Even those ancient strategists Sun Wuzi, Wu Qi and Sima Rangju* could do no better than this if they were here!"

"Don't flatter me," said Cao Cao. "I hope to benefit by your criticism too."

Then they went together to see the naval camp. There were twenty-four entrances to this with warships drawn up as ramparts and small boats within. There were channels to pass to and fro and the vessels were in good order.

Pang Tong said with a laugh, "Your reputation as a

---

* These men lived in the sixth, fourth and sixth centuries B.C. The writings of the first two are classics of military strategy.

commander is well deserved, Prime Minister!" Then pointing to the south he cried, "Ah, Zhou Yu! Your doom is at hand!"

Much elated, Cao Cao took him back and asked him into his tent. Drinking together they talked of the arts of war, and Pang Tong waxed eloquent, his words flowing like water. His host, filled with admiration, showed him marked respect.

Then Pang Tong, pretending to be tipsy, asked, "Have you good physicians in your army?"

Cao Cao asked the reason for this question.

"Your marines are prone to illness; you need good physicians for them."

The fact was that some of Cao Cao's men, unused to the climate here, had succumbed to disease. They kept vomiting and many of them had died. This was a source of anxiety to their commander; so when his guest mentioned the matter, he naturally sought his advice.

Pang Tong said, "Your naval training is excellent. Unfortunately there is one thing lacking."

"What is that?"

"I have a plan to cure all your naval forces so that you can be sure of victory."

Delighted, Cao Cao asked to be told this plan.

Pang Tong said, "On this river you have rising and falling tides as well as frequent winds and storms. Your men from the north are unused to ships, and the motion makes them sick. If you put all your vessels, large and small, in rows of thirty or fifty, their sterns and bows fastened with iron chains and covered with planks, even horses can travel on them safely, let alone men. With your fleet made fast in this way, you need no longer fear the winds and storms or the rising and falling tides."

Cao Cao rose from his seat to thank him, saying, "If not for this masterly plan, I should never have been able to defeat the armies of Wu."

"My ideas are foolish and shallow," said Pang Tong. "It is up to you to decide."

At once Cao Cao issued orders to his blacksmiths to lose no time in forging great chains and nails to fasten the ships together. And his men, hearing this, were glad.

Then Pang Tong said to Cao Cao, "I know many able men in the south who bear Zhou Yu a grudge. Let me go and win them over to you. For when Zhou Yu is alone with no one to help him, you can certainly defeat him. And once he is beaten, Liu Bei is powerless."

"If you can do us this great service, I shall ask the emperor to make you a chief minister."

"I am not after rank or riches, but simply want to help the people. When you cross the river, I hope you will be merciful."

"I am the instrument of Heaven's will. I should not dream of killing the common people."

Then Pang Tong asked for a decree to guarantee the safety of his clan.

"Where do they live?" asked Cao Cao.

"By the river bank. With such a decree they will be safe."

Cao Cao had the decree drawn up and having signed it he gave it to Pang Tong, who thanked him, saying, "I trust you will attack as soon as I have gone, before Zhou Yu gets wind of this."

Cao Cao agreed, and then Pang Tong took his leave.

When he reached the river and was about to embark, a man in a Taoist's gown and bamboo hat seized hold of him.

"What a nerve you have!" he said. "Huang Gai has himself beaten so that he may pretend to desert, and Kan Ze brings a false letter offering to surrender. Now you further propose this business with chains, so that you can burn up the entire fleet. These wicked schemes of yours may take Cao Cao in, but not me!"

Pang Tong was scared out of his wits.

> Though the men of the southeast could plot and
> scheme,
> There were able men in the northwest as well.

To know who this stranger was, you must read the next chapter.

CHAPTER 48

Cao Cao Feasting on the Yangzi Makes a Song

The Northern Force Attacks in Chained Ships

Pang Tong whirled round, aghast, only to find that the speaker was his old friend Xu Shu. Reassured, he looked round and saw no one else was near. "If you give me away," he said, "you will be the death of the people of eighty-one prefectures south of the Yangzi!"

Xu Shu retorted with a laugh, "What of the lives of Cao Cao's eight hundred and thirty thousand men?"

"Do you really mean to wreck my scheme, then?"

"I have always wanted to repay Liu Bei's kindness. And, because Cao Cao caused my mother's death,* I have sworn never to advise him any more. Why then should I wreck your scheme, brother? But I have followed Cao Cao's army here, and if it is defeated how am I to escape in the indiscriminate slaughter? Show me a safe way out and I promise to shut my mouth and keep out of the way!"

Pang Tong laughed. "For a man of your intelligence, that shouldn't be hard."

"Still I wish you would make some suggestion."

Then Pang Tong whispered something into his ear which pleased Xu Shu, who thanked him. After that Pang Tong took his leave and rowed back to the south bank.

That night Xu Shu secretly sent men to spread rumours in the camp. The next day the soldiers gathered

---

* Xu Shu had served under Liu Bei, but Cao Cao kept his mother in the north and forged a letter in her name ordering him to enter Cao Cao's service. When Xu returned to his mother and she learned why he had come, she hanged herself.

in threes and fours, heads together, their tongues busy wagging. And a scout reported to Cao Cao that Han Sui and Ma Teng of Xiliang were rumoured to have rebelled and to be advancing against Xuchang. Startled by this news, Cao Cao promptly summoned his advisers and said, "My one anxiety on this expedition has been Han Sui and Ma Teng in the rear. Now this rumour has spread through the army. Though there may be no truth in it, we must be on our guard."

At once Xu Shu stepped forward to speak. "I have lived on your bounty, Prime Minister, and done nothing in return. Give me three thousand horsemen and I shall go straight to the San Pass and guard it. You shall know at once of any emergency."

"If you will do this, I shall have no more worry," said Cao Cao, very pleased. "There are already troops at the pass, who will also be under your command. I shall give you three thousand men and Zang Ba as your vanguard. Go as fast as you can, without a moment's delay!"

Xu Shu took his leave and set off with Zang Ba. This was Pang Tong's plan for securing his old friend's safety.

Xu Shu's departure took a weight off Cao Cao's mind. After riding out to inspect his fortresses, he went to his naval camp, boarded a large ship and had his commander's flag hoisted on the mast. On both sides, from the upper deck, could be seen strong fortifications manned by a thousand archers. It was the fifteenth of the eleventh month, in the thirteenth year of the Jian An period.* The day was sunny and the water

* A.D. 208.

calm. Cao Cao ordered a feast on board for his officers that evening. When dusk fell, the moon rose over the eastern hills making all as bright as day. The Yangzi under the moonlight seemed a length of white silk. The Prime Minister sat there in state surrounded by hundreds of armed attendants in bright embroidered silk, while officers, civil and military, were seated in due order.

Cao Cao looked at the Nanping Hills, lovely as a painting, Chaisang in the east, Xiakou in the west, Mount Fan in the south, and Wulin in the north. Elated by the splendid prospect, he said to his officers, "Since devoting my forces to the just cause of ridding the Han empire of evil influences, I have vowed to cleanse all the land within the Four Seas and pacify the whole world. Now only the Yangzi Valley remains unsubdued. With my million veterans and all you gentlemen to help me, I have no doubt of success. Once the Lower Yangzi Valley is conquered and the empire at peace, together we shall enjoy prosperity and honour, living in happiness and tranquillity."

All his officers rose from their seats to thank him, saying, "We hope for a speedy victory. All our lives we shall shelter under your good fortune!"

In high good humour, Cao Cao called for more wine and they drank till midnight. Then, very merry, he pointed to the south bank, saying, "Zhou Yu and Lu Su do not know the will of Heaven. But now some of their men are on our side, working against them from within. Heaven is aiding us!"

"Do not speak of that, Prime Minister," cautioned Xun You, "or the secret may leak out."

Cao Cao only laughed and answered, "I can trust

you, gentlemen, and my attendants as well. What harm is there in mentioning this?" Pointing to Xiakou he went on, "Liu Bei and Zhuge Liang are mere ants, yet the fools want to challenge Mount Tai!" Then turning to his officers he said, "I am fifty-four this year. If I subdue the Yangzi Valley, I have one desire. Lord Qiao was a good friend of mine in the old days, and I know his two daughters are lovely beyond compare; but they were married to Sun Ce and Zhou Yu. I have recently built the Tower of the Bronze Bird by the River Zhang. If I subdue the Yangzi Valley, I shall take these two beauties to this tower to comfort my declining years. Then all my wishes will be satisfied." With that he laughed heartily.

As Cao Cao was talking and laughing, he heard crows cawing in their southward flight.

"What makes them caw at night?" he asked.

His attendants answered, "They have mistaken the bright moonlight for dawn. So they fly cawing from the trees."

At that Cao Cao laughed again. He was now quite drunk. Grasping his lance, he took his stand at the prow, poured a libation of wine into the river, and drained three brimming cups. Then lowering the lance he said to his officers, "With this lance I have vanquished the Yellow Turbans, captured Lü Bu, destroyed Yuan Shu, conquered Yuan Shao and penetrated deep into the northern wastes as far as Liaodong. I have ranged the whole empire, not failing in my great task. This scene today stirs me to the depths. I will sing a song, and you can join in the chorus." And so he sang:

Songs should go with wine,
For man's life is short
As the morning dew;
How much time has passed!
Deeply moved at heart,
I cannot forget my grief;
The one thing to banish care
Is Du Kang's* brew.
Blue is the scholar's gown.
Deep my admiration;
I ponder and look around;
All my thoughts are of you.
Stags cry as they crop
On wormwood in the wilds;
I have honoured guests,
Sound citherns and flutes!
Bright is the moon,
Revolving without end;
My heart is full of care,
Which will never cease.
Friends cross fields and meadows
To come to me;
We feast and make merry,
And think of friendships past.
Bright the moon and few the stars,
Crows are southward bound;
Three times they circle the trees,
But can find no place of rest.
The mountain can never be too high,
Nor the ocean too deep.

---

*Known in legend as the first man to brew wine.

The Duke of Zhou* stopped his meal to welcome
  guests,
And all men flocked to him.

He sang and the officers joined in the chorus. They
were all very merry except one man who approached
him and said, "On the eve of battle, when men must
risk their lives, why do you utter such ill-omened
words?"

Cao Cao saw that the speaker was Liu Fu, prefect of
Yangzhou, a native of Xiang County in the Principality
of Pei. This Liu Fu had begun his career at Hefei,
where he had ruled a prefecture, rallied all those who
were running away, set up schools, made the soldiers
till the land, and succeeded in restoring order. He
had served Cao Cao for many years and had rendered
valuable service.

Holding his lance at the level, Cao Cao asked, "What
did I say that was ill-omened?"

"You spoke of crows flying southward under a bright
moon and few stars, circling the trees three times yet
finding no resting place. This is a bad omen."

Cao Cao flared up and shouted, "How dare you try
to spoil my pleasure?" Thrusting with his lance, he
killed Liu Fu on the spot, to the horror of all the assembled. So the feast broke up.

The next day, recovered from the effects of wine,
Cao Cao was full of remorse. When Liu Fu's son Liu
Xi asked for the body of his father for burial, Cao Cao
shed tears. "Yesterday I was drunk," he said. "I
should never have killed your father, but it is too late

* An outstanding statesman of the eleventh century B.C.

for regret. Bury him with the honours of a chief minister." He sent soldiers to escort the coffin back that same day for burial.

The following day his naval commanders, Mao Jie and Yu Jin, came to report, "All the vessels, large and small, have been chained together and our flags and weapons are ready. Please give the order to set sail."

Cao Cao took his place in a large ship in the centre of the squadron, where all his officers were gathered to receive orders.

The different units of the land and naval forces were distinguished by flags of five different colours. The flag of the main naval force under Mao Jie and Yu Jin was yellow, that of the vanguard under Zhang He red, the rearguard under Lü Qian had a black flag, the left force under Wen Pin a green one, and the right force under Lü Dong a white one. The vanguard of the cavalry and infantry led by Xu Huang had a red banner, the rearguard led by Li Dian a black one, Yue Jin's left force a green one, and Xiahou Yuan's right force a white one. Xiahou Dun and Cao Hong were in charge of liaison between the land and naval forces, while Xu Chu and Zhang Liao were responsible for troop movements during battle. All the officers were assigned to different units.

After Cao Cao had issued his orders, drums were sounded three times in the naval camp, and the ships sailed out by different ways. There was a strong northwest wind that day, yet the vessels with their sails hoisted charged through the waves as securely as on dry land. The northerners exercised vigorously aboard with spears and swords, and the different squadrons kept to their appointed places, while more than fifty small boats plied to and fro inspecting the advance.

Cao Cao, watching the manoeuvres from his platform, was delighted to think he had found the way to certain victory. He ordered the ships to furl sail and they returned to the camp in perfect order.

Back in his tent, Cao Cao told his advisers, "If Heaven were not on my side, should I have got this marvellous plan from the Phoenix Fledgling? By chaining the boats together, we can cross the river as if it were dry land."

Cheng Yu said, "It is true that chaining makes them secure; but in case of attack by fire we should find it hard to get away. This is the danger."

Cao Cao laughed. "You look well ahead, yet there is something you have overlooked."

"Cheng Yu is right," said Xun You. "Why do you laugh at the idea?"

Cao Cao replied, "Attack by fire depends largely on the wind. Now this is the middle of winter, when only the west and north winds blow, not those from the east or south. We are on the northwest, the enemy on the south bank. If they use fire, they will destroy themselves. So we have nothing to fear. Had this been the tenth month, I should have taken precautions."

This convinced all his officers, who exclaimed, "The Prime Minister is more far-sighted than any of us."

Looking round at the assembly, Cao Cao said, "Our men from the north are not used to boats. If not for this plan, how could we cross the dangerous Yangzi?"

Then two officers stepped forward and declared, "Though we come from the north, we are accustomed to the water. Give us twenty boats and we shall go straight to capture the enemy's flags and drums. That will show that we of the north can fight on water too."

The speakers were Jiao Chu and Zhang Nan, two of Yuan Shao's former officers.

"I doubt if you, coming from the north, can succeed," said Cao Cao. "The men of these parts are thoroughly at home on the river. This is no game but a matter of life and death."

Still the two protested loudly, "If we fail, we are willing to suffer any punishment!"

"All the large ships are chained together. That leaves only small boats, each of which holds no more than twenty men. They would be little use in a fight."

"It would not be a remarkable feat if we used big ships," said Jiao Chu. "Let us have a score of the small boats, half for Zhang Nan and half for myself. We shall go straight to the enemy's camp today, seize a flag, kill a commander and come back!"

"I'll give you twenty boats and five hundred picked troops armed with lances and powerful crossbows. At daybreak tomorrow we shall send out the large vessels to awe the enemy from a distance, and Wen Pin shall go with thirty boats to cover your return."

Then the two officers went away satisfied.

The next morning food was prepared at the fourth watch. By the fifth watch all was ready. When drums and gongs sounded in the naval camp, the ships moved out and took up their positions on the river. All along the Yangzi green and red banners fluttered. Then Jiao Chu and Zhang Nan set off with twenty scouting boats for the south bank.

The forces on the south bank had heard the din and drumming the previous day and seen Cao Cao's naval manoeuvres in the distance. Scouts reported this to Zhou Yu, who climbed to the top of a hill to watch; but Cao Cao's troops had already withdrawn. This morning there was another thunderous drumming, and when scouts climbed to high ground to have a look, they saw small boats bounding towards them over the waves. They hastily reported this to headquarters. Zhou Yu called for volunteers to engage the enemy, and Han Dang and Zhou Tai offered themselves. Zhou Yu was pleased and ordered his different commanders to be vigilant and not move into action rashly.

Han Dang and Zhou Tai sailed out separately, each with five scouting boats.

Meanwhile the small craft of bold Jiao Chu and Zhang Nan were bearing down on them swiftly. Wearing armour, his lance in his hand, Han Dang stood in the prow of his boat. Jiao Chu, who was ahead of Zhang Nan, ordered his men to shoot once they came within range, but Han Dang warded off the arrows with his shield. And when Jiao Chu attacked with his lance, with one thrust Han Dang killed him.

Zhang Nan was coming up with great shouts when Zhou Tai intercepted him. The northern officer was standing in the prow with his lance, while his men were shooting wildly. When the two boats were still some seven or eight feet apart, Zhou Tai, his shield in one hand, a sword in the other, leapt on to the enemy's boat. One sweep of his sword and Zhang Nan toppled into the river. Then Zhou set about killing the rest of the crew. The other boats turned and rowed hard for the north bank. Han Dang and Zhou Tai pursued them as fast as they could. In midstream, Wen Pin's squadron came up, and the battle was on again.

Zhou Yu with some of his officers was standing on a hill to watch the northern warships, which were deployed in good order with their different banners and ensigns. Then he saw Wen Pin engage Han Dang and Zhou Tai, who attacked so hard that the northerners could not withstand them but turned to retire with the southerners after them. Not wanting his commanders to get too far into enemy waters, Zhou Yu hoisted a white flag and sounded gongs to recall them. Then Han and Zhou brought their boats back.

From the hilltop Zhou Yu could see that the enemy's ships across the river were withdrawing into their camp. He turned and said to his officers, "The northern vessels are packed as closely as reeds, and Cao Cao is very wily. How can we defeat him?"

Before anyone could answer, the flagpole of the yellow banner in the centre of the enemy fleet snapped in the wind and fell into the river. Zhou Yu laughed aloud. "That's a bad omen for them!"

That same instant a strong wind sprang up, making waves beat against the shore. Zhou Yu's banner flapped against his cheek, and a thought flashed through his mind. With a sudden cry he fell backwards, coughing up blood. His men hastened to lift him up, for he had fainted.

> Sudden laughter, a sudden cry;
> Hard for men of the south to beat those of the north!

To know what became of Zhou Yu, you must read the next chapter.

CHAPTER 49

Zhuge Liang Prays for Wind at the Altar of Seven Stars
At Sanjiangkou Zhou Yu Sets Fire to the Enemy Fleet

After watching from the hilltop for some time, Zhou Yu suddenly coughed up blood and fell unconscious. He was carried back to his tent, where his officers coming to inquire after him looked at each other in dismay and said, "Our enemies are more than a million, and they are like ravening beasts. But now our commander is ill, what if Cao Cao attacks?" Hastily sending a report to Sun Quan, they summoned a physician.

Lu Su was very worried and went to tell Zhuge Liang of Zhou Yu's sudden seizure.

"What do you make of it?" asked Zhuge Liang.

"It's a stroke of good luck for Cao Cao, a calamity for us."

Zhuge Liang said with a smile, "I know how to cure him."

"If you do, that will be a great thing for our state."

He took Zhuge Liang with him to see Zhou Yu, and going in first found the commander in bed, his head covered by a quilt.

"How do you feel now, general?" asked Lu Su.

"I have a pain in my heart and dizzy spells."

"What medicine have you taken?"

"I feel too nauseated to swallow anything."

"Just now I saw Zhuge Liang, who says he can cure you. I left him outside. Would you like to try his treatment?"

Zhou Yu asked him to bring Zhuge Liang in and made his attendants help him sit up in bed.

"I haven't seen you for some days," said Zhuge Liang. "I never thought you would fall ill."

" 'A man is the plaything of fate.' No one is safe."

Zhuge Liang chuckled. "Yes, and sudden changes in Nature are unpredictable, too."

Zhou Yu changed colour at this and uttered a groan.

"Is your heart restless and anxious?" asked Zhuge Liang.

"It is indeed!"

"You must take a cooling draught to calm yourself."

"I have done, but it was quite useless."

"First regulate the humours, then your breathing will become regular and you will be cured."

Suspecting that Zhuge Liang knew what was troubling him, Zhou Yu asked, "What medicine must I take for that?"

Zhuge Liang laughed. "I have a prescription which should help."

"I wish you would tell me."

Then Zhuge Liang asked for a pen and paper, sent away the attendants and wrote down these words, "To defeat Cao Cao you must use fire. Now all is ready, but there is no east wind."

He handed this paper to Zhou Yu, saying, "This is my diagnosis of your illness."

When Zhou Yu saw this he was taken aback and thought, "Zhuge Liang is truly amazing! Since he knows what is troubling me, I might as well tell him the truth." He said with a laugh, "If you know the cause of my illness, please tell me how to cure it. The case is growing serious."

"Small though my talents are," said Zhuge Liang, "I once knew a magician who taught me how to summon winds and rain. If you want a southeast wind, you must build an altar on the Nanping Hills, calling it the Altar of Seven Stars. It should be nine feet high with three tiers, surrounded by a hundred and twenty men holding flags. Then I will use magic at the altar to make a strong southeast wind blow for three days and three nights. Would that help your campaign?"

"One night of wind would do, let alone three days and three nights. But the matter is very urgent. Speed is essential!"

"I will call up the wind on the twentieth of the eleventh month, if you like, and make it end on the twenty-second."

Zhou Yu was so pleased that he got up at once, quite cured, and sent five hundred picked troops to the hills to build the altar. Another hundred and twenty men with flags were dispatched to guard it and wait for further instructions.

Zhuge Liang took his leave and rode off with Lu Su to look for a suitable site in the Nanping Hills. He made the soldiers take red earth from southeast of the hill to build the altar. It was two hundred and forty feet across, with three tiers each three feet high, nine feet in all. On the bottom tier he set flags symbolizing the twenty-eight constellations: on the east seven green flags with the sign of the grey dragon of the east, on the north seven black flags with the sign of the dark tortoise of the north, on the west seven white flags with the sign of the white tiger of the west, on the south seven red flags with the sign of the red sparrow of the south. On the second tier, in groups of eight, were sixty-four yellow flags corresponding to the sixty-four trigrams. On the top tier stood four men wearing chaplets, dark silk robes, phoenix coats, broad belts, red sandals and square-cut skirts. The one at the left front carried a long pole surmounted by chicken feathers to show when there was a wind; the one at the right front carried a long pole bearing a belt with the symbol of the seven stars to show the direction of the wind. The man at the left rear carried a sword, the man at the right rear an incense-burner. Below the altar, ranged round it, were four and twenty men holding flags, umbrellas, halberds, lances, yellow spears with yak tails, white hatchets, red pennants and black ensigns.

On the twentieth Zhuge Liang, having bathed and fasted, put on a priestly gown and went barefoot with loosed hair to the altar.

He told Lu Su, "Go back to the army and help Zhou Yu make his dispositions. Don't be surprised, though, if my prayers go unanswered."

After Lu Su had left, Zhuge Liang forbade the guards at the altar, on penalty of death, to leave their posts, talk or whisper to each other, or show the least alarm. Then he slowly ascended the altar for a final inspection, after which he burned incense, filled a vessel with holy water, looked up to the sky and prayed. He left the altar, returning to rest in his tent, and told the soldiers to take their meals in turn. He mounted and descended the altar three times that day, but no southeast wind arose.

Meanwhile Zhou Yu had asked Cheng Pu, Lu Su and his other officers to wait in their tents till a southeast wind sprang up, when they could dispatch their forces. At the same time he sent a request to Sun Quan for reinforcements. Huang Gai had prepared twenty fire-ships, their prows studded with large nails, which were loaded with reeds or straw soaked in fish oil topped with inflammables like sulphur and saltpetre. These ships were covered with black material and oil-cloth. In their prows were green dragon flags, and at their sterns small boats were fastened. All were waiting, ready for the order to sail.

Gan Ning and Kan Ze were keeping Cai He and Cai Zhong aboard their ship, drinking with them every day and not allowing a man to go ashore. They were so closely guarded by the forces of Wu, that not a drop of water could have leaked through, as they held themselves in readiness for Zhou Yu's signal.

As Zhou Yu conferred in his tent with his officers, scouts reported that Sun Quan's fleet had moored eighty-five *li* away to await developments. Lu Su was sent to tell the officers and men to have their ships, weapons, sails and oars quite ready. The instant the order came, they must go into action. Any disobedience would be punished by martial law. All hearing this order made ready, rubbing their hands and preparing eagerly for battle.

Night was falling, yet the sky was still clear and there was not the least breeze. Zhou Yu said to Lu Su, "Zhuge Liang didn't know what he was talking about. A southeast wind in mid-winter? Impossible!"

Lu Su said, "I don't think Zhuge Liang makes empty boasts."

Towards the third watch they suddenly heard the sound of wind, and the flags began to flutter. When Zhou Yu went out to look, the tassel on his banner was streaming towards the northwest. In no time there was a strong southeasterly wind.

Zhou Yu exclaimed, "Why, the fellow has the power to change the course of Nature: he is more than human! If we let him live, he will be the ruin of our state. I had better kill him now to avoid trouble later." He sent at once for his tribunes Ding Feng and Xu Sheng, and told them to take a hundred men each, one party by water and the other by land, to the altar in the Nanping Hills. There, without asking questions, they were to seize and behead Zhuge Liang. They would be rewarded when they brought back his head.

The two accepted these orders. Xu Sheng and a hundred men armed with swords and axes set off by boat, while Ding Feng with a hundred bowmen went on horseback to the hills. The southeast wind blew in their faces all the way.

Ding Feng's party was the first to arrive. He saw the guards with their flags standing in the wind. But when he dismounted and marched with drawn sword up the altar, Zhuge Liang was nowhere to be seen. Taken aback, he questioned the guards, who told him, "He has just left."

As he started hurriedly down to make a search, Xu Sheng's boat arrived, and the two men met on the bank.

There a soldier told them, "Yesterday evening a small, fast boat moored just inside the bay. A few moments ago Zhuge Liang, his hair loosed, stepped aboard. The boat has gone upstream."

Ding and Xu set off in pursuit by land and water. Xu put on all sail to take full advantage of the wind, and presently they sighted a boat ahead. Then, standing in the prow, he shouted, "Stop, adviser! The commander wants to see you."

Zhuge Liang, standing in the stern, laughed heartily.

"Go back and tell your commander to make good use of his men. I am off to Xiakou for a while, but hope to see him again another day."

"Please wait a little," urged Xu Sheng. "This business is urgent."

"I know what it is. Your commander can't endure me and has sent you to kill me. That's why I took the precaution of asking Zhao Yun to meet me. It's no use your chasing me any further."

Since the other boat had no sail up, Xu Sheng pursued it hard. But as he drew near, Zhao Yun appeared in the stern, fitting an arrow to his bow. "I am Zhao Yun!" he shouted. "My orders were to come and fetch our adviser. What do you mean by chasing us like this? With one arrow I could kill you, but between allies that might look unfriendly. I'll just show you what I can do!"

As he spoke, his arrow flew to cut through their rigging. The sail toppled into the water and the boat swung round. Then Zhao Yun hoisted sail on his own craft, and the fair wind carried it rapidly off out of reach of its pursuers.

Ding Feng on the bank hailed Xu and said, "Zhuge Liang is without an equal for uncanny foresight. And Zhao Yun is a match for ten thousand men. Remember what he did at Changban Slope in Dangyang?* All we can do is go back and report this."

So they went back and told Zhou Yu how Zhuge Liang had arranged beforehand to be met. Zhou Yu

---

* When Cao Cao attacked Jingzhou, Zhao Yun who was serving under Liu Bei fought very bravely at Dangyang against Cao Cao's pursuing troops and covered Liu Bei's retreat with success.

was staggered. "This man is so infernally crafty, I cannot have a moment's peace day or night!" he cried.

"Wait till Cao Cao is beaten to deal with him," said Lu Su.

Then Zhou Yu issued orders to his officers. He bade Gan Ning take Cai Zhong and his men along the south bank. "Using the banners of the northern army, go straight to Wulin where Cao Cao keeps his supplies. Then strike deep into the enemy camp, and signal by fire when you reach your destination. Leave Cai He behind. I have other uses for him."

Next he ordered Taishi Ci, "Take three thousand men straight to Huangzhou to cut off enemy reinforcements from Hefei. As soon as you meet Cao Cao's forces, signal by fire. When you see a red banner, that will be Sun Quan coming to relieve you."

These two forces had the farthest to go, so they set off first. Then Lü Meng was sent with three thousand men to Wulin to help Gan Ning by setting fire to Cao Cao's ramparts. Another three thousand men, led by Ling Tong, were to cut through Yiling and go to Lü Meng's aid when they saw the fire signal there. A fifth party of the same size under Dong Xi was to capture Hanyang and attack Cao Cao from Hanchuan. They would be reinforced by three thousand troops with white banners under Pan Zhang.

When these six forces had set off, Huang Gai made his fire-ships ready and sent a soldier with a message to Cao Cao, saying that he would go over that very night. Four squadrons commanded by Han Dang, Zhou Tai, Jiang Qin and Chen Wu were assigned to support Huang Gai. Each squadron had three hundred vessels with twenty fire-ships in front. Zhou Yu and Cheng Pu would direct operations from their large galley, Xu Sheng and Ding Feng would act as escorts on both sides, while Lu Su, Kan Ze and others were left to guard the camp. Zhou Yu's expert disposal of his troops filled Cheng Pu with admiration.

Then a messenger came from Sun Quan with the army tally to announce that Lu Xun, at the head of the van, was advancing towards Qizhou and Huang-zhou, followed by Sun Quan himself. Zhou Yu thereupon sent men to the Western Hills and Nanping Hills to signal and hoist flags at the time appointed. All being ready, they waited for dusk to go into action.

Let us turn back now to Liu Bei, who was waiting at Xiakou for Zhuge Liang's return. A fleet arrived with Liu Qi, who had come for news. Liu Bei asked him to the ramparts and when they were seated said, "A southeast wind has been blowing for some time, and Zhao Yun has gone for Zhuge Liang. I am rather worried because they are not back yet."

His guard pointed towards Fankou, saying, "A boat in full sail is coming this way. It must be our adviser."

The two commanders hurried down to meet the boat, and soon Zhuge Liang and Zhao Yun came ashore, to the great joy of Liu Bei.

After an exchange of greetings, Zhuge Liang said, "There is no time to report on other matters. Are your cavalry and warships ready as we planned?"

"Ready long ago, just waiting for your instructions."

Zhuge Liang accompanied them to the headquarters, where he told Zhao Yun, "Take three thousand cavalry across the river by a short cut to Wulin, and lay an ambush in the dense forest. After the fourth watch tonight, Cao Cao will be escaping that way. When his troops arrive, start a fire. Even if you cannot kill them all, you will destroy a good half."

"There are two ways to Wulin," said Zhao Yun. "One leads to Nanjun, the other to Jingzhou. Which path do you think he will take?"

"Nanjun is too dangerous for him. Cao Cao will not dare take that road. He will make for Jingzhou so that he can retreat towards Xuchang."

Zhao Yun left to carry out his instructions. Then Zhuge Liang told Zhang Fei to take three thousand men across the river, cut the road to Yiling and lay an ambush in the Gourd Valley. "Cao Cao will not dare go to South Yiling but will go to North Yiling," he said. "He will halt there tomorrow after the rain for a meal. When you see the smoke from his fires, set the valley ablaze. Even if you fail to capture Cao Cao, you will win a great victory."

When Zhang Fei too had left, Zhuge Liang told Mi Zhu, Mi Fang and Liu Feng to embark and give the finishing blows to the enemy fleet and to capture all the weapons they could.

After they had gone, Zhuge Liang rose from his seat and said to Liu Qi, "Wuchang is a strategic point. Go back there and station your troops in the harbour. Some of Cao Cao's defeated soldiers will retreat there and you can capture them. But don't leave the city!"

Then Liu Qi took his leave.

Last of all, Zhuge Liang said to Liu Bei, "You, my lord, can station your troops at Fankou and watch the battle from the height. You will see Zhou Yu win a great victory tonight."

Guan Yu, who had long been waiting his turn, had

been completely ignored. Losing patience, he now said loudly, "I have fought under my sworn brother all these years and never lagged behind. Now we are going to fight a great battle, but I am given nothing to do! What does this mean?"

Zhuge Liang smiled and said, "Don't take offence. I would like you to guard a most important point, but I have some scruples about asking you."

"What scruples? I wish you would tell me."

"Cao Cao once entertained you so generously* that you must feel some gratitude to him. In his defeat, he will flee along the Huarong Road, and if I post you there you may let him pass. That is why I hesitate to send you."

Guan Yu protested, "How can you doubt me like that? True, Cao Cao treated me well; but by killing Yan Liang and Wen Chou in battle and helping him raise the siege of Baima, I have repaid him. If I meet him today, I certainly shan't let him pass."

"What if you do?"

"You can punish me according to martial law!"

"Very well. Put that in writing."

Guan Yu did so and asked, "What if Cao Cao doesn't pass that way?"

"I can sign a pledge too."

Guan Yu was delighted.

Zhuge Liang went on, "You can stack wood and

---

* When Cao Cao attacked Xuzhou, Guan Yu, surrounded by enemy troops, lost contact with Liu Bei and was forced to surrender. But Cao Cao treated him with courtesy. Later, when Guan Yu learned of Liu Bei's whereabouts, he left Cao Cao to return to his sworn brother.

grass on high ground on the road to Huarong, and set fire to it to lure Cao Cao on."

"If he sees smoke, he will know there is an ambush and keep away."

Zhuge Liang smiled. "Don't you know that in strategy you should combine truth and falsehood? Cao Cao is a good strategist; this is the only way to fool him. When he sees the smoke, he will think it a ruse and will certainly take that way. But don't be too soft-hearted!"

Accordingly Guan Yu left with Guan Ping, Zhou Cang and five hundred swordsmen to lay an ambush on the road to Huarong.

Liu Bei said, "Brother Guan Yu sets great store by friendship. If Cao Cao really takes the Huarong Road, I am afraid he may let him go."

"I have studied the signs in the skies at night, and Cao Cao is not fated to perish yet. It will be as well to let Guan Yu do this kind deed."

"Surely no other man sees as far as you!" said Liu Bei.

Then, leaving Sun Qian and Jian Yong on guard, the two of them went to Fankou to see how Zhou Yu conducted the battle.

Cao Cao in his camp was conferring with his officers while waiting for news from Huang Gai. When a strong southeast wind sprang up, Cheng Yu reported it, saying, "A southeasterly wind is blowing. We must take precautions."

But Cao Cao laughed and said, "The winter solstice is the time when spring starts to revive. During the moment of change, there may naturally be a southeast wind. That is nothing to be alarmed about."

Then scouts reported the arrival of a small boat from the east with a messenger bringing a secret note from Huang Gai. Cao Cao sent for the man, who presented the letter. It said, "Zhou Yu kept such a strict watch that I could not get away before. Now some grain is being shipped here from Lake Boyang, and I am in charge of the convoy. I am now in a position to start things going. I will try to kill a few well-known officers of Wu and bring you their heads when I come. Expect me at midnight. The boats with the green dragon flags are my grain ships."

Exulting, Cao Cao went with his officers to the naval camp and boarded a large ship to watch for Huang Gai's coming.

As dusk approached, Zhou Yu sent for Cai He and ordered soldiers to bind him. When the spy protested his innocence, Zhou Yu said, "How dare you come here pretending to be a deserter? I need a victim to sacrifice to my flag. For that I shall take your head."

Seeing that denial was useless, Cai He shouted, "Your officers Kan Ze and Gan Ning were in this too!"

"They joined your plot by my orders!" said Zhou Yu.

It was too late for Cai He to repent. Zhou Yu had him taken to the black flag by the river. There he poured a libation, burned sacrificial paper and with one sweep of his sword beheaded the spy, sacrificing his blood to the flag.

Then the fleet received the order to advance. Huang Gai was on the third fire-ship. He had a breast-plate on and a sword in his hand. Written large on his flag were the words, "Huang Gai, General of the Vanguard." And so with a fair wind they sailed towards the Red Cliff.

The strong easterly wind was making the waves pitch and toss. Cao Cao from his camp was watching the opposite shore. When the moon rose over the river, countless golden serpents seemed to be rolling in the waves. With the wind in his face, Cao Cao laughed aloud, sure of success.

Suddenly a soldier pointed to the river and said, "Look at all those sails heading up this way with the wind!"

Cao Cao climbed up higher to watch. Then his scouts reported that all the boats had green dragon flags and one carried a great banner with the name Huang Gai.

"Yes, he has come over." Cao Cao laughed. "Heaven is on our side!"

As the boats drew nearer, Cheng Yu, who had been watching closely, said, "This must be a trick. Don't let them come too near." When Cao Cao demanded the reason, he explained, "If there were grain in them, those boats would be deep in the water. But as you can see, they are light and float easily. Tonight there is a strong southeast wind. If they mean mischief, how are we to stop them?"

At once Cao Cao saw the truth of this and asked, "Who will go and intercept them?"

Wen Pin said, "I know the river well. Let me go." With that he leapt into a small craft and signed to a dozen or so scouting boats to go with him. Standing in the prow of his boat he shouted, "By order of the

Prime Minister, you southern boats are to come no nearer! Cast anchor there in midstream!"

His soldiers yelled to them to lower their sails. But while they were shouting a bowstring twanged and Wen Pin fell with an arrow through his left arm. Thrown into confusion, all his boats withdrew.

Huang Gai's squadron was now two *li* only from the enemy fleet. He waved his sword and the leading ships burst into flame. The fire was fanned by the wind, and the twenty boats sped like arrows. The smoke billowing from them blotted out the sky. They dashed against Cao Cao's fleet, setting light to it too. And since the northern vessels were chained together they could not get away.

A signal was given on the other bank, and all the fire-ships converged on Sanjiangkou. The wind spread the conflagration far and wide till a lurid glare lit up the earth and sky. When Cao Cao turned towards the shore to look at his tents, some were already ablaze.

Huang Gai leapt into a small boat with a few oarsmen, and shot through the flames and smoke in search of Cao Cao. Cao Cao, seeing his danger, decided to go ashore; and Zhang Liao bringing up a light boat helped him into it. The large vessel was already on fire as Zhang Liao with ten men or more escorted him swiftly to the bank.

Huang Gai had seen a man in red leave the flagship. Knowing that this must be Cao Cao, he urged his boat on and brandishing his sword shouted, "Stop, you rebel! Here comes Huang Gai!"

Cao Cao cried out in dismay, but as Huang Gai approached Zhang Liao drew his bow and let fly an arrow. The roaring of the wind and flames drowned the twang of the bowstring, and with the arrow through his shoulder Huang Gai fell into the water.

> From peril of burning he fell into peril of drowning;
> The scars of his beating still fresh, he was wounded anew!

To know whether Huang Gai lived or died, read the next chapter.

CHAPTER 50

Zhuge Liang's Prediction Comes True at Huarong
Guan Yu in His Kindness Releases Cao Cao

After shooting Huang Gai so that he fell into the river,
Zhang Liao got Cao Cao ashore and found horses for
immediate flight. By then the whole army was in utter
confusion. As Han Dang pressed through the smoke
and flames to attack Cao Cao's naval camp, his soldiers
told him, "A man is clinging to the rudder and shouting your name!" Han Dang listened carefully and
heard the cry, "Han Dang! Save me!"

"Why, that is Huang Gai!" he cried and promptly
had him pulled aboard.

Huang Gai had broken off the arrow in his shoulder,
leaving only the tip embedded in his flesh. Han Dang
quickly pulled off his friend's wet clothes, removed the
arrow-head with a knife, and tore up a flag to bandage
the wound. Then he gave him his own robe and sent
him back by another boat to their camp for treatment.
Huang Gai was such a good swimmer that although he
had fallen in full armour into the river, and the water
was bitterly cold, he had escaped drowning.

It was a mighty battle indeed that day at the Red
Cliff! The river was a mass of flames, and battle cries
reverberated from the banks. The forces of Han Dang
and Jiang Qin attacked from the west of the Red Cliff,
those of Zhou Tai and Chen Wu from the east. In the
centre was the main fleet led by Zhou Yu, Cheng Pu,
Xu Sheng and Ding Feng. The fighters followed up the
destruction by fire, and the fire lent its fierceness to the
fighters. Spears and arrows took a heavy toll of Cao

Cao's men. Countless others were burned to death or drowned in the river.

Leaving the battle on the river, let us turn to the shore. Gan Ning made Cai Zhong lead him through the northern camp, then cut him down from his horse with one sweep of his sword and set fire to the grass. When Lü Meng, some way off, saw the flames in Cao Cao's headquarters, he followed Gan Ning's lead and set fire to a dozen more places. Pan Zhang and Dong Xi did the same elsewhere, raising a great din and thunder of drums all around.

Cao Cao and Zhang Liao with about a hundred horsemen galloped through the burning forest — everywhere was ablaze. Presently Mao Jie, who had rescued Wen Pin, joined them with a dozen more horsemen. Cao Cao ordered them to find a way out, and pointing ahead Zhang Liao said, "There is more open ground in Wulin. Let us go that way!"

As they headed for Wulin, a party of the enemy came after them, calling, "Halt, you traitor!" In the light of the flames, they saw Lü Meng's name on the flag. Cao Cao urged his men on, leaving Zhang Liao to hold Lü Meng off.

But presently more torches gleamed ahead and another force charged out of the valley crying, "Here is Ling Tong!" Cao Cao was nearly paralysed with fright when a third party interposed itself from one side, and the newcomers cried, "All is well, Prime Minister! Xu Huang is here!" While Xu Huang battled with Ling Tong, Cao Cao fled to the north.

When more cavalry was sighted on the slope ahead, Xu Huang reconnoitred and found the officers in command were Ma Yan and Zhang Yi, who had served under Yuan Shao but come over to Cao Cao. They had three thousand men and horses encamped here; but the blazing fires all round had made them afraid to move. This was a stroke of luck for Cao Cao, who ordered a thousand men to clear the road while the rest remained as his guard. This reinforcement put fresh heart into him. Ma Yan and Zhang Yi galloped forward, but before they had gone ten *li* they heard battle cries and another force appeared, the leader of them shouting, "Here is Gan Ning!" Before Ma Yan could engage him, Gan Ning had felled him from his horse. Then, spear in hand, Zhang Yi charged; but Gan Ning raised a mighty cry and catching Zhang Yi off guard cut him down too. This was hastily reported by the others to Cao Cao, who hoped that his Hefei troops would come to his aid. But Sun Quan was barring the road to Hefei and when he saw the fire on the river and knew that his side was winning, he ordered Lu Xun to give the pre-arranged signal. At once Taishi Ci joined forces with Lu Xun to charge, and Cao Cao had to flee towards Yiling.

On the road he met Zhang He and told him to cover the retreat. He galloped hard till dawn when, turning back, he saw that the fires seemed fainter. Somewhat reassured, he asked where he was. His men told him: west of Wulin and north of Yidu. It was mountainous and densely wooded country, at the sight of which he threw back his head and laughed. When his officers asked the cause of his mirth, he said, "Zhou Yu's carelessness and Zhuge Liang's folly. Had I been in command of their troops, I should have laid an ambush here. Then we should have been in trouble."

While he was still speaking, drums thundered on

both sides and flames shot up. Cao Cao nearly fell off his horse, he was so startled. And out from one side dashed more men, the foremost crying, "I am Zhao Yun! I have waited a long time by order of our adviser!"

Leaving Xu Huang and Zhang He to resist Zhao Yun, Cao Cao made off hastily through the smoke and fire. Zhao Yun did not pursue him, but captured all the flags. So once more Cao Cao escaped.

It was brighter now, but dark clouds were hanging low and the southeast wind was still blowing. Suddenly there came a heavy downpour of rain which soaked through their clothes and armour. But they pressed on through the rain till they were famished. Then Cao Cao made his men seize food from the villages and find kindling to light a fire. Before they could prepare a meal, however, another force came up from behind. Cao Cao was beginning to panic, when he saw to his relief that it was Li Dian and Xu Chu escorting his advisers.

Ordering his men to move on, he asked, "What lies ahead?"

They answered, "On this side, the road to South Yiling; on that, the track through the hills to North Yiling."

"Which is the shorter way to Nanjun and Jiangling?"

"The way through Gourd Valley to South Yiling."

Cao Cao decided to take this second way. By Gourd Valley, his troops were too hungry to go any further and the horses too were worn out. A number had fallen by the roadside. So Cao Cao called a halt. Some of his men had cooking pans and some had taken rice from the villages. They chose a dry spot by the hills to light fires and cook rice or roast strips of horseflesh. Wet clothes were taken off to dry in the wind, while the horses were unsaddled and loosed to graze.

Then Cao Cao, seated in a clearing, threw back his head and laughed again.

His officers said, "When you laughed just now at Zhou Yu and Zhuge Liang, out came Zhao Yun and we suffered heavy losses. What are you laughing at now?"

"At those two men's lack of foresight. In their place, I should have laid another ambush here to wait quietly for our exhausted troops. Then we might have escaped with our lives, but not without heavy losses. I am laughing because this never occurred to them."

As he was speaking, the men before and behind him cried out in alarm. Terrified, Cao Cao jumped on his horse without even stopping to buckle on his armour. Many of his men had no time to catch their mounts, for in a flash flames and smoke enveloped the valley, and out came a troop commanded by Zhang Fei. Levelling his spear as he sat in the saddle, Zhang Fei cried, "Cao Cao, you traitor, where do you think you are going?"

The sight of Zhang Fei struck fear into them all. Xu Chu rode up bareback to engage him, and Zhang Liao and Xu Huang galloped to join in the fray. A skirmish began, and Cao Cao was the first to flee. Some of his officers managed to follow him. Zhang Fei gave chase, but Cao Cao rode so hard that soon his pursuers were outdistanced. When he looked at his officers, however, most of them were wounded.

As they went on a soldier reported, "There are two roads ahead. Which shall we take?"

Cao Cao asked, "Which is the shorter?"

"The high road is smoother but more than fifty *li* longer than the by-way to Huarong. But that is so narrow and rough that the going is hard."

Cao Cao sent men up the hill to reconnoitre. They came back to report, "Smoke is rising at several points along the track by the hill, but the highway is quiet."

Cao Cao ordered them to take the by-way.

"Where there is smoke there must be troops," said his officers. "Why take that road?"

Cao Cao said, "One of the rules of strategy is that appearances can never be trusted. Zhuge Liang is so crafty that he would light fires there so that we dare not take the track through the hills. I am certain he has laid an ambush on the highway. But we won't fall into his trap."

They said, "You have wonderful judgement, Prime Minister. None of us is a match for you."

So they took the Huarong Road.

By this time Cao Cao's men were collapsing from hunger, and their horses were utterly spent. The badly burnt were hobbling along on crutches, those wounded by arrows and spears were dragging their feet. They were drenched and had lost most of their accoutrements. Their weapons and flags were in complete disorder. In the confusion of flight on the Yiling road, most of them had ridden off bareback, leaving behind their saddles, reins and clothing. It was now the coldest time of winter, and their wretchedness defied description.

Soon the troops in front halted, and when Cao Cao asked the reason he was told, "The hilly track ahead is narrow and this morning's rain has filled the pits in it. Our horses are bogged down in the mud."

Cao Cao cried angrily, "When soldiers come to hills

they cut a way through; when they come to streams they bridge them. Who ever heard of an army stopped by mud?"

He ordered the old, weak and wounded to follow on slowly behind, while the able-bodied repaired the road with earth, timber, grass and reeds. They must lose no time, and any disobedience would be punished by death.

So the troops had to dismount and fell trees or bamboos by the roadside to fill up the pits. And for fear lest they be overtaken, Cao Cao ordered Zhang Liao, Xu Chu and Xu Huang with a hundred swordsmen to expedite the work by killing any who were slow.

By now the men were utterly famished and spent, all falling by the wayside. When the next order came to move on, many of them had perished. Cries of misery were heard the whole of the way.

"What is this wailing?" raged Cao Cao. "Life and death are decreed by fate. Off with the head of anyone who wails!"

One-third of his men had dropped behind, one-third had died on the road, so that only one-third was left to follow him.

This difficult stretch passed, the going became easier. Looking back, Cao Cao observed that he had barely three hundred riders left, none of them fully equipped. When he urged them to make haste, they replied that the horses were at the end of their tether and must rest a while.

"Very well then, after we reach Jingzhou," said Cao Cao.

They marched on for a few more *li*, when Cao Cao flourished his whip and laughed again.

"What are you laughing at now?" asked his officers.

"Zhou Yu and Zhuge Liang are always said to be so crafty," he answered. "But to my mind they are incompetent. If they had ambushed us here, we should all have been captured."

Before he had finished, a signal sounded, and on both sides five hundred swordsmen appeared. The leader who barred their way was Guan Yu, wielding his Green Dragon sword and astride his Red Hare steed. Cao Cao's men were frightened out of their wits and gazed at each other in utter consternation.

"Since it's come to this," said Cao Cao, "we must fight to the death!"

His officers protested, "Even if we are not afraid, our horses are worn out. How can we fight?"

Cheng Yu said, "I know Guan Yu. He behaves arrogantly to those above him, but is kind to those below. He will injure the strong but never bully the weak. He knows how to show gratitude or bear a grudge, and he has always kept faith. You treated him well in the past, Prime Minister. Make a personal appeal to him and we might go free."

Accordingly, Cao Cao rode forward to bow to Guan Yu. "How are you, general?" he asked.

Guan Yu, bowing in return, replied, "I have been waiting for Your Lordship here for some time on the orders of our adviser."

"My army is defeated and my situation desperate," said Cao Cao. "I have come to a sorry pass. I hope you will remember our long-standing friendship."

"You treated me well in the old days," admitted Guan Yu. "But by killing Yan Liang and Wen Chou and helping you out of your difficulty at Baima, I have paid back my debt of gratitude. I cannot let private feelings interfere with my public duty now."

"Don't you remember how you crossed the five passes and killed the six officers? A gentleman should have a sense of justice. You have made a careful study of the *Zhou Annals*. You must recall the story of Yugong Zhisi and his pursuit of Zizhuo Ruzi."*

Now Guan Yu had a keen sense of honour. The thought of Cao Cao's past kindness and the slaying of those officers could not fail to move him. Besides, his heart bled for Cao Cao's woebegone men, who looked ready to burst into tears. He reined back his horse and ordered his troops, "Spread out!" Obviously he meant to give them a chance to slip through. When Cao Cao saw this, he and his officers dashed through the cordon. By the time Guan Yu turned round again, they had gone. Guan Yu uttered a cry, at which the rest of Cao Cao's men slipped from their horses to kneel weeping on the ground. Guan Yu pitied them with all his heart and just as he was wondering what to do, up galloped his old friend Zhang Liao. At sight of him, Guan Yu's heart melted, and heaving a long sigh he let them all pass.

After Cao Cao's escape at Huarong, when he came to the end of the valley and looked back, all that remained to him was twenty-seven horsemen. That evening they reached Nanjun, where they saw blazing torches ahead

---

* They were both famous archers of ancient times. During a battle Yugong Zhisi was sent to overtake Zizhuo Ruzi, who being ill was unable to defend himself. "I learned archery from your pupil," said Yugong Zhisi. "I cannot use your skill to harm you." So he knocked off the tips of four arrows and returned after shooting these.

and troops barring the way. Cao Cao cried out in despair, "This is the end!" But the scouts of the other party galloped towards them and he found to his joy that these were the troops of Cao Ren. The latter, arriving presently, explained that although they had heard of the army's defeat they had not dared to leave their post but had simply come out a short distance to meet them.

"I nearly missed seeing you altogether!" said Cao Cao.

They were taken to Nanjun to rest, and presently Zhang Liao arrived, testifying to Guan Yu's kindness. Most of Cao Cao's officers were wounded, and he ordered them to rest. Cao Ren brought wine to cheer him; but as he feasted with his advisers the tears ran down his cheeks.

They said, "When fleeing from the tiger's lair, you showed no fear. Now you have come to this city where your men have food, your horses forage. This is the time to prepare for your revenge. Why do you weep?"

Cao Cao said, "I am lamenting the loss of Guo Jia.* Had he been alive, I should not have suffered this great defeat." Beating his chest, he groaned aloud and exclaimed, "Ah, my friend Guo Jia! What a loss your death was!" His advisers were shamed into silence.

The next day Cao Cao told Cao Ren, "I am going back to Xuchang to raise another army to take revenge. I want you to defend Nanjun for me. I have a sealed plan here which I shall leave you. Don't open it unless you are hard-pressed. But if you are desperate follow

---

* One of Cao Cao's chief advisers, who died of sickness before the Battle of the Red Cliff.

its instructions. Then the armies of Wu will not dare
to attack Nanjun again."

"Who will defend Hefei and Xiangyang?" asked Cao
Ren.

"Your task is to defend Jingzhou. I shall send Xiahou Dun to hold Xiangyang. As Hefei is most important, I am making Zhang Liao my commander there
with Yue Jin and Li Dian to assist him. In case of
emergency, send me word at once!"

Having made these arrangements, Cao Cao rode off
with his followers to Xuchang, taking with him the officers of Jingzhou who had gone over to his side. Cao
Ren on his part sent Cao Hong to defend Yiling and
Nanjun against any attack by Zhou Yu.

After Guan Yu let Cao Cao escape, he led his men
back. By this time all the different forces had returned
to Xiakou with their spoils of horses, weapons, money
and grain. Guan Yu alone had not captured a single
man or horse but had come empty-handed to report to
Liu Bei. Zhuge Liang was celebrating the victory with
his master when Guan Yu's arrival was announced. He
hastily left his seat and went to welcome him, winecup
in hand.

"Congratulations, general!" he cried. "You have
done a great deed and rid the world of a great evil. I
should have ridden out to congratulate you."

Guan Yu was silent.

"Are you angry because we didn't come out to meet
you?" asked Zhuge Liang. And turning to the attendants, he demanded, "Why didn't you report this earlier?"

Guan Yu said, "I have come to ask to be put to
death."

"Do you mean that Cao Cao never took the Huarong Road?"

"He did. But, fool that I am, I let him escape."

"What officers and men have you captured?"

"None."

"Obviously the memory of Cao Cao's kindness made you let him go deliberately," said Zhuge Liang. "But since you signed a pledge, you will have to be punished according to martial law." He ordered the guards to take Guan Yu out and kill him.

> For friendship's sake he risked death;
> Men yet unborn will admire his gallantry.

To know what became of Guan Yu, you must read the next chapter.

On *The Three Kingdoms*

Chen Minsheng

THE Three Kingdoms, by Luo Guanzhong of the 14th century, is the first long novel in classical Chinese literature. Its rich content, brilliantly constructed plot and masterly characterization marked a new departure in the development of Chinese fiction. The book depicts the political and military struggle between feudal rulers of China and reflects the historical conditions of nearly a hundred years from the end of the second to the end of the third century.

This was an age of great confusion and unrest. By the end of the second century, the Eastern Han Empire was tottering. The peasant revolts which swept through nearly the whole country were brutally suppressed by the armed forces of the big landlords, who went on to annex land and become strong and independent, then started to attack and pillage each other. These clashes led by degrees to the rise of the Three Kingdoms. The prime minister to the Han court, Cao Cao, held the vast territory of the north and established the kingdom of Wei; Liu Bei, a descendant of the imperial house, occupied the strategic region in the southwest and there set up the kingdom of Shu; while Sun Quan, who came from a powerful family, held the wealthy southeast and founded the kingdom of Wu.

This period, when warring chieftains were carving up the empire, produced a great number of wise, courageous men and gave rise to countless stirring tales of their exploits, many of which were recorded in *The History of the Three Kingdoms*, written by Chen Shou in the third century, and the annotations to this history by Pei Songzhi as well as the collection of anecdotes *New Social Talk* by Liu Yiqing which appeared in the fifth. As time went by these legends grew more numerous and richer in content, as we can see from the poems by Li Shangyin and Du Mu of the Tang Dynasty, which in some respects suggest the episodes and characters in *The Three Kingdoms*. Between the 10th and the 13th centuries there were story-tellers who specialized in tales about the Three Kingdoms. In the 14th century an illustrated edition of a *chante-fable* on the subject was published. At about this time a number of operas about the Three Kingdoms also appeared. Legends about the Three Kingdoms were already popular throughout the country.

The illustrated *chante-fable*, the first written work of literature dealing with the Three Kingdoms still extant and one of the earliest prototypes of the great novel, played an important role in the development of this cycle of stories. Though only a sketchy story-teller's script or "prompt book", it possessed certain significant characteristics; the story-tellers made full use of historical facts but were not restricted by them, for they made bold improvisations to express their own likes and dislikes, creating fairly readable scripts.

Chen Shou's history and these various anecdotes, legends and prompt books, then, were the basis and raw material of *The Three Kingdoms*, one of the

world's great novels.   Little is known about its author, Luo Guanzhong, who lived between 1330 and 1400.
It is merely recorded that he came from Taiyuan in the
province of Shanxi and was a quiet man who made few
friends.   He joined in a revolt to overthrow the Yuan
Dynasty; after the fall of the dynasty he retired from
public life to devote his time to writing historical novels
and dramas.

The earliest edition we have of his novel was printed
in 1494.   It consists of twenty-four books of ten sections
each, every section headed by a seven-word line of verse
which serves as title.   During the 16th century an an-
notated edition was brought out by the well-known philosopher Li Zhuowu.   This is not divided into books,
but two sections of the original have been combined to
form a chapter, and each chapter has as its heading two
lines of verse.   The form and structure of classical Chinese novels owe much to this, for it started a tradition
which has been handed down through the centuries.

By the middle of the 17th century Mao Zonggang and
his father had further improved the novel by rewriting a
few episodes, making certain additions, cutting certain
repetitious details, and rearranging some chapters or
changing some verses.   The present popular edition is
based on this text.   So this great work had evolved for
centuries before it reached its final form.

Based to a large extent on historical fact, this novel
reflects all the ramifications of the contest for power
among various ruling cliques during the Three Kingdoms period, vividly bringing out the sharpness of these
conflicts.   The fierce struggles for selfish interests left a
mark on all those involved, affecting every aspect of

their life — family, friends and marriage. Those in power showed unparalleled cruelty and ferocity. The whole country was in a turmoil and the lot of the common people was wretched indeed. It was against such a vast and complex background that this epic work was written. Chinese readers, comparing this book with a later masterpiece, *Outlaws of the Marsh*, have passed the verdict: "*Outlaws of the Marsh* teaches courage, while *The Three Kingdoms* teaches wisdom." In other words, men down the ages have always regarded this novel as a source-book of life and history.

The author in this novel created more than four hundred characters with different personalities and the work embodies his own political ideal — benevolent rule and opposition to despotism. The struggle between the two factions of Liu Bei and Cao Cao is treated, with a wealth of human documentation, as a struggle between a kindly ruler and a despot, a good man and a tyrant. So the conflict in the story unfolds and deepens through the struggles between these two groups, while the conflict with Sun Quan's faction is described as secondary; sometimes Sun Quan allies with Liu Bei against Cao Cao, at others he helps Cao Cao against Liu Bei. By this treatment the complex struggle among these political factions comes to possess a typical significance; stress is laid on its main features, while a clear and logical picture and one of absorbing interest is presented.

The author shows his hatred for treacherous schemers and warlords whose ambition knew no bounds in his successful portrait of Cao Cao. All that is evil and hateful in rulers of the feudal society is epitomized in him. Hypocritical and crafty, willing to stoop to the basest machinations, Cao Cao adopts a pose of humanity and justice to win men to his side. After wantonly murdering an innocent man, he laments bitterly and gives his victim a sumptuous burial to show his fairness and benevolence. Once, escaping from the capital, he is well treated by an old friend of his father called Lü, but he suspects that Lü is going to betray him and kills the man's whole family; later he discovers his mistake, but to prevent Lü from taking revenge he kills the old man too. His motto in life is "It is better for me to injure others than to let any other man injure me." However, Luo Guanzhong does not simply make Cao Cao an out-and-out villain. His penetrating portrayal of Cao Cao's wickedness and cruelty is supplemented by equally vivid descriptions of the man's extraordinary ability and courage, so that Cao Cao as a character appears both complex and thoroughly authentic. The remarkable character of Cao Cao will live as long as Chinese literature.

The author shows a partisan spirit too when it comes to presenting Liu Bei, Guan Yu, Zhuge Liang, Zhang Fei and others whom he endows with such qualities as loyalty, patriotism, courage and wisdom.

Liu Bei, for instance, is a humane, enlightened ruler who loves the people, helps those in distress and works untiringly to pacify the state. Of course, in this respect the author was influenced by the orthodox view of history of that time. Liu Bei, a descendant of the House of Han, wants to restore the Han empire and therefore he represents the side of right; whereas Cao Cao, prime minister to the Han emperor, has contrived to usurp the throne and is therefore disloyal and a traitor. Historians and critics today hold divergent views on this question, but it is perhaps worth pointing out that the ideas expressed in the stories about the Three Kingdoms came into being over a long period of time and were the outcome of very real problems. The Han people had suffered for long years from foreign aggression as well as from despotic rule. The common people's own experience and their deep observation of life made it natural that they should champion Liu Bei and condemn Cao Cao for his many evil deeds. This was actually a reflection of the people's patriotism, their demand for a better and more stable government and their opposition to despotism and oppression. Obviously, in that historical period it was, to a certain extent, a reflection of the people's aspirations.

Liu Bei's adviser Zhuge Liang and his sworn brother Guan Yu, both of whom stand highly in the author's regard, have also had a very strong influence on later generations owing to the skill with which they are presented.

Zhuge Liang's extraordinary wisdom and foresight and Guan Yu's conspicuous courage and dignity have won the admiration and love of readers through the centuries. More important still are the moral qualities which they symbolize: Zhuge Liang's selfless devotion and loyalty and Guan Yu's unswerving sense of justice and goodness to Liu Bei. Many unforgettable episodes in the novel lay stress on these moral attributes, and by so doing add to the stature of Liu Bei.

The author's view of these men was naturally conditioned by his age. For example, in the Battle of the Red Cliff he regards Guan Yu as gallant and kind because he lets Cao Cao go, while Zhuge Liang is described as a man who has powers to summon the wind at will. But these instances of prejudice and superstition are after all unimportant and cannot seriously detract from the greatness of this masterpiece.

The 120 chapters of *The Three Kingdoms*, totalling over 700,000 words, deal mainly with various campaigns, battles and skirmishes; but these are described and treated differently, without any repetition. In the course of describing these fierce and involved battles, the author also depicts complex human relationships between the ruler and his ministers, between father and son, between brothers, friends, or husband and wife, while there are passages presenting the life of hermits in the hills, feasts and celebrations, marriages, the writing of poems and so forth. In this way the spirit of the characters is more profoundly revealed, and a rich picture of historical reality is given. The story revolves around wars, which are dealt with to show a host of characters. The descriptions of war in this novel are outstanding in classical Chinese literature, while the characters in the book are known throughout China.

The section dealing with the Battle of the Red Cliff is one of the finest in the book for its detailed, profound portrayal of the complexity and sharp contradictions in a campaign. It takes eight chapters, starting with Zhuge Liang's argument with Sun Quan's advisers and ending with Guan Yu's release of Cao Cao. It deals not merely with fighting but with the tact and wisdom of Zhuge Liang. Cao Cao is attacking Sun Quan and Liu Bei, but this section is concerned largely with the secondary conflict between Liu Bei and Sun Quan; and Zhuge Liang's decisive role throughout the whole campaign and at the crucial moment is emphasized. One subtle and interesting episode after another brings out his extraordinary wisdom. He joins in the campaign alone and uses Sun Quan's forces to achieve a great victory for Liu Bei.

The author's skill is shown above all by the way in which he uses these episodes to draw character. When Cao Cao is advancing on the Yangzi Valley at the head of 830,000 men, the officers of the south are alarmed and cannot decide whether to make peace or fight. Zhuge Liang has a clear idea of the situation, however; he analyses the strength and weakness of the three sides and takes the initiative, never worrying because Liu Bei's force is weak. Sun Quan hesitates, on the other hand, feeling unequal to resisting so powerful an enemy. Zhou Yu has a good grasp of the situation; while treating different factions politely, he despises those who have panicked and makes careful plans to worst the enemy; yet when he pits his wits against Zhuge Liang, his limitations, pettiness and over-confidence are revealed. Again, Cao Cao is shown as a proud man who despises his enemy and counts on his superior strength to win the war and conquer the whole empire; but his weakness is utilized and he falls repeatedly into his enemy's traps until he is badly defeated. As this dramatic story develops, all the characters in it spring to life.

Although *The Three Kingdoms* covers such a vast range of political and military struggles, the author shows discrimination in his choice of episodes and great attention to detail in his characterization. For example, in the Battle of the Red Cliff, Zhuge Liang, Zhou Yu and Lu Su all have political acumen; but Luo Guanzhong contrasts the attitude of these three men to the main conflict — the attack on Cao Cao's forces —

to reveal their different characteristics. Lu Su is used to bring out his two friends' wisdom and foresight, while the description of Zhou Yu reveals the broadmindedness and shrewdness of Zhuge Liang. Again, the pretended defection of Cai Zhong and Cai He, which appears to take Zhou Yu in, but which he actually uses for his own purpose, is followed by that of Huang Gai and Kan Ze, which at first arouses Cao Cao's suspicions but eventually fools him; the scene in which Zhou Yu fools Jiang Gan by pretending to be asleep is followed by that in which Jiang Gan falls into Zhou Yu's trap by trying the same trick. These similar actions have such different results that they shed light on the mood, temperament and situation of the different characters involved. Then there are many fine touches of detail exemplifying the skill with which the author handles his plot. For instance, Huang Gai's loyalty is first suggested during Zhuge Liang's debate with the advisers, to be emphasized later in the crucial scenes when he is beaten and when he takes his fire-boats up the river. All this throws Huang Gai's character into sharp relief. This attention to detail undoubtedly strengthens the artistic impact of the work.

The Three Kingdoms exerted a tremendous influence on the novels which followed it and many later writers modelled their historical novels on this work, which also supplied the theme for other forms of literature and drama.

All the tactics and strategy described in this novel, the offensive and defensive measures employed, the reasons for the rise and fall of kingdoms and the other historical experience embodied in it have much influenced later generations. It is said that Li Zicheng and

Zhang Xianzhong who led the 17th-century peasant revolt at the end of the Ming Dynasty learned much from this novel, as did some leaders and generals of the Taiping revolution. And countless others have admired the heroes of this novel or used the characters in it as a yardstick for behaviour in real life. *The Three Kingdoms* can without exaggeration be described as a textbook on life in feudal China.

Wu Cheng'en

The Flaming Mountain
(An excerpt from *Pilgrimage to the West*)

Pilgrimage to the West

CHAPTER 59

Tripitaka Is Stopped by the Flaming Mountain
Monkey Tries to Get the Palm-Leaf Fan

MANY the strains sprung from one common stock,
Boundless the store of the sea;
And vain are men's myriad fancies,
For every sort and kind blend into one.
When at last the deed is done, the task accomplished,
Perfect and bright Truth is manifested on high.
Then let not your thoughts wander east or west,
But hold them well in check
And smelt them in the furnace
Till they glow red as the sun,
Clear, brilliant and resplendent
To ride the dragon at will.

Our story tells how the monk Tripitaka accepted as his disciples Monkey, Pigsy and Sandy, how having overcome doubts and curbed unruly thoughts they joined forces to journey with one accord towards the West.

Time sped like an arrow, the sun and the moon flew like shuttles. Sultry summer passed once more into late, frosty autumn. Look!

> Light clouds are scattered,
> The west wind blows hard;
> Storks cry in distant valleys,
> The frosted forest is a tapestry;
> Chill and desolate the scene,
> Across far hills and further streams.
> Wild geese come to the northern pass,
> Swallows return to the south,
> While travellers lonely on the road lose heart
> And the monks' robes are cold.

As the monk and his three disciples travelled on, little by little the heat became intense. Tripitaka reined in his horse to say, "This is autumn now; what makes it so hot?"

Pigsy answered, "Don't you know? There is a kingdom in the west called Sicily where the sun sets. Men usually call it the 'Brink of the Sky'.* About four or five every afternoon the king sends men up the city wall to beat drums and blow horns to drown the seething noise of the ocean. For the sun is the true Fiery Principle, and when it falls into the Western Ocean it hisses and seethes like fire plunging into water. If there were no drumming and bugling to fill their ears, the children in the city would be killed by the din. It's so sweltering

---

* This legend was taken from earlier Chinese accounts based on Arabic sources. Here Sicily is confused with a legendary region in the west called by the Arabs Djabulsa or the Land of the Setting Sun.

here, I think we must have reached the place where the sun sets."

Monkey burst out laughing and said, "Don't talk like a fool! We're a long way from Sicily. If we keep changing our minds like our master and dawdle like this, even if we travelled from childhood till old age and had three lives, we'd never get there."

"If this isn't the place where the sun sets, brother, why should it be so confoundedly hot?" asked Pigsy.

Sandy said, "It must be freakish weather, an autumn heat-wave or something of the sort."

As they were arguing, they saw by the roadside a manor house with a red-tiled roof, red brick walls, a gate painted red and red lacquered benches — the whole building was red. Tripitaka dismounted and said, "Monkey, go and ask the people in that house the reason for this fearful heat."

Then Monkey laid aside his gold-hooped staff, tidied himself, assumed a scholarly air and went down the road to have a look at the gate. An old man suddenly came out, and this was what he looked like —

> He wore a linen gown neither yellow nor red,
> A straw hat neither green nor black;
> He held a gnarled bamboo cane neither crooked
>   nor straight,
> And was shod in leather boots neither new nor old.
> Copper-red his face, silver-white his beard,
> Long shaggy eyebrows covered his blue eyes
> And his teeth flashed gold when he smiled.

This old man, looking up, was taken aback to see Monkey. Gripping his cane tight, he shouted, "What monster are you? What are you doing outside my gate?"

Monkey bowed and said, "Don't be afraid, sir. I'm no monster. I've been sent by the Great Tang Emperor of the East to find Buddhist scriptures in the West. We and our master have just reached your worthy district. I've come to ask why it is so hot here and what the name of this place is."

The old man, reassured, said with a smile, "Forgive me, friar. My eyes played a trick on me and I did not see you were a monk."

"That's quite all right," said Monkey.

"Where is your master?"

"There to the south, standing in the road."

"Please ask him over."

Monkey waved cheerfully to the rest, whereupon Tripitaka approached with Pigsy and Sandy leading his white horse and carrying the baggage. They all bowed to the old man who, pleasantly surprised by Tripitaka's handsome looks and the unusual appearance of Pigsy and Sandy, invited them in to rest, telling his household to serve tea and prepare a meal.

Tripitaka, hearing this, stood up to thank him and ask, "May I inquire, sir, how it is that your honourable district has grown so hot even in autumn?"

The old man answered, "This unworthy place is called the Flaming Mountain. We have no spring or autumn here. It is hot in all four seasons."

Tripitaka asked, "On which side is this Flaming Mountain? Does it block the way westward?"

"There's no going west," said the old man. "That mountain is sixty *li* from here, right in the way you would have to go. And its flames reach out eight hundred *li* so that not a blade of grass can grow round about. A man with a head of copper and body of iron would melt if he took that road."

At this Tripitaka paled and dared ask no more.

Just then a young fellow pushing a red wheelbarrow stopped outside the gate and cried, "Cakes for sale!"

Monkey pulled out a hair and changed it into a copper with which to buy a cake. The lad took the money and with no further ado whipped the steaming cloth cover from his wheelbarrow and handed a cake to Monkey. That cake was as hot as burning charcoal or red molten iron in a furnace. Just watch him shift it from one hand to another! "Phew!" he exclaimed. "It's roasting! I can't eat this!"

The lad laughed, "If you're afraid of heat, this is no place for you. That's how hot things are in these parts."

"That doesn't make sense, young fellow," retorted Monkey. "The proverb says: Without heat and cold no crops will grow. If this place is so sweltering all the time, where did you get the flour for your cakes?"

"To find that out, you must pay a respectful visit to the Iron Fan Fairy."

"Why, what has the fairy to do with it?"

"This Iron Fan Fairy has a palm-leaf fan. One swish of that fan will put out the fire; another swish will make a breeze; a third will bring rain. That's how we sow and reap in due season and get our crops. If not for that, I assure you, not a blade of grass could grow."

Then Monkey hurried inside and gave the cake to Tripitaka, saying, "Take it easy, Master. There is no need to worry yet. When you've eaten this cake I'll explain why."

Tripitaka offered the cake to his host, who said, "I

haven't served you any tea or food yet: how can I accept this from you?"

Monkey laughed, "Don't bother about tea and food, sir. Just tell me where the Iron Fan Fairy lives."

"Why do you ask?"

"That pedlar just now told me that this fairy has a palm-leaf fan. One swish of that fan will put out the fire, another swish will make a breeze; a third will bring rain. That's how you sow and reap your crops. I want to borrow that fan to put out the fire so that we can go past and you can get harvests to feed yourselves."

'That may be so," replied the old man. "But since you have no offerings I doubt whether the holy one would help you."

"What offerings does she require?" asked Tripitaka.

The old man answered, "Folk here make their request every ten years with four pigs, four sheep, red silk, flowers, the choicest fruit of the season, chickens, geese and good wine. After purifying ourselves we go with humble hearts to the fairy mountain. There we prostrate ourselves and beg the fairy to come out of the cave and put out the fire."

"Where is the mountain?" asked Monkey. "What's the place called? Is it far? Wait while I go and borrow the fan."

"It lies to the southwest," said the old man. "Its name is the Mountain of Emerald Clouds and on it you'll find a fairy cave called Palm-Leaf Cavern. The journey there and back takes pilgrims from here a whole month. The distance is nearly one thousand four hundred and sixty *li*."

"That's all right," said Monkey with a smile. "I'll be back in no time."

"Wait!" cried the old man. "You must have some tea and food first and prepare some rations. You'll need a couple of people to go with you too. That's a lonely road infested with wolves and tigers and the journey takes more than one day. This is no joke!"

Monkey laughed, "No need, no need! Off I go." And with that he vanished.

The old man was amazed. "Heavens!" he exclaimed. "So he's one of these immortals that ride on clouds."

We need not describe the redoubled respect with which this family now treated Tripitaka. Let us accompany Monkey, who in no time arrived at the Mountain of Emerald Clouds and hiding his divine aura started searching for the cave. Presently he heard the sound of felling wood and saw a woodcutter in the forest. Hastening forward Monkey heard him chant:

> Faintly through clouds I glimpse the familiar woods,
> The path is lost among sheer cliffs and brambles;
> I see the morning rain on the western hills,
> On my way back the southern stream has risen.

Monkey accosted him with a bow. "Greetings, brother!"

The woodcutter put down his axe to return the bow and asked, "Where are you going, friar?"

"Can you tell me whether this is the Mountain of Emerald Clouds?" When the woodcutter said that it was, Monkey continued, "I hear there is a Palm-Leaf Cavern belonging to the Iron Fan Fairy. Where would that be?"

The woodcutter said with a smile, "There is such a

cavern, but there is no Iron Fan Fairy. There is only a Princess Iron Fan, also called Rakshasa."

"Is she the one said to have a palm-leaf fan which can put out the flames of the Flaming Mountain?"

"That's right, that's right. Because the goddess has this magic fan which can help the local people by putting out the flames, they call her the Iron Fan Fairy. We here have no need of her and know her only as Rakshasa, the wife of the powerful Ox Demon King."

When Monkey heard that, he lost colour in dismay. "Up against an enemy again!" he thought. "That Red Boy we captured was said to be their son. When we met his uncle in Poer Cave on Jieyang Mountain, he refused us water and wanted to take revenge. Now here I am up against the mother — how am I to borrow the fan?"

Seeing Monkey deep in thought, heaving long sighs, the woodcutter said with a smile, "Friar, what can worry a holy man like you? If you take this path east, less than five or six *li* will bring you to Palm-Leaf Cavern. You don't have to worry."

"I can take you into my confidence," said Monkey. "I am the first disciple of Tripitaka, who has been sent by the Tang Emperor of the East to find Buddhist scriptures in the West. A year or so ago in Fire-Cloud Cave we had words with the princess' son, Red Boy. Now we want to borrow her fan, I'm afraid she may refuse out of spite. That's what's worrying me."

"Just watch your step, friend," said the woodcutter. "Simply ask for the fan and say nothing about the past. I'm sure you'll get it."

"Thank you for your advice, brother." Monkey bowed. "I'm off."

Leaving the woodcutter he went straight to Palm-Leaf Cavern. The double gate was firmly closed and the scenery around was beautiful. Undoubtedly, that was a lovely spot!

> Rocks formed the bones of the mountains,
> The essence of the earth.
> The mist held last night's moisture,
> Moss made a new, fresh green;
> High peaks outdid the islands of Penglai,
> The quiet and scent of flowers made a fairy world,
> Wild storks nested on tall pines
> And orioles called to each other from fading willows;
> A time-hallowed, unearthly place was this,
> The bright-plumed phoenix sang in a green plane tree,
> The grey dragon lurked in the running stream,
> Vines drooped above winding paths,
> Creepers climbed over rocky steps;
> On emerald cliffs monkeys hailed the rising moon,
> On tall trees birds saluted the clear blue sky;
> Bamboos on both sides cast shade cool as rain,
> Flowers on the path made a thick, patterned carpet;
> At times white clouds drifted up from distant valleys
> To wander aimlessly after the breeze.

Monkey stepped forward and called, "Brother Ox! Open the gate!"

Then the gate grated open and out came a maid with a flower basket in her hand, a hoe over her shoulder.

Her dress was plain and bare of any adornment, her face radiant with piety. Monkey advanced, his palms pressed together in a salute, and said, "May I trouble you, maid, to announce me to the princess? I am a monk on my way west to find Buddhist scriptures, but I cannot cross the Flaming Mountain and have come here to ask for the loan of the palm-leaf fan."

"Tell me your monastery and your name, so that I can report to my mistress," said the maid.

"I come from the East," answered Monkey. "I am the monk Sun Wukong."*

The maid turned and went in to kneel before Rakshasa. "The monk Sun Wukong from the East is outside the cave, madam," she said, "he wants to see you to borrow the palm-leaf fan so that he can cross the Flaming Mountain."

To Rakshasa the name Sun Wukong was like salt sprinkled on fire or oil added to flames. She flushed crimson, her heart swelled with anger and she swore, "That vile ape! So he's here, is he!" Calling for her armour and weapons, she put on her helmet and breast-plate, seized two swords of blue steel and sallied forth. Monkey slipped to one side to have a look at her.

> A flower-patterned scarf she had
> And silk robe with cloud designs;
> The double tiger-sinews about her waist;
> Barely disclosed her embroidered skirt beneath;
> Three inches long her arched phoenix-beak slip-
>   pers,
> Dragon-tassels had her gilded greaves;

---

* Monkey's Buddhist name.

> Grasping her swords she shouted in her rage,
> Fierce as a goddess from the moon.

Stepping out of the gate she cried, "Where is Sun Wukong?"

Monkey stepped forward and bowed. "Here, sister-in-law! Greetings."

Rakshasa snorted with rage. "Who's your sister-in-law? Who wants your greetings?"

"The Ox Demon King of your honourable house was my sworn brother, one of seven sworn brothers," said Monkey. "Now that I learn you are his wife, lady, shouldn't I address you as my sister-in-law?"

"Vile ape! If you were our sworn brother, would you injure my child?"

"Your child?" Monkey pretended ignorance.

"Yes, my son Red Boy, the Holy Child King of Fire-Cloud Cave in the Valley of Withered Pines on the Howling Mountain. You trapped him. I was looking for you to pay you back, and now you've delivered yourself into my hands. Don't think I'm going to let you off!"

"Come, that's not reasonable, sister-in-law," protested Monkey with a smile. "You can't blame me. Your son captured my master and wanted to steam him or boil him. Luckily Guan Yin carried Red Boy off and saved my master. Now he is with Guan Yin as the angel Sudhana. He's become a genuine bodhisattva, deathless and pure, and will live as long as the sun and moon, as long as heaven and earth endure. You should be thanking me for preserving him instead of blaming me — that's most unfair!"

"You smooth-tongued baboon!" scolded Rakshasa.

"My son may not be dead, but can he come back to me? Shall I ever see him again?"

"That's not difficult." Monkey laughed. "If you want to see your son, sister-in-law, just lend me your fan to put out the fire so that I can escort my master on his way. Then I'll go to Guan Yin and ask her to send him to see you and return the fan. You can see then whether he's been harmed or not. If he's been hurt in the least, you'll have cause to blame me. If he looks in better condition, you ought to thank me."

"Hold your tongue, you devil! Stretch out your head and let me take a few slashes at it. If you can stand the pain, I'll lend you the fan. If not, I'll send you all the sooner to Hell."

With folded hands, Monkey went up to her, laughing. "Say no more, sister. Here's my head. You can whack at it till you're tired. You'll have to lend me the fan."

Without another word, Rakshasa swung her swords and rained down a dozen resounding blows on his head. When Monkey did not turn a hair, the princess took fright and turned to fly.

"Where are you going, sister?" he cried. "Hurry up and lend me the fan."

"I don't lend my treasure," she answered.

"If you won't lend it, see how you like a dose of Brother Sun's cudgel!"

The Monkey King seized her with one hand, with the other plucking the staff from inside his ear. He swung it once and it grew as thick as a bowl. Rakshasa pulled free and raised her swords to resist. Then Monkey attacked with his staff. So there at the foot of the Mountain of Emerald Clouds both sundered their bonds of

friendship, black hatred in their hearts. And what a
fight that was!

> The woman was a monster,
> Hating Monkey, eager to avenge her son;
> Though Monkey, too, was angry,
> He spoke her fair when the road west was blocked,
> Asking patiently, he asked for the loan of the
>   palm-leaf fan,
> Making no parade of his strength.
> In her folly Rakshasa attacked him,
> Yet the Monkey King remembered the ties between
>   them.
> But how can a woman prevail against a man?
> Women, when all is said, are the weaker sex.
> Mighty his iron staff with its hoops of gold,
> And swift her gleaming swords with the blue
>   blades;
> Each struck at the other's head and face,
> Contending hard with no respite,
> Parrying blows left and right.
> Warding off attacks before and then behind;
> They were fighting with all their might
> When the sun sank in the west;
> Then Rakshasa waved her fan —
> One swish of that fan and even the gods were
>   afraid!

Rakshasa fought Monkey till evening fell and she
knew she could not win, for his staff was heavy and he
wielded it with great skill. Thereupon she took out the
palm-leaf fan and waved it. At once a cold wind
sprang up and Monkey, unable to stop, was blown

straight out of sight. Then Rakshasa returned in triumph to her cave.

Monkey floated up and away. Though he strained left and right he was powerless to come down, like a leaf whirled off by a gale or a fallen petal swept head-long by a stream. A whole night he hurtled through the sky, not till daybreak did he alight on a mountain top, where he flung both arms round a crag. After some time, when he had recovered a little, he looked careful-ly about him and saw that this was the Lesser Sumeru Mountain.

"What a shrew!" He let out a long sigh. "How did she get me here? I remember coming to this place a year or so ago to ask the Bodhisattva Ling Ji to rescue my master by overcoming the Yellow Whirlwind Monster. The Yellow Whirlwind Mountain was more than three thousand *li* to the south. Since I've come back from the west, this must be goodness knows how many tens of thousands of *li* to the southeast. Let me go down and ask the bodhisattva my best way back."

The clear note of a temple bell broke into his thoughts and he hurried down the slope straight to the monas-tery. The priest at the gate recognized him and went in to announce, "That furry-faced god who came the year before last to ask you to subdue the Yellow Whirlwind Monster is here again."

Ling Ji, realizing who it was, hastily rose from his seat and went out to greet Monkey. He invited him in, saluted him and said, "Congratulations! Are you back already with the sutras?"

"Not yet," said Monkey. "No, we're still a long way from that."

"If you haven't succeeded yet, what brings you back to these wild mountains of ours?"

"The other year you were kind enough to overcome the Yellow Whirlwind Monster for us. Since then we've met with many more hardships on our way. Now we've reached the Flaming Mountain and can get no further. The local people told us about an Iron Fan Fairy with a palm-leaf fan which can put out the fire, so I made a special trip to see her. She turned out to be the Ox Demon King's wife and Red Boy's mother. She blames me for making her son one of Guan Yin's attendants and bears me a grudge because she'll never see him again. Instead of lending me the fan, she fought me. And when she found my staff too powerful for her, she waved her fan at me and sent me flying all the way here before I managed to stop. I've taken the liberty of calling at your monastery to ask my way back. How far is it from here to the Flaming Mountain?"

"That was Rakshasa or Princess Iron Fan," said Ling Ji with a laugh. "That precious palm-leaf fan of hers has divine powers for it was created by the Universe after the Primordial Chaos. Since it is the essence of the Primary Female Principle, not only can it put out fires but if waved at a man it will send him flying eighty-four thousand *li* before its wind drops. From here to the Flaming Mountain is little more than fifty thousand *li*. You stopped because you know how to ride the clouds. Most people wouldn't have come down so soon."

"This is terrible!" exclaimed Monkey. "How is my master going to cross that region?"

"Set your mind at rest," replied the bodhisattva.

"Your coming here is a sign that Tripitaka's luck is good and that you will succeed."

"How shall we succeed?"

"In the past when Buddha taught me, gave me a wind-calming pill and a flying-dragon wand, I used the wand to overcome the Yellow Whirlwind Monster, but I haven't yet used the pill. I'll give it to you so that she won't be able to blow you away; then you can get the fan and put out the fire, and after that you will succeed."

As Monkey bowed his thanks, the bodhisattva took a silk pouch from his sleeve and tucked the wind-calming pill inside Monkey's collar, where he had it sewn firmly in place. Then he saw Monkey to the gate saying, "I shan't entertain you now. Head northwest to reach the mountain where she lives."

So Monkey left Ling Ji and somersaulted through the clouds straight back to the Mountain of Emerald Clouds, arriving there in next to no time. He banged on the gate with his iron staff and shouted, "Open up! Open up! I've come to borrow the fan."

The panic-stricken maid inside rushed to report to her mistress, "That man is back again to borrow the fan!"

Alarmed to hear this, Rakshasa thought, "That wretched ape certainly knows a trick or two! My treasure fans men eighty-four thousand *li* without stopping. How did he manage to get back so soon? This time I'll wave my fan at him two or three times, so that he can't find his way back."

She hastily got up, buckled on her armour and picked up her two swords. Reaching the gate she shouted, "So you aren't afraid of me, Monkey! You've come back to be killed."

Monkey laughed. "Don't be so mean, sister! You must lend it to me. After I've helped my master Tripitaka to cross the mountain, I'll send it back without fail. I'm a very honest gentleman, not one of those fellows who never returns what he borrows."

"You scoundrelly baboon! The idea!" swore Rakshasa. "What impudence! You haven't yet paid for taking away my son, and now you want to borrow my fan — not likely! Stand your ground and have a taste of my swords."

Monkey, no whit dismayed, parried with his staff. After six or seven clashes, Rakshasa's arms were tired while Monkey was still vigorous and invincible. Since the battle was going against her, Rakshasa took out her fan and waved it at him, but Monkey stood immovable as a rock. Putting away his staff he said with a smile, "This time things have changed. Fan as hard as you please. If I budge, I'm no true man."

She fanned again and yet again, but sure enough Monkey did not move. Then Rakshasa lost her head and putting away her magic fan turned and fled into the cave, making fast the gate behind her.

When Monkey saw that she had closed the gate, he decided to play a trick. Having taken the wind-calming pill from his collar and put it in his mouth, he transformed himself into a tiny gnat and squeezed through a crack in the gate. He heard Rakshasa call, "I'm thirsty. Hurry up and bring the tea!" Then the maid attending her brought a pot of fragrant tea and poured out a full bowl with bubbles on top. In high spirits, Monkey swooped to hide under the bubbles. Since Rakshasa was parched she drained the bowl in two gulps and Monkey found himself inside her belly, where he resumed his own form. Then he called at the top of his voice, "Sister, lend me your fan!"

Pale with fright, Rakshasa asked her maids if the gate were locked. Assured that it was, she said, "If the gate is locked, how do I hear Monkey shouting inside my room?"

The maids told her, "His voice is coming from inside you, madam."

Rakshasa demanded, "What magic are you up to, Monkey?"

"I have never worked magic in all my life," said Monkey. "This is genuine honest skill. I am enjoying myself in your honourable belly and may now say I know you inside out. I find you are hungry and thirsty, so here's a bowl of tea for you." With that he stamped so hard that Rakshasa felt an excruciating pain in her belly and fell groaning to the ground. "Don't stand on ceremony, sister!" Monkey continued. "Here's some cake to stay your hunger." And he butted with his head till she felt an excruciating pain in her chest. She rolled on the ground, her face waxen and her lips white, screaming, "Spare me, brother! Spare me!"

At that Monkey stopped plaguing her and said, "So now you recognize your brother-in-law, eh? For the sake of Brother Ox I'll spare your life. Hurry up and give me the fan."

"I will, I will, brother! Come out and take it."

"You must show me the fan before I'll come out."

Rakshasa told a maid to fetch the palm-leaf fan and Monkey saw it from her throat. He said, "Since I'm sparing you, sister, so as not to make a hole in your belly

I'll come out through your mouth. Open your mouth three times."

As she complied, Monkey flew out in the form of a gnat to alight on the palm-leaf fan. Not knowing this, Rakshasa went on opening her mouth and calling, "Come out, brother!"

Then Monkey resumed his true shape and picked up the fan. "Here I am!" he cried. "Thanks for the loan!" He strode off, while the maids hastened to open the gate and let him out.

Having turned his cloud eastwards again, in no time at all Monkey came down beside the red brick wall. Pigsy exclaimed in pleasure at the sight, "Here's Brother Monkey, master! He's back!"

Then Tripitaka, Sandy and the old man came out to welcome him and lead him inside. Monkey showed them the fan and asked, "Is this the fan, sir?"

The old man answered, "That's it."

Tripitaka said in high delight, "You have done extremely well. You must have gone to a great deal of trouble to get this treasure."

"The trouble is nothing," said Monkey, "but do you know who this Iron Fan Fairy is? None other than the wife of the Ox Demon King and the mother of Red Boy. They call her Rakshasa or Princess Iron Fan. When I went to her cave to borrow the fan, she brought up old grievances and whacked me several times with her swords. And as soon as I frightened her with my staff, with one wave of her fan she sent me flying all the way to the Lesser Sumeru Mountain. Luckily I met the Bodhisattva Ling Ji who gave me a wind-calming pill and showed me the way back to the Mountain of Emerald Clouds and Rakshasa. This time when she fanned me again and I didn't move, she went into her cave. So I changed into a gnat and flew in too, and when she called for a drink I hid under the bubbles in her tea and jumped around in her belly till the pain was too much for her and she begged me again and again to spare her life, promising to lend me the fan. I let her off then and took the fan, which I shall return when we've crossed the Flaming Mountain."

When Tripitaka heard this he was most thankful. They said goodbye to the old man and proceeded west for forty *li* or so till the heat became almost intolerable. Sandy swore that his feet were scorched and Pigsy complained of blistered soles, while the horse trotted faster than usual, unable to keep its hooves on the ground for long. Soon it became impossible to go further.

"You had better dismount now, master," Monkey said. "While you stop here I shall go to put out the fire. After the wind and rain, when the ground is cooler, we can cross the mountain together."

Then Monkey raised the fan, approached the flames and fanned with all his might. The flames only blazed up higher. He fanned again and the flames increased a hundredfold. He fanned a third time and they soared up ten thousand feet and started to burn him. Though he jumped back fast, the hair on his thighs was singed. He promptly ran back to Tripitaka, shouting, "Turn back, quick! Turn back! The fire is coming this way." Tripitaka climbed into his saddle and with Pigsy and Sandy they hastened east for more than twenty *li* before they halted.

Then Tripitaka asked, "What happened, Monkey?"

Monkey threw down the fan. "It's no use, it didn't work. That woman fooled me."

When Tripitaka heard this, his heart sank and he knitted his brow in dismay, unable to hold back the tears. "What shall we do?" he lamented.

Pigsy asked, "Brother, why were you in such a hurry to make us turn back?"

"The first time I fanned, the flames blazed up," said Monkey. "The second time I fanned, the fire grew even fiercer. And the third time the flames shot up ten thousand feet high. If I hadn't made off double-quick I'd have no hair left!"

Pigsy laughed. "You're always boasting that no thunderbolt or fire can harm you. How is it you're so afraid of fire today?"

"You fool, what do you know?" retorted Monkey. "I was on my guard before, so I came to no harm. But today I was so eager to put out the flames that I didn't recite any charm to ward off fire or use any magic to protect myself. That's why all the hair has been burnt off my thighs."

Sandy asked, "What shall we do now with this great blaze cutting our road to the West."

Pigsy said, "Let's find a way where there's no fire."

Tripitaka asked, "In which direction is there none?"

"There's no fire in the east, south or north," answered Pigsy.

"Where are the Buddhist scriptures?" asked Tripitaka.

"In the west," was Pigsy's reply.

Tripitaka said, "The only way I want to go is that which leads to the scriptures."

Sandy said, "There are flames where the scriptures are, and where there are no flames there are no scriptures either. We can neither go forward nor back."

While the master and his disciples were disputing at cross purposes, someone called to them, "Don't worry, holy ones! Have something to eat before making any decision."

They turned to see an old man in a long cape, a crescent-shaped hat and hob-nailed boots, who was holding a dragon-head wand. Behind him was a demon with a nuzzle like the beak of a hawk and broad cheeks like a fish. This demon had on its head a bronze pot full of steamed bread and cakes, cooked millet and rice.

Approaching them from the west, the old man bowed and said, "I am the local god of the Flaming Mountain. I know that Saint Monkey is helping a holy monk in his pilgrimage and that you are unable to advance. I have come to offer you some food."

"Never mind the food," said Monkey. "When can the fire be put out so that my master can pass this place?"

"To put out the fire, you must borrow Rakshasa's palm-leaf fan," said the local deity.

Monkey picked up the fan from the road. "Here it is," he said. "But the fire burnt higher than ever when I fanned it."

The local god examined the fan and laughed. "This isn't it. Rakshasa fooled you."

"How can I get the genuine one?" asked Monkey.

The local deity bowed and said with a smile, "To borrow the genuine fan, you must first find the Prince of Mighty Strength."

If you want to know the reason for this, you must hear what is related in the next chapter.

CHAPTER 60

The Ox Demon Calls Off a Fight and Goes to a Feast
Monkey Makes a Second Attempt to Get the Fan

The local god said, "The Prince of Mighty Strength is the Ox Demon King."

"Was this fire started by the Ox Demon King?" asked Monkey. "Is that why it's called the Flaming Mountain?"

"No, no," said the local deity. "I don't dare tell you unless you promise not to be angry."

"Go on," said Monkey. "Why should I be angry?"

Then the local deity said, "You were the one who started this fire, sir."

"Where was I at the time?" demanded Monkey angrily. "What nonsense is this! Am I the sort of person that starts fires?"

"I see you don't recognize me. There used to be no mountain here; but five hundred years ago when you played havoc in heaven, the god Er Lang captured you and took you to the Taoist Patriarch, who put you in the Eight Trigram Furnace. When they opened the furnace you kicked it over and a few bricks fell down here, still flaming, and turned into the Flaming Mountain. In those days I was the priest in charge of the furnace in Tushita Palace. To punish me for not keeping better watch, the Patriarch sent me here to be the local god of the Flaming Mountain."

When Pigsy heard this he swore, "So that explains your get-up! You're a Taoist priest turned local deity."

Still somewhat sceptical, Monkey asked, "Tell me, then, why I have to find the Prince of Mighty Strength?"

The local god answered, "He is Rakshasa's husband. Some time ago he left her and went to Cloud-Reaching Cave in the Mountain of Gathering Thunder. A fox king there after living for ten thousand years had died leaving a daughter, Princess Marble Face. This girl had property worth millions but no husband; and two years ago, impressed by the power of the Ox Demon King, she invited him to be her husband and made over all her property to him. So the Ox Demon King has left Rakshasa for some time, never going back. If you find him, you can ask for the real fan. Then you can put out the fire and continue on your way with your master. You will be doing the local people a good turn by getting rid of the Flaming Mountain for ever. And I shall be forgiven and allowed to go back to Heaven to the Taoist Patriarch."

"Where is this Mountain of Gathering Thunder?" asked Monkey. "Is it far from here?"

"It is over three thousand *li* north of here."

Then Monkey told Sandy and Pigsy to take care of their master, and asked the local god to keep watch there. The next instant he had vanished. In no time he reached a mountain which towered to the sky. Descending from the clouds to alight on a peak, he looked about him. That was a magnificent mountain!

> Its summit soared up to the azure sky,
> Its great roots reached down to the Nether Stream;
> The sun shone warm in front of it, the wind blew
>   cold behind it;
> The plants on its sunny side knew nothing of
>   winter.
> The ice on its windy side never melted in summer;

Mountain brooks flowed eternally into Dragon
    Pool,
And hillside flowers bloomed early by Tiger Cave;
Springs flowed from a thousand sources like flying
    jasper,
Flowers bloomed all together like outspread
    tapestry;
Here were twisted trees on twisted mountain
    ridges,
Gnarled pines beside gnarled rocks;
Peaks, crags, precipices, chasms,
Sweet flowers, rare fruit, red vines, purple bam-
    boos,
Green pines and verdant willows;
Unchanging was the bloom in every season,
Immortal as the dragon it endured.

After surveying this scene, Monkey plunged down
from the peak to explore the mountain. He was at a
loss for the way when he saw in the shade of the pines
a girl swaying gracefully towards him with a sprig of
fragrant orchid in her hand. He hid behind a grotesque
rock to have a good look at her. What was she like,
this girl?

Hers was the beauty that makes kingdoms fall,
Lingering her lotus steps;
Hers was the loveliness sung in days of old,
Like a blossom that can speak, like jade but
    sweeter;
Her black hair was piled up high,
Her eyes were limpid as an autumn pool;
Beneath her skirt tiny arched slippers peeped,

From her sleeves fluttered tapering fingers;
With crimson lips and sparkling teeth,
She seemed the goddess who comes with rain and
  clouds;
Smooth as the River Jing, fair as Mount Emei,
She was lovelier than the fairest maids of Chengdu.

As the girl slowly approached the rock, Monkey bowed and said softly, "Where are you going, lady?"

At the sound of his voice the girl looked up in surprise. Frightened by Monkey's unprepossessing appearance, she faltered, "Who are you? Why should you ask?"

Monkey thought, "I had better not tell her about our search for scriptures and the magic fan, because she may be in league with the Ox Demon King. I'll pretend I'm here to see him."

Since he was silent, the girl changed her tune and asked sharply, "Who are you? How dare you accost me?"

Monkey bowed and answered with a smile, "I come from the Mountain of Emerald Clouds. Being new to your honourable district, I don't know the way. May I ask you whether this is the Mountain of Gathering Thunder?" When she replied that it was, Monkey continued, "And where is Cloud-Reaching Cave?"

"Why do you ask?"

"I have come from Princess Iron Fan of Palm-Leaf Cavern on the Mountain of Emerald Clouds to fetch home the Ox Demon King."

At that the girl was very angry. Flushing up to her ears, she swore, "The stupid bitch! The Ox Demon King has lived here with me for less than two years and I have given him a great store of jewels, gold and silver, brocade and silk, supplying him every month with firewood and rice so that he can enjoy himself just as he pleases. Is she utterly without shame that she still wants him back?"

Realizing that this was Princess Marble Face, Monkey drew out his staff and swore, "Bitch yourself! You bought the Ox Demon King with your family property, buying yourself a husband, you shameless slut! How dare you call others names?"

The frightened girl lost her head and darted off, running away in terror. Monkey followed, shouting, and once past the shady pines he found the entrance to the cave. The girl ran in and slammed the gate behind her. Monkey put away his staff and stopped to look round. It was a lovely spot.

> Dense woods, steep precipices,
> Were clothed with shady creepers and sweet orchids;
> Brooks splashed like tinkling jade through tall bamboos,
> The smooth rocks deftly billowed fallen petals;
> Mist shrouded distant hills, sun shone on clouds,
> Dragons and tigers roared, storks and orioles sang;
> Loveliness so secluded,
> For ever bejewelled with flowers,
> Was a match for the fairy cavern of Mount Tiantai,
> Fair as the magic islands of Penglai.

Let us leave Monkey enjoying the scenery while we follow the girl. Running until she was in a lather of sweat and panting for fright, she rushed into the Ox

Demon King's library where she found him quietly studying a volume on alchemy. She flounced angrily on to his lap, scratching her cheeks and wailing. With a smile the Demon King said, "Don't look so cross, sweet. What is it?"

The girl stamped and scolded, "This is all your fault, you monster!"

"What have I done now?" he asked with another smile.

"Because I was left an orphan, I married you for your protection. You had a name for courage, yet I find you are nothing but a useless, hen-pecked fellow."

The Ox Demon King took her in his arms and said, "Now, my love, what have I done wrong? Just tell me and I can apologize."

"I was strolling outside in the shade just now, picking orchids, when I was suddenly accosted by a jutting jawed hairy-faced monk. I nearly died of fright. As soon as I'd recovered enough to ask who he was, he told me Princess Iron Fan had sent him to fetch the Ox Demon King back. When I had something to say to that, he swore at me and chased me with a stick. If I hadn't run fast, the fellow would have killed me! You're the cause of all this trouble! You'll be the death of me!"

Not till the Ox King made a formal apology and used many endearing terms and blandishments did his concubine stop sulking. Then he assured her emphatically, "My sweet, I have no secrets from you. Palm-Leaf Cavern is a quiet, out-of-the-way spot and my wife who has studied the Truth since she was young is now a regular saint. In fact my household is so strict and correct that we don't even keep a page boy. How could she send this man with the jutting jaw? Take my word for it, he's a monster from elsewhere who has come here in her name to see me. Let me go and have a look at him."

Then the Ox Demon King strode out of the library to put on his armour in the hall. Taking up an iron staff he went out of the gate. "Who is making a disturbance out there?" he shouted.

Monkey observed that the Ox had changed a great deal in the last five centuries.

> His iron helmet gleamed like polished silver,
> His golden armour was covered with embroidered
>   velvet;
> He was shod in pointed, white-soled deer-skin
>   boots,
> And his belt of twisted silk had a lion-head buckle.
> His eyes were mirror-bright.
> Red rainbows his eyebrows,
> A scarlet bowl his mouth,
> Rows of copper plates his teeth;
> When he roared, the mountain deities took fright;
> When he stirred, the foul fiends trembled;
> Known through all the Four Seas as the World
>   Destroyer,
> Styled the Demon King of the West for his mighty
>   strength.

Monkey straightened his clothes to advance and make a deep bow. "Do you remember me, brother?" he inquired.

Returning his bow, the Ox Demon King said,

"Aren't you Monkey Sun Wukong, the Paragon of Heaven?"

"That's right. I haven't paid my respects to you for a long time. I found out your whereabouts just now from a woman. I must congratulate you — you're looking very well."

"Hold that smooth tongue of yours!" swore the Ox Demon King. "I heard that after playing havoc in Heaven you were captured and imprisoned by Buddha under the Mountain of Five Peaks. Not long ago you were released from your punishment to escort Tripitaka on a pilgrimage to the West to find Buddhist scriptures. Why did you harm my son Red Boy at Fire-Cloud Cave in the Valley of Withered Pines on the Howling Mountain? I was just wondering how to pay you back, and here you come looking for me!"

Monkey bowed and said, "Don't blame me for what wasn't my fault, brother. Your son captured my master, meaning to eat him, and there was nothing I could do. Luckily Guan Yin rescued Tripitaka and prevailed on your son to mend his ways, so that now he is the angel Sudhana with a higher status than yours, enjoying perfect bliss, complete freedom and eternal youth. What's wrong with that? In what way am I to blame?"

"You with your glib tongue!" swore the Ox Demon King. "You may deny injuring my son, but why did you bully my dear concubine and chase her all the way home?"

Monkey laughed. "When I couldn't find you, brother, I asked a woman the way. I had no idea she was your second wife. Since she answered me rudely, I may have spoken sharply and frightened her. I hope you'll overlook it."

"In that case, for old times' sake I'll let you off."

"I am overwhelmed by your generosity," said Monkey. "But I have another favour to ask. I really must beg your help."

"Wretched Monkey, don't you know when you're well off?" swore the Ox. "Don't pester me but go while the going's good. How dare you ask my help?"

"I'll tell you the truth," said Monkey. "I'm escorting Tripitaka on his pilgrimage West, and our way has been blocked by the Flaming Mountain. I learned from the local people of your respected wife Rakshasa's palm-leaf fan. When I went to your place yesterday to borrow it, she wouldn't lend it to me. So I've come to beg your help. I hope in the great goodness of your heart you will come with me to your wife and at all costs lend me that fan to put out the flames. I shall return it to you as soon as I've escorted my master across the mountain."

At this the Ox Demon King flew into a passion. Grinding his teeth, he swore, "What insolence! So you want the fan, do you! No doubt you've already insulted my wife and, when she refused you, you came to find me. You chased my concubine too! The proverb says: Don't insult a friend's wife or bully his concubine. You've done both, you impudent ape! Come here and let me have a whack at you!"

"If you want to fight, brother, I'm not afraid," said Monkey. "But I'm in earnest about borrowing your magic fan. Won't you please lend it to me?"

"If you can win three rounds against me, I'll tell my wife to lend it. If not, I'll kill you to avenge myself."

"Right you are, brother," said Monkey. "I have been so remiss, not calling on you all this time, that I don't know how you fight now compared with the old days. Let's have a try."

Without a word the Ox Demon King raised his iron mace and smashed it down. Monkey parried with his gold-hooped staff. It was a grand fight that followed.

> A gold-hooped staff, an iron mace —
> In rage they break off their friendship.
> One says, "You wretched ape, you ruined my son!"
> The other, "Don't be angry; your son is an angel."
> One shouts, "How dare you come to seek me out?"
> The other says, "I came to ask a favour."
> One wants the fan to safeguard Tripitaka,
> The other is too niggardly to lend it.
> They bandy words, forgetting their old friendship,
> Enraged to be so ill-used.
> The Ox King's mace is like a darting dragon,
> Monkey's staff would put demons to flight;
> First they battle at the foot of the mountain,
> Then soar into the clouds
> To display their might in mid-air,
> Revealing their skill in a bright aura of light;
> Their weapons clash before the gate of Heaven,
> But neither combatant can worst the other.

They battled more than a hundred times, yet neither could defeat the other. At the height of the fray, a voice called from the mountain peak, "Lord Ox, the prince, my master, sends you his greetings. He hopes you will come early to the feast."

The Ox King warded off Monkey's staff with his mace. "Stop a minute, Monkey!" he cried. "Wait till I come back from a feast with a friend." With that he descended from the clouds and went to his cave to tell

Princess Marble Face, "My love, that fellow with the jutting jaw is Monkey Sun Wukong. I've given him such a drubbing with my mace that he'll hardly dare come back. So don't you worry. I'm off now to drink with a friend." Then he unbuckled his armour, put on a black velvet coat and went out to mount his Golden-Eyed Wave-Cleaving Steed. Having ordered his followers to guard the cave, he rode off northwest through the clouds.

Monkey watching from a high peak wondered, "Who is this friend of the Ox and where is the feast? Suppose I follow him?" He shook himself and changed into a breeze to go after the Ox. In no time they reached a mountain where the Ox King vanished. Resuming his own form, Monkey alighted on the mountain after him. He found a deep, clear pool and beside it a stone tablet on which was inscribed in massive characters: The Pool of Emerald Waves, Craggy Mountain. Monkey thought, "The old Ox must have dived into this pool. No doubt the monster here is a water-serpent, dragon, fish, turtle, tortoise or alligator. I'll pop in too and have a look." He made a magic pass, recited a spell and shook himself, changing into a crab about thirty-six pounds in weight. He jumped with a splash into the pool and sank straight to the bottom. There he was confronted by a finely carved arch, under which was tethered the Ox King's Golden-Eyed Steed. The other side of the arch was completely dry. Monkey crawled inside and looked carefully around. He heard music from one direction, and this is what he saw:

A vermilion palace like those upon the earth,
With pearly arches, golden tiles, jade lintels

Tortoise-shell screens and coral-studded balus-
     trades;
An auspicious aura glowed round the lotus throne,
Lighting up heaven above and earth below.
This was no palace of the sky or ocean,
But a place lovelier than the fairy isles;
In that high hall the hosts and guests were feasting,
Officials great and small wearing crowns and
     pearls;
Fairies were summoned to bring ivory dishes,
Immortal maidens tuned their instruments,
Whales sang and huge crabs danced,
Turtles played pipes, an alligator sounded drums,
The pearl at the dragon's neck shed light on the
     feast,
Strange hieroglyphics graced the kingfisher screen,
Lobster-antennae curtains hung in the halls,
All manner of instruments made heavenly music,
Resounding strains lingered among the clouds,
The green-headed perch strummed the cithern,
The red-eyed mussel fluted,
The mandarin fish presented venison,
The dragon's daughter wore a gold phoenix tiara;
They fed on rare, celestial fare
And drank the heady, heavenly elixir.

The Ox King was in the seat of honour with three
or four serpent monsters beside him and in front an old
dragon accompanied by his sons, grandsons, wife and
daughter, all of them drinking very merrily. Monkey
was going straight up to them when the old dragon
saw him and ordered: "Catch that lawless crab!" The

dragon sons and grandsons rushed forward and seized Monkey.

Then in human speech Monkey begged, "Spare me! Spare me!"

The old dragon demanded, "Where are you from, crab? How dare you break into our hall and scuttle about so wildly before our honoured guest? If you want to live, out with the truth!"

Then Monkey spun them a tale and it was this:

> I have lived all my life in the lake,
> With my cave beside the cliff,
> After long years I have attained my wish,
> My title is Sidewise Scuttling Knight in Armour.
> Crawling through grass and mud
> I have never learned manners;
> Now, ignorant of etiquette, I have trespassed —
> I crave Your Lordship's pardon.

When the other monsters at the feast heard this, they bowed to the old dragon and said, "This is the crab knight's first visit to our palace, and he does not know how to behave. We hope Your Lordship will pardon him."

The old dragon having agreed, the monsters ordered, "Let this fellow go. Next time he will be beaten. He may wait outside."

Monkey assented and fled straight out to the arch, where he reflected: "The Ox King is fond of drinking: it will be a long time before the feast breaks up. Even then, he won't lend me the fan. I had better steal his Golden-Eyed Steed and pass myself off as him to deceive that woman Rakshasa. In that way I can get the fan and see my master over the mountain."

So Monkey took his own form, untethered the Golden-Eyed Steed, leapt into the saddle and rode out through the water. Once out of the pool, he changed himself into the semblance of the Ox King, and urging his mount through the clouds in no time reached Palm-Leaf Cavern on the Mountain of Emerald Clouds.

"Open the gate!" he called.

The two maids inside opened the gate and seeing it was the Ox King went in to announce: "Our master is here, madam."

Rakshasa hastily arranged her cloudy tresses and hurried out on lotus feet to welcome him. Monkey, having alighted and tied up the Golden-Eyed Steed, went boldly ahead with the deception; and Rakshasa, unable to detect the imposture, led him in by the hand, bidding her maids prepare seats and serve tea. The whole household was on its best behaviour now that the master was back.

After the customary greetings had been exchanged the sham Ox King said, "We have not seen each other for a long time, madam."

"I hope all has gone well with you," responded Rakshasa, adding, "you are so fond of your new wife that you have deserted me. What brings you back to-day?"

Monkey laughed, "Desert you? How could I? But after Princess Marble Face took me into her family we have been busy with household affairs and many friends have called, delaying my return for a long time. We have acquired a new property, though." Then he continued, "Recently I heard that Monkey Sun Wukong who is escorting Tripitaka has come to the Flaming Mountain. I am afraid he may try to borrow the fan.

I hate that fellow for the injury he did our son, which we have not yet avenged. So if he comes, send word to me. I shall catch him and cut him into ten thousand pieces to work off our anger."

To this Rakshasa replied with tears, "Great king, it is said that a man without a wife has no one to look after his property, while a woman without a husband has no one to protect her. I nearly lost my life at the hands of that ape."

Monkey, pretending to be outraged, swore, "When did the scoundrel leave?"

"He hasn't gone yet. Yesterday he came to borrow the fan, and in the hate I bear him for injuring our son I buckled on my armour, seized my swords and went out to teach the wretch a lesson. He let me strike him and kept addressing me as his sister-in-law and referring to you as his sworn brother."

"Yes, five hundred years ago we were sworn brothers. There were seven of us."

"I swore at him and I struck him," Rakshasa continued. "But the wretch neither argued nor fought back. Then I fanned him away with my fan. But he managed somehow to find a wind-calming method, for this morning he was back shouting at the gate. And this time when I waved the fan he didn't move, and when I swung my swords at him he fought back. Finding his staff too heavy for me, I ran inside and closed the gate, but he contrived to get into my belly and nearly killed me. I had to call him Brother and give him the fan."

At that Monkey beat his breast in mock regret. "What a pity, what a pity! You shouldn't have done that. How could you give him our treasure? That's really too bad."

Rakshasa laughed. "Don't be angry, my lord. The

fan I gave him was a fake. I had to trick him to get him out of the way."

"Where is the real fan?" asked Monkey.

"Don't worry. It's safe with me."

Rakshasa told her maids to bring wine to celebrate the Ox King's return. Then she offered a cup to him, saying, "You have a new wife now, my lord, but I hope you won't forget your old one. Try some of our home-made wine."

Monkey had to accept the cup, but with a smile he of-fered it to her, saying, "You must drink first, madam. I have been away a long time managing my new prop-erty and I am grateful to you for supervising the household. Let me express my gratitude."

Rakshasa drained the cup, refilled it and handed it to him remarking, "There is an old saying that a wife is her husband's helpmate. You are my prop and sup-port — what thanks do you owe me?"

This little ceremony over, they sat down to drink. But Monkey, not liking to break his fast, simply ate a little fruit as he chatted with her. Several cups of wine made Rakshasa merry and rather amorous. She cuddled up to Monkey, holding his hand and murmuring softly to him, rubbing his shoulder and whispering endearments as she held the cup first to his mouth and then to hers and fed him fruit from her own lips. Monkey, pretending a fondness he did not feel, chatted, laughed and returned her caresses.

> Wine makes for poetry and sweeps grief away,
> A cure for every ill;
> A stickler for etiquette will relax after drinking,
> A woman will lose her restraint and laugh out loud;

Red as the peach she blushes,
Pliant as the willow she sways;
Her tongue is loosened, she begins to flirt;
Sometimes she smooths her hair with slender fingers,
Sometimes she shakes a sleeve, arches a foot;
She bends her powdered neck, sways from the waist;
Though not a word is said of love's delight,
Her breast is half revealed, her gown undone,
And tipsily swaying,
She darts forth amorous looks from languishing eyes.

When Monkey saw that she was thoroughly tipsy, he asked, "Where did you put the real fan? You must be careful, Monkey is a wily creature. Don't let him steal it by a trick."

With a smile Rakshasa took the fan from her mouth. It was no larger than an apricot leaf. She handed it to him, saying, "Here it is!"

Monkey took it rather sceptically. "How can such a small fan put out a fire?" he wondered. "This may be another fake."

When Rakshasa saw him brooding over the fan, she nestled closer and laid her cheek against his. "Put away the treasure and let us drink, darling," she said. "What's on your mind?"

Monkey seized this opportunity to ask, "How can such a tiny thing put out flames that have spread over eight hundred *li*?"

Too drunk to be suspicious, Rakshasa reproached him, "My lord, we have been parted for two years, and no doubt all the pleasure you've had day and night with Princess Marble Face has so bewitched you that you've forgotten your treasure. Surely you know that if you put your left thumb on the seventh red thread of the handle and call out: He-hi-ho-she-shi-shu-hu! the fan will grow twelve feet long. This fan has such marvellous powers that it can put out even eighty thousand *li* of flames."

Monkey promptly memorized the incantation and put the fan in his mouth. Then he rubbed his face, resumed his own form and cried fiercely, "Look, Rakshasa! Am I your husband? Aren't you ashamed of the way you've been flirting with me?"

When she saw that it was Monkey, Rakshasa knocked over the table in her panic and fell to the ground, quite overcome with shame. "Oh, this will be the death of me!" she wailed.

Not caring what became of her, Monkey shook her off and strode out of Palm-Leaf Cavern. Thus, unmoved by female beauty, returning exultant, he leapt on to a cloud and soared to the summit of the mountain where he took the fan from his mouth and did as he had been told. Laying his left thumb on the seventh red thread of the handle he chanted: He-hi-ho-she-shi-shu-hu! Sure enough, the fan at once became twelve feet long. He held it up and examined it carefully. This was certainly different from the bogus fan: it emitted a sacred aura, and its thirty-six red threads merged into the handle like veins. Since Monkey had asked only how to make the fan larger, not how to make it smaller, he had to carry it bulky as it was on his shoulder as he returned by the path he had come.

Meanwhile the Ox Demon King after feasting with

the other monsters at the bottom of the Pool of Emerald Waves went out to find his Golden-Eyed Steed had disappeared. The old dragon called the monsters together and asked, "Who has taken away Lord Ox's Golden-Eyed Steed?"

The monsters kneeling replied, "None of us would dare do such a thing. We were all at the feast presenting wine and dishes or singing and making music together. Not one of us came here."

"Our own people would not dare do this," said the old dragon. "But did no stranger come here?"

The young dragons answered, "The only stranger was that crab monster who came as we were starting the feast."

When the Ox King heard this, the truth dawned on him. "No further investigation is needed," he said. "Earlier on when you sent to invite me, I was with Monkey Sun Wukong. He is escorting the monk Tripitaka to look for Buddhist scriptures but they have been stopped by the Flaming Mountain. When I refused to lend him my palm-leaf fan we came to blows, but neither side worsted the other. I left him to come to your feast. Monkey is always up to some mischief or other. He must have transformed himself into a crab to come here for news and stolen my steed to go back to my wife and try to get the fan by a trick."

The monsters hearing this were greatly perturbed. "Is that Monkey who played such havoc in heaven?" they asked.

"That's the one," said the Ox King. "If any trouble crops up on your way to the Western Heaven, try to steer clear of him."

"What shall we do about your steed?" asked the old dragon.

The Ox King laughed. "Don't worry. You'd better go back. I'll catch him up."

Cleaving the waters he left the bottom of the pool and rode on a murky cloud straight to Palm-Leaf Cavern on the Mountain of Emerald Clouds, where Rakshasa could be heard stamping, beating her breast and shrieking. The Ox King pushed open the gate and found his Golden-Eyed Steed tethered in the yard. He called out, "Madam, where is Monkey?"

At sight of him the maids fell to their knees. "The master is here!" they cried.

Rakshasa seized him and butted him with her head. "Plague take you!" she scolded. "How could you be such a fool as to let Monkey steal your Golden-Eyed Steed and take your form to trick me?"

Through clenched teeth the Ox King asked, "Where has the wretch gone?"

Beating her breast, Rakshasa cried, "That villainous ape tricked me out of the fan and went off in his true form. I am bursting with anger!"

"Take good care of yourself and don't worry. I shall catch him up and get the fan from him. Then I'll flay him alive, grind his bones to powder and take out his heart and liver to avenge you!" He shouted to the maids, "Bring me my weapons!"

"They aren't here, sir," they said.

"In that case, bring me the princess' weapons."

So the maids brought him Rakshasa's swords. The Ox King stripped off the black velvet coat he had worn to the feast and fastened his inner jacket tightly about him.   Then, brandishing both swords, he left Palm-Leaf Cavern and ran towards the Flaming Mountain.

> The fond wife took Monkey for her heartless husband,
> The fierce Demon King goes forth to seek his foe.

If you want to know what the upshot was, you must listen to what is related in the next chapter.

CHAPTER 61

Pigsy Helps to Defeat the Demon King

Monkey Makes a Third Attempt to Get the Fan

Soon the Ox Demon King came in sight of Monkey walking happily along with the fan over one shoulder. Taken aback, the Demon King said to himself, "So the ape has even learned how to use the fan! If I demand it outright, he's sure to refuse. And if he fans me with it, I'll be blown eighteen thousand *li* away, which would no doubt suit him very well. I've heard that Tripitaka is waiting for him on the road with his two other disciples, Pigsy and Sandy, whom I met when they were monsters. I had better take the form of Pigsy to deceive him in his turn. Monkey is so pleased with himself now that he won't be on his guard."

Now the Ox King could also assume seventy-two different forms and had mastered the same arts of warfare as Monkey except that he was clumsier, less agile and dexterous. Having put away his swords and chanted a spell, he shook himself and changed into the semblance of Pigsy. He made straight for Monkey, calling out, "Here I am, brother!"

Monkey was in the highest spirits. As the proverb says, a cat who has won a fight exults like a tiger. He was too full of his achievements to examine the approaching figure carefully, but seeing what seemed to be Pigsy he called out, "Where are you off to, brother?"

The Demon King spun him this yarn, "You've been away so long that our master was afraid the Ox King had proved too much for you and you were finding it hard to get his magic fan. He told me to look for you."

Monkey laughed. "Don't you worry. I've got it."

"How did you get it?"

"That old Ox and I battled about a hundred rounds, but neither could beat the other. Then he left me to go to the bottom of the Pool of Emerald Waves in Craggy Mountain to feast with a bunch of serpent and dragon monsters. I trailed him there, having changed into a crab, and stole his Golden-Eyed Steed. Then in the form of an ox I went back to Palm-Leaf Cavern to fool that woman Rakshasa, and after we'd played at husband and wife for a while I managed to get the fan from her by a trick."

The Ox King said, "We're grateful for all the trouble you've taken. You must be tired out. Let me carry the fan."

The idea that this Pigsy was a fraud had not even crossed Monkey's mind. So he handed over the fan.

The Ox King knew how to put away the fan. As soon as it was in his hands he chanted an incantation to make it shrink back to the size of an apricot leaf, while at the same time he resumed his own form. "Vile ape!" he swore. "Do you know me?"

At this sight, Monkey reproached himself bitterly. With an oath he stamped his foot and shouted, "Hah! The archer who's been shooting wild-geese all his life has had his eye pecked today by a gosling!" In his rage he swung his iron staff hard against the Ox King's head. The Ox waved his fan. But Monkey, when changing himself into a gnat to slip into Rakshasa's belly, had put the wind-calming pill in his mouth and it had slipped into his stomach. So now his whole body was strong, his whole frame was firm, and hard as the Ox King fanned he could not be moved. The Demon King was disconcerted. Thrusting the fan into his mouth he raised his swords and fought back. The two of them battled desperately in mid-air.

> Sun Wukong, the Paragon of Heaven,
> And the Ox Demon King, the World Destroyer,
> All for the sake of the palm-leaf fan
> Made trial of their strength in battle.
> For once wily Monkey slipped up
> And was outwitted by the bold Ox King.
> Now one attacks ruthlessly with his gold-hooped staff,
> The other wields his blue blades skilfully;
> Monkey in his might emits a coloured halo,
> The Ox King in his rage sheds a bright light;
> They fight bravely, fired with hatred.
> Gnashing their teeth in fury.
> Dust rises till the earth and sky grow dark;
> A sand-storm swirls till ghosts and deities hide.
> One shouts, "How dare you trick me!"
> The other: "How dare you lay hands on my wife!"
> They bandy high words in their passion,
> "For deceiving my wife," says the Ox King,
> "You shall suffer punishment at the hands of the law."
> The clever Monkey and the fierce Ox King
> Will brook no argument but fight to the end;
> Hard they thrust with staff and swords —
> Whoever slackens for an instant will go to Hell.

Let us leave them locked in battle and return to Tripitaka waiting at the roadside. The sweltering heat of the flames combined with his anxiety and thirst made him ask the local god, "Can you tell me, respected deity, how powerful this Ox Demon King is?"

"Very powerful indeed, with a great store of magic," replied the local deity. "Monkey will find a worthy opponent in him."

Tripitaka said, "Monkey is a swift traveller, who can usually cover two thousand *li* in no time. I can't think why he has been gone a whole day, unless he is fighting with the Ox King." He called to Sandy and Pigsy, "Which of you, Wuneng and Wujing, will go to meet Monkey? If you find him fighting some enemy, you can help him to get the fan to put an end to this heat. Then we can cross the mountain and go on our way."

"It's getting late," said Pigsy. "I'd gladly go and meet him, but I don't know the way to the Mountain of Gathering Thunder."

"I know the way," said the local deity. "If Lord Sandy will keep the master company, I'll go with you."

Tripitaka welcomed this suggestion. "That is extremely kind of you," he said. "When our task is done we shall show our gratitude."

Then Pigsy bestirred himself, tightened the belt over his black silk coat, took up the rake which served him as a weapon and rode eastwards on the clouds with the local god. As they journeyed they heard loud battle cries and felt a wild gust of wind. Pigsy stopped the clouds and saw Monkey embroiled with the Ox King.

The local deity cried, "Go ahead, Lord Pigsy!"

Then Pigsy clutching his rake bellowed, "Here I am, brother!"

"You fool!" swore Monkey. "You've spoilt the whole show."

"The master told me to come and find you," said

Pigsy. "Because I didn't know the way we spent some time discussing what to do, till the local god offered to bring me here. I may be late, but how have I spoilt the show?"

"I'm not blaming you for being late," said Monkey. "This confounded Ox has no sense of what is right. I got the fan from Rakshasa, but he took your form and said he had come to meet me. I was feeling so pleased that I passed the fan to him. Then he showed his true form and we started fighting here. That's why I said you spoilt the show."

At this, Pigsy was very angry. Brandishing his rake, he swore at the Ox King, "Plague on you, you bloated ox! How dare you pass yourself off as me to deceive my brother and spoil our relationship?" He started striking out wildly.

Now the Ox King was too tired after fighting all day with Monkey to resist Pigsy's fierce onslaught with his rake. He turned to flee. But the local god of the Flaming Mountain led a ghostly army to block his way and said, "Prince of Mighty Strength, we entreat you to stop fighting! The monk Tripitaka is on his way to find scriptures in the West and all the deities are on his side. His quest has been announced to Heaven, Earth and the Nether Regions and won universal support. Give us your fan now quickly to put out the flames so that he can cross the mountain safely. Otherwise Heaven will visit its wrath upon you."

"Do be reasonable, local deity!" said the Ox King. "That scurvy ape has kidnapped my son, bullied my concubine and deceived my wife. To get even with him for all these wicked deeds I am itching to swallow him up and turn him into dung for the dogs to eat. I am certainly not going to lend him my treasure."

While they were parleying, Pigsy came up and swore, "You pain in the neck! Hand over that fan at once if you want your life spared!" The Ox King had to swing round and fight Pigsy again with his swords. Then Monkey came with his staff to Pigsy's aid. It was a tremendous contest!

> The pig spirit, the ox monster
> And the immortal monkey who went up to Heaven —
> The Truth must be steeled in battle,
> With the Earth Element and Primal Cause;
> The rake's nine teeth are sharp,
> The double blades are pliant,
> The iron staff is a formidable weapon,
> And the Earth God lends a hand.
> The three elements contend together in turn,
> Each exerting its magic power;
> Gold comes when the Ox is made to till the earth,
> Wood is at rest when the Pig returns to the furnace,
> When the mind is absent, Truth is not to be found;
> To keep the spirit within, Monkey must be harnessed.
> Wild is the clamour, painful is the quest,
> As three weapons clash together;
> The rake and swords are used with an ill purpose,
> The gold-hooped staff is raised with good intent;
> They fight until the stars and moon hide their light
> And a chill mist darkens the sky!

The Ox King battled bravely and stubbornly, fight-

ing each step of the way. A whole night they contended, neither side giving ground, till it was dawn again.
They were now just in front of Cloud-Reaching Cave
on the Mountain of Gathering Thunder, and the deafening din made by these three combatants, the local deity
and his ghostly troops roused Princess Marble Face,
who asked her maids to find out the cause of this disturbance. The small monster at the gate reported, "Our
master is fighting that man with the jutting jaw who
came yesterday, a long-snouted, big-eared monk and
the local god of the Flaming Mountain."

When Princess Marble Face heard this, she ordered
her garrison officers great and small to go to her husband's aid with lances and swords. A hundred or so
were mobilized in all, and they trooped forth eagerly,
brandishing spears and staffs as they called to the Ox
King, "Great prince, we have been sent by our mistress
to aid you!"

"Splendid!" exulted the Ox King.

When these monsters charged with their weapons,
Pigsy taken unawares could not withstand them and
fled in defeat trailing his rake after him. With one
somersault Monkey leapt out of the fray, while the
ghostly troops scattered too. So the Ox King was the
victor. He went back to the cave with his monsters and
made fast the gate behind him.

"That's a brave rogue!" said Monkey. "He fought
me from yesterday afternoon till tonight, and I couldn't
beat him. Then luckily the two of you came to help me.
But though we fought one whole night and half a day,
he showed no sign of exhaustion. Those small monsters

of his seemed a pretty tough lot too. Now he has closed
his gate and won't come out. What shall we do?"

Pigsy said, "Brother, you left our master at about ten
o'clock yesterday morning, but you didn't start fighting
till the afternoon. Where were you in between?"

"After leaving you I came straight to this mountain,"
said Monkey. "I met a young woman and when I spoke
to her I found she was his favourite concubine Princess
Marble Face. I frightened her with my iron staff so
that she ran into the cave to fetch the Ox King. He
shouted and argued with me for a while, after which
we came to blows. A couple of hours later he was invited to a feast and I followed him to the bottom of the
Pool of Emerald Waves in Craggy Mountain, where I
changed myself into a crab to overhear their talk. Then
I stole his Golden-Eyed Steed and went back to Palm-
Leaf Cavern in the Mountain of Emerald Clouds in the
semblance of the Ox King. I tricked Rakshasa out of
the fan and when I went out and tried her magic I made
the fan grow big but couldn't make it small again. As
I was walking away with it on my shoulder, he came
along in your shape and got the fan back by a trick.
That took quite a few hours."

Pigsy replied, "As men say, 'When a boatload of
beancurd capsizes into the sea, brine returns to brine.'
If we can't get the fan, how can we help our master to
cross this mountain? Let's turn back and try some other
way."

"Don't be upset or lose heart," urged the local god.
"It's no good talking about turning back; even going by
a devious path shows a lack of virtue. The ancients
said, 'Never take a by-path.' How can you think of

turning back? Your master is sitting on the right road waiting eagerly for you to succeed."

"Quite right," agreed Monkey firmly. "Don't talk like a fool, Pigsy! The local god is right. We must persevere."

> We must fight it out, showing our skill;
> Watch me use my transformations!
> Coming West I have found no rival,
> The Ox is simply one form taken by the mind,
> And now we are meeting together;
> But first we must contend for the magic fan,
> With coolness put out the flames
> And break through the void to reach Buddha.
> When the deed is done we shall go to paradise
> And feast in bliss the immortals.

When Pigsy heard this, he took heart and said eagerly:

> Quite right! Let us go, let us go,
> Whether the Ox wills it or no!
> The Wood Element becomes a Pig,
> The Ox returns to the Earth;
> The Metal Element is Monkey;
> When one fight there will be peace.
> The palm-leaf fan signifies Water,
> When the flames are out all will be done;
> Day and night we must press on without rest,
> When success is won we shall go to the feast.

So the two went forward with the local god at the head of his ghostly troops. With their rake and iron staff they smashed down the front gate of the Cloud-

Reaching Cave. The officers guarding the gate shook with fear and dashed inside to report, "Great prince, Monkey and his men have broken our gate!"

The Ox King was in the middle of describing the fight to Princess Marble Face and cursing Monkey. This news threw him into a passion. Hastily donning his armour he seized his iron mace and rushed out, swearing, "Vile ape! Who do you think you are? How dare you make this disturbance at my gate and break it in?"

Pigsy stepped forward and swore, "Stinking old hide! Who are you to call other people names? Stand your ground and look out for my rake!"

"Filth-guzzling swine!" swore the Ox King. "You're beneath my notice. But send that baboon here at once!"

"Old bag of hay!" cried Monkey. "Yesterday I counted you as my sworn brother, but today we are enemies. Take a blow from my staff!"

The Ox King put up a fearless resistance and this time the battle raged even more fiercely. The three mighty ones grappled together. What a fight!

> The rake and iron staff with miraculous might
> Led the ghostly troops to fight;
> The Ox revealed a fierceness, strength and power
> Matched nowhere under heaven.
> The rake and staff dealt strong blows,
> The iron mace worked wonders of bravery,
> Ding-dong! the weapons clashed,
> Thrusting, parrying, yet neither side giving way
> As they contended for supremacy.
> Earth was their reinforcement,
> Wood and Earth were tempered together.

Those two demanded, "Lend us that palm-leaf
fan!"
This one retorted, "You deceived my wife,
Pursued my concubine, injured my son
And have made fresh trouble at my gate!"
Monkey cried, "Beware of my staff — it will flay
you alive!"
And Pigsy, "Mind my rake — it will riddle your
carcase!"
But the Ox Demon was no whit afraid
And swung his iron mace to resist.
Blow followed blow like clouds and rain
Scattering mist and wind.
With hatred in their hearts they fought,
Determined to destroy the enemy,
Resisting and parrying, they did not weaken.
The two brothers attacked in concert;
The Ox King withstood single-handed with his
mace;
Three or four hours they fought,
Till at last the Demon King gave ground.

The three battled recklessly for about a hundred
rounds. Pigsy's stubborn temper was roused and with
Monkey to back him he lashed out wildly with his rake.
The Ox King could not withstand such an attack and
turned to flee to his cave, but the local god and his
ghostly troops barred the way.

"Halt, Prince of Mighty Strength!" they cried. "We
are here."

When the Ox saw that he could not slip inside and
that Pigsy and Monkey would soon be upon him, he
tore off his armour in haste, threw down his mace and

with a shake changed himself into a swan to fly up into the sky.

Monkey laughed. "See Pigsy, the old Ox has fled!"

That fool Pigsy did not know what had happened and neither did the local god and his troops. They were staring this way and that up and down the mountain when Monkey pointed a finger, "Isn't that him flying up there?"

Pigsy answered, "That's a swan."

"That's what the old Ox has changed into," explained Monkey.

"In that case, what shall we do?" asked the local god.

"Fight your way into the cavern, both of you. Wipe out all the monsters there and destroy his lair to cut off his retreat. I'm going to pit my transformations against his."

Pigsy and the local deity agreed and started storming the cavern.

Then Monkey put away his gold-hooped staff, recited a spell and with one shake of his body transformed himself into a hawk. He shot into the clouds, then swooped down on the swan, seizing its neck and pecking at its eyes. The Ox King, well aware that this was Monkey, hastily flapped his wings and became an eagle, wheeling back to attack the hawk. Monkey changed into a black vulture to chase the eagle, upon which the Ox King changed into a white stork and with a shrill cry flew south. Monkey halted, shook his plumage and turned into a crimson phoenix crying aloud. At sight of the king of birds whom all feathered creatures must obey, the stork swept down the cliff and became a musk-deer lazily nibbling grass at the foot of the hill. But Monkey also folded his wings and changed into a ravening tiger which with tail outstretched rushed to catch the deer to devour it. The Ox King in panic changed into a spotted leopard and rounded on the tiger, but in face of this onslaught Monkey shook his head and became a gold-eyed lion with a roar like thunder and a head strong as iron, which flung itself against the leopard. The Ox King hastily changed into a bear and rushed to grapple with the lion. Then Monkey rolled on the ground and became an elephant with a trunk like a serpent and tusks like bamboo shoots, which curled its trunk to seize the bear. At that, with a laugh, the Ox King showed his true form. He was a huge white bull whose head towered high as a hill, whose eyes darted light, whose two horns were like iron pagodas and whose teeth seemed a row of sharp swords. He measured more than ten thousand feet from head to tail and about eight thousand feet in height. "Damn you!" he bellowed at Monkey. "What can you do now?"

Monkey decided to show his real form too. Taking out his gold-hooped staff and straightening his back, he shouted, "Grow!" At once he became ten thousand feet tall with a head like Mount Tai, eyes like the sun and moon, mouth like a pool of blood and teeth like gates. Raising his iron staff high, he lunged at the Ox King's head. The Ox sprang forward to gore him. The shock of battle shook the mountains and made earth and heaven quake. As the following verses will testify:

> Evil grows ten thousand feet when Truth grows one foot high,
> The Monkey of the mind is hard put to it to subdue him;

> To extinguish the blazing fire of the Flaming
> Mountain,
> The coolness of the magic fan is needed.
> Firmly the Yellow Dame supports the Dark
> Patriarch;
> With care the Wood Mother wipes out the mon-
> sters;
> The Five Elements in accord, Truth is achieved;
> Free from evil, the mind purified, the Western
> Heaven is attained.

The two of them made great trial of their magic powers as they contended in mid-air, till all the passing spirits and deities, the Six Cyclic Gods and Eighteen Guardian Angels came to hem in the Ox King. Nothing daunted, he thrust east and west with his straight, gleaming iron horns, then lashed south and north with his erect spiky tail. Monkey fought him face to face while the other deities gave aid from the side. The Ox King in desperation rolled on the ground and resumed his previous form to escape back to Palm-Leaf Cavern. Thereupon Monkey also changed back to his normal size and gave chase with the other deities. When the Ox King dashed into the cave and closed the door, refusing to come out, they besieged the whole of the Mountain of Emerald Clouds. As they were about to storm the cavern gate, Pigsy and the local god came up noisily with the ghostly troops. Monkey asked them, "What happened at Cloud-Reaching Cave?"

Pigsy said laughing, "I killed the mistress of that old Ox with my rake, and when I stripped off her clothes I found she was a white-faced wild cat, while her monsters were donkeys, mules, calves, bulls, jackals, foxes, stags, goats, tigers, deer and the like. I killed the lot of them. I also burned all the living quarters in the cavern. The local god told me he has another home here. That's why we've come."

"Well done, brother! Congratulations." applauded Monkey. "I competed at transformations with that old Ox for nothing, for I couldn't beat him. Then he changed back into an enormous white bull and I grew until I filled heaven and earth. I was fighting him when the gods came down and surrounded him. Then he resumed his usual form and went into the cave."

Pigsy asked, "Is that Palm-Leaf Cavern?"

"That's right, where Rakshasa lives."

"Then why not smash our way in and kill them to get the fan?" demanded Pigsy with an oath. "Why let them sit there having a pleasant chat?"

At that, foolish Pigsy showed his might and smashed at the gate with his rake. Crash! Part of the rocky cliff and the gate caved in.

The maid inside hastily informed the Ox King, "Master, someone outside is smashing our front gate!"

The Ox King, who had reached shelter panting, was just telling Rakshasa of his fight with Monkey over the fan. This news threw him into a frenzy. He spat out the fan and handed it to his wife, who, holding it, pleaded with tears in her eyes, "Great king, why don't you give this fan to Monkey so that he calls off his forces?"

The Ox King replied, "Though this is a small thing, madam, I bear him a deep grudge. Just wait here while I fight it out with him."

Once more the Ox King buckled on his armour, chose two swords and sallied forth. He found Pigsy bashing in the gate with his rake. Without a word, the Ox King raised his swords and fell on Pigsy, who warded him off with his rake and fell back a few steps. As he left the gate, Monkey came up with his staff. Then the Ox King rode on the wind away from his cavern and battled with Monkey over the Mountain of Emerald Clouds. Soon he was surrounded by all the gods and the ghostly troops of the local deity too. That was another fine fight!

> Clouds hide the world, mist veils the universe;
> Cold blasts of wind swirl sand and dust;
> His towering rage is like the angry waves,
> Once more he whets his swords and puts on
>   armour;
> His hatred, ocean deep, grows fiercer yet!
> To gain his end, Monkey ignores old friendship,
> To win the fan, Pigsy too shows his might;
> The gods and angel hosts pursue the Ox,
> Whose two hands have no rest
> As he wards off attacks from left and right
> Even the passing birds cannot fly above them,
> The fish cease swimming and sink deeper down;
> Spirits lament, the earth and sky grow dark,
> Dragons and tigers take fright, the sun is dimmed.

The Ox King battled desperately for more than fifty rounds. Then, unable to resist further, he fled north. There he was stopped by the Vajra Po Fa of Mimo Cliff on Mount Wutai, who shouted, "You can't pass this way, Ox Monster! Buddha has given me orders to spread nets in heaven and on earth to capture you."

At that moment up came Monkey, Pigsy and the other

deities. The Ox King hastily turned and fled south. There he was stopped by Vajra Sheng Zhi of Qingliang Cavern in Mount Emei, who shouted, "I am waiting to capture you by order of Buddha!"

Dismayed, his limbs faltering, the Ox King sped east. There he was stopped by Vajra Ta Li of Moer Cliff in Mount Sumeru, who shouted, "Where do you think you are going, old Ox? I have orders from Buddha to capture you."

The Ox King recoiled in fear and fled west. There he was stopped by Vajra Yong Zhu of Jinxia Ridge on Mount Kunlun, who shouted, "Where are you going? I have been instructed by the Buddha of the Temple of the Great Thunder Voice in the Western Heaven to halt you here. I won't let you slip through my fingers!"

The Ox King, trembling with fear, regretted his folly too late. He was surrounded by Buddha's troops and heavenly angels who had spread a great net from which there was no escape. As he was in this desperate plight, Monkey came up with his men and the Ox King rode upwards on a cloud.

This time his way was barred by the Heavenly Prince Li and his son Nezha at the head of yaksas and giants who shouted, "Stop! We have orders from the Jade Emperor to subjugate you."

In desperation the Ox Monster shook himself and changed once more into a huge white bull to gore the prince with his iron horns, while the prince swung his sword at him. By this time Monkey had caught up again.

Nezha called out, "Excuse us for not bowing to you, since we have armour on. Yesterday my father and I saw Buddha and reported to the Jade Emperor that the monk Tripitaka had been stopped by the Flaming Mountain and Monkey Sun Wukong could not overcome the Ox Monster. The emperor ordered my father to bring angels to help you."

"The fellow knows quite a bit of magic!" said Monkey. "Now he's changed into such a hulking brute, what shall we do?"

"Don't worry." Nezha laughed. "Watch me capture him."

With a cry Nezha changed himself into a god with three heads and six arms, and leaping on the enemy's back he swept his sword and cut off the bull's head. But then as he put down his sword to greet Monkey, from the neck of the bull sprouted another head, its mouth belching black smoke, its eyes throwing off golden sparks. Nezha hacked again, but as fast as one head fell another grew in its place. A dozen blows he struck and a dozen heads sprouted one after another. Then Nezha brought out his flaming wheel and hung it on the bull's horns, making the magic fire blaze so fiercely that the Ox was burned and tossed his head and tail, bellowing with pain. This time he could not change his shape again, however, for he was caught under the prince's magic mirror.

"Spare me!" he pleaded. "I surrender to Buddha."

"If you want to be spared," said Nezha, "give us that fan without any more delay."

"My wife has it," said the Ox.

Hearing this, Nezha uncoiled his rope for binding monsters and astride the Ox's back seized its muzzle, put the rope through and so drove it along. Meanwhile Monkey assembled the four Vajra Kings, the Six Cyclic Gods, the Guardian Angels, the Heavenly Prince and the Giants, as well as Pigsy, the local deity and his ghostly troops. Thronging around the white bull, they went back to Palm-Leaf Cavern.

The Ox Monster called, "Wife, bring out the fan to save me!"

At this Rakshasa quickly divested herself of her jewels and coloured garments, and dressed in a white robe with hair knotted like a nun she came out carrying the twelve-foot fan. At the sight of all the angels, the Heavenly Prince and his son Nezha, she dropped to her knees and kowtowed, crying, "Spare us, Buddha! We'll give this fan to Brother Sun to accomplish his mission."

Monkey came forward at that and took the fan. Then, riding on bright clouds, they all headed eastwards.

Let us now return to Tripitaka and Sandy who, standing and sitting by turns, had been waiting for Monkey all this time and were very worried because he did not come back. Suddenly they saw the sky fill with auspicious clouds which covered the ground with light, while deities of every description came floating towards them. "Sandy," cried Tripitaka in dismay. "What divine army is that coming this way?"

Sandy recognizing the host said, "Master, there are the four great Vajra Kings, the Guardian Angels, the Six Cyclic Gods and other deities. The one leading the Ox is Prince Nezha, the one holding the mirror is the Heavenly Prince his father. Brother Monkey is carrying the palm-leaf fan, followed by Brother Pigsy and the local deity with other guardian angels."

When Tripitaka heard this, he put on his monk's cap and cape and went forward with Sandy to welcome the angels, to whom he offered these thanks, "I have no virtue or ability and am deeply indebted to you for taking such trouble to come here."

The four Vajra Kings replied, "Congratulations, holy monk! Your task is nearly accomplished. We have been sent by Buddha to assist you. You must persevere in your efforts and not slacken in your search for Truth."

Tripitaka kowtowed as he received these instructions.

Then Monkey took the fan and approached the mountain. He fanned with all his might and the fire on the Flaming Mountain went out, leaving it dark without a single spark. He fanned a second time and a cool breeze sprang up. He fanned a third time and the sky became overcast while a light rain started to fall. As the following verse will testify:

Eight hundred *li* the Flaming Mountain stretches;
The whole world knows of that great conflagration;
Fire makes it hard to achieve the philosopher's stone,
The Truth is darkened in that smoke and flame;
The borrowed palm-leaf fan brings rain and dew,
And help is brought by hosts of heavenly angels.
The rampant Ox returns to Buddha's yoke;
Fire and water merge and all things are at peace.

So now, freed from heat and worry, Tripitaka could set his mind at rest. They thanked the Vajra Kings who returned each to his sacred mountain. The Six Cyclic Gods soared to guard the sky, the other deities scattered, and the Heavenly Prince and his son led the Ox back to Buddha. Only the local deity was left waiting there with Rakshasa.

Monkey asked, "Well, Rakshasa, why aren't you gone? What are you standing here for?"

On bended knees Rakshasa pleaded, "Be merciful I beg you, and return me the fan!"

"Ungrateful bitch!" swore Pigsy. "Isn't it enough that we spared your life? How can you ask for the fan? If we take it across the mountain, we can sell it to buy some cakes. After all the trouble you've caused us, why should we give it back to you? It's raining, you'd better go."

Rakshasa kowtowed and said, "You promised before that after the fire was out you would give it back. I am sincerely sorry for all that has happened and our foolhardiness which made you mobilize such a host. I have already attained human form but not reached sainthood yet. After seeing the revelation of the True Form, I shall never dare to act wilfully again. If you will give me the fan, I promise to make a fresh start and go to cultivate virtue and study the Truth."

The local deity interposed, "Lord Monkey, since this woman knows quite well how to put out the fire, why not get rid of it once and for all before returning her the fan? Then I can live here in peace and you will be doing a good turn to the local people, who may offer sacrifice to me. That would be a kind deed."

Monkey said, "I heard from the local people that after the fire is put out by fanning they can get in a year's harvest, but then the fire starts again. How can we put it out for good and all?"

"If you want to put out the flames for good," said Rakshasa, "just fan forty-nine times in succession. Then the fire will never start again."

Hearing this, Monkey took the fan and fanned with

all his might forty-nine times, there came a great down-pour of rain on the mountain. That fan was certainly a wonderful thing, for rain fell only where there had been flames; elsewhere the sky was blue. Since they were standing in a place without flames, they avoided a drenching. After spending the night there, they saddled the horse the next morning, made ready their luggage and returned the fan to Rakshasa.

Monkey told her, "I'm giving you back the fan so as not to be accused of breaking my word. But don't start any trouble now that you have it. I'm letting you off lightly because you've already attained human form."

Rakshasa took the fan and recited an incantation, whereupon it became as small as an apricot leaf and she put it in her mouth. Then she thanked them and went off quietly to cultivate Truth. Later she attained saint-hood too and her name is kept in Buddhist canons.

When Rakshasa and the local deity had thanked for their kindness and seen them off, Monkey, Pigsy and Sandy escorted their master on his way, cool and re-freshed in body, with a spring in their step.

> Warring Elements unite to form the Truth,
> Water and Fire at peace, the Great Deed is ac-
> complished.

If you want to know how many years it was before they returned to the East, listen to what is told in the next chapter.

Pilgrimage to the West
and Its Author

Wu Zuxiang

PILGRIMAGE to the West is a great mythical romance in the treasury of Chinese classical literature. Its distinctive artistic appeal is the result of a synthesis of remarkably magnificent fantasy and a profoundly rich realistic content.

The only other Chinese classical novels which can compare with *Pilgrimage to the West* in their strong influence on the masses are *The Three Kingdoms* and *Outlaws of the Marsh*. Though *Pilgrimage to the West* reached its final form as a novel more than a hundred years later than the other two, these three masterpieces underwent a similar process of development. They were all to a greater or lesser extent based on historical events, which were passed down as legends for centuries among the people, becoming the oral literature of folk artists, and eventually being given their final form by outstanding writers. Works which come from the people and have gone back to the people, they are splendid examples in classical literature of collaboration between professional writers and folk authors.

The historical basis of *Pilgrimage to the West* is as follows: In A.D. 628, the second year of the Zhen Guan period of the Tang Dynasty, the monk Xuan Zang, aged twenty-seven, reached the kingdom of Magadha in India after passing through more than fifty kingdoms to the west of China and overcoming many dangers and difficulties on the way. He studied the Buddhist canons in the monastery of Nalanda, and after seventeen years succeeded in acquiring 657 Buddhist texts to present to the Tang court. The travels and adventures of this young monk aroused tremendous admiration and interest among his contemporaries as well as later generations; and this, combined with the propaganda by Buddhists, was responsible for the gradual evolution of a popular legendary tale embodying the people's dreams and aspirations. From the time of the Tang and Song Dynasties, story-tellers adopted this as their theme, further amplifying it and introducing more supernatural elements. We still have an incomplete text of a story-teller's prompt-book printed in the Song Dynasty entitled *The Chante-Fable of the Monk Tripitaka of the Great Tang Dynasty and His Search for Buddhist Scriptures.** This tells of Tripitaka's pilgrimage through many strange lands, and in it appears the figure of Friar Monkey who, with his great magic powers and skill in both literature and military arts, helps the monk to overcome the perils on the way, assisted in this by the God of the Deep Sand who also possesses supernatural powers. This text of little more than ten thousand words reveals the early outline of the main story of the present *Pilgrimage to the West.*

---

* Tripitaka (San Zang) is Xuan Zang's honorary Buddhist title.

Friar Monkey was developed in the novel into the hero Monkey Sun Wukong, while the God of the Deep Sand became Sandy, one of the four pilgrims who went out in search of scriptures. This prompt-book, moreover, contains several important episodes in *Pilgrimage to the West,* as for example the story of the Valley of Fire and the Country of Amazons. The Valley of Fire episode was the early form of the adventure of the Flaming Mountain.

During the Yuan Dynasty (1271-1368), not a few plays made use of the incidents in the story of this pilgrimage. A famous example is Wu Changling's *Pilgrimage to the West.* By now the plot and characters are much more highly developed than in the Song Dynasty *chantefable.* In addition to Monkey and Sandy, we now have Pigsy as well as such characters as Red Boy and Princess Iron Fan. At the same time these tales were written into prose romances. Thus the *Yong Le Encyclopaedia* compiled in 1403 at the beginning of the Ming Dynasty contains the story of Wei Zheng who in a dream killed the dragon of the River Qing, and notes that this was taken from *Pilgrimage to the West.* This episode in more than a thousand words is fairly close to Chapter 10 of the present version of *Pilgrimage to the West.*

However, the man who rewrote the story of the pilgrimage, making of it a truly great work of art, was Wu Cheng'en (c. 1500-1582) of the Ming Dynasty. He was the son of a small tradesman in Huaian Prefecture on the north bank of the Yangzi. His family, which had once produced scholar-officials, was poor when he was young. He was a good student, brilliant and highly gifted. He was also lively, fond of making jokes and writing satires. Although he won a certain reputation in his district, he never did well in the official examinations. He stayed for fairly long periods in Nanjing, where he lived on the money he made by writing essays and contributions from friends. At the age of sixty he was appointed assistant magistrate of Changxing County, but because he would not flatter his superiors and did not get on well with them he left the post before long and returned to his own district where he lived to be over eighty. *Pilgrimage to the West* was the work of his last years, carried out at home after his retirement. His family origin and experience had made him discontented with the utterly corrupt politics and social life of his time. His love for folk legends and his familiarity with these rich and colourful stories provided him with a means to vent his feelings and express his ideal, to attack the society of his time and hold it up to ridicule.

Wu Cheng'en made certain important changes in the story of the pilgrimage. First, he transformed the main theme of the story, raising to a higher level the popular account of the pilgrimage and transforming the folk story which had a strong religious flavour into a mythical novel with a clearer, richer and more profound realist social significance. In this connection we should note that the formerly admired hero Tripitaka was relegated to a secondary position, becoming relatively an object of criticism and ridicule; while the real hero is Monkey, the rebel against authority who exterminates evil spirits, symbolizing the hero of the people's dreams. Secondly, while presenting a great variety of clear and vivid artistic images, including gods, saints and monsters, Wu Cheng'en embodied in this work the specific historical features and contents of a particular society; while in handling his scenes and episodes, he freely exposed the society of the day. His criticism and satire is steeped in wit and humour. Thirdly, he skilfully selected a number of characters and episodes from other popular folk legends and myths, adding these to the skeleton of the original story and integrating them with the central theme. His sources were Buddhist and Taoist legends as well as ordinary folk tales.

The mystic utterances interspersed throughout the novel represent the confused and hazy ideas about the so-called unity of the three religions — Confucianism, Buddhism and Taoism — which were prevalent in the upper strata of the society of that period. Wu Cheng'en wrote these passages ironically.

2

Pilgrimage to the West has 100 chapters. The first seven describe how Monkey is born, seeks sainthood and attains immortality, how he masters seventy-two transformations and such magic arts as riding the clouds and somersaulting through the air. To win freedom and become the master of his fate, he makes havoc in the Dragon King's Palace, in Hell and in Heaven, waging revolutionary struggles against the so-called Three Spheres which symbolize the feudal powers, until the Jade Emperor was forced to give him the title of the Paragon of Heaven. After winning a series of glorious victories he is finally defeated when in a contest with Buddha he bounds 108,000 *li* away to the end of Heaven in one somersault, but comes back only to discover that he has gone no further than Buddha's palm. So he is made captive under the Mountain of Five Peaks, which is a transformation of Buddha's hand, and cannot move. The 5 chapters from Chapter 8 onwards describe the reason for Tripitaka's pilgrimage to the West and the preparations. The 80-odd chapters following Chapter 13 make up the main bulk of the novel with the story of the 81 perils which the pilgrims encounter on their way to the Western Heaven. Tripitaka, passing the Mountain of Five Peaks, rescues Monkey Sun Wukong from beneath it and makes him his disciple to help him to exterminate evil spirits and overcome the dangers on the road. After some fights on Monkey's part a pig monster and a water monster become Tripitaka's disciples too — Pigsy and Sandy. These are the four pilgrims who go to seek for scriptures, and they also subdue a dragon which is changed into a horse for Tripitaka. On their journey they meet with dangers great and small. There are many involved interludes and the incidents are connected as far as possible so that the whole work appears very well organized. Thus this novel which purports to have the quest for Buddhist scriptures as its main theme is actually a book about vigorous fights to overcome perils and difficulties, with Monkey as its chief protagonist, while the search for the scriptures is deliberately ignored. In fact when the pilgrims reach the realm of Buddha in the Western Heaven and obtain the scriptures the novel is concluded.

Of course, this mythical story of a pilgrimage with Monkey as the chief character like all other ancient myths reflects the people's desire to conquer and to master nature. This is not merely the significance of the various magic powers and feats of Monkey; all the gods and saints and many monsters and evil influences also signify the forces of nature expressed in fanciful forms.

It goes without saying that the mythical Monkey Sun Wukong is a complex character. In the first 7 chapters, Monkey is a rebel passionately seeking freedom, urgently demanding change, daring to challenge and oppose whichever authority that rules over the universe and determines fate. No matter how great the authority of the gods and saints, how exalted their position, how high their dignity, no matter what wonderful magic powers they possess, in their fight with Monkey they all stand revealed as useless cowards who panic shamefully. In these descriptions, which are a bitter satire on the gods and saints, Wu Cheng'en pays the warmest tribute to every act of defiance and revolt on the part of the rebel and to his victories. It is precisely in this attitude he takes to express his likes and dislikes that the writer gives full rein to his astonishing imaginative powers.

In one sense, Monkey resembles the revolutionary masses of that period: he carries on brave and effective struggles against the feudal rule yet he cannot break through the domination of this system. Though one somersault will carry him 108,000 *li* away, he cannot leave the palm of Buddha's hand or avoid being imprisoned beneath the Mountain of Five Peaks. This handling of the subject is not due solely to the fatalistic ideas of the writer himself.

But Monkey is not one to surrender tamely after defeat. He helps Tripitaka travel West to find Buddhist scriptures not because he has submitted to the powers of Heaven or is going against his own will. It would be more correct to say that he is sent to help Tripitaka search for scriptures because as a result of his brave struggles the gods and saints realize his invincible strength, recognize his resolute and noble qualities and are forced to respect him. They have to let him go forth and fight in another just cause. Monkey, for his part, helps Tripitaka of his own free will. When fighting the gods and saints before, he lacked a clear goal and purpose. His slogan when he made havoc in Heaven was simply, "This year is the Jade Emperor's turn; next year, mine." He fails because although he opposes the existing rule he can propose nothing new; but unwilling to admit defeat he persists in seeking what he considers to be the truth or the ideal. It is this deep-seated need in his heart that makes him help the monk to seek the scriptures. His energies are actually concentrated on destroying the monsters and forces of evil on the way; he is not sure himself how much genuine interest he has in finding the scriptures, and the novel does not go into any detail about this either.

Because Monkey puts his yearning for the ideal into the task of safeguarding Tripitaka in his search, he shows the greatest enthusiasm and determination, brings his courage and wisdom into full play and overcomes countless difficulties and obstacles, revealing incomparable optimism and heroism. Monkey's essential spirit while making havoc in Heaven and escorting the monk on his pilgrimage is consistent throughout.

If we examine Monkey in this story of the pilgrimage, we notice four things about his relationship with others. First, he is fighting most of the time against monsters who represent forces of evil which clash directly with his own aspirations. So his fight to exterminate them is a just one, and no matter how arduous the struggle

Monkey always triumphs in the end. Secondly, in his fight against the monsters Monkey is often assisted by the gods and saints; but it does not follow simply from this that Monkey during the pilgrimage is entirely on the side of the gods, acting as a stooge of the ruling powers of Heaven. It is very clear from many passages in the book that on the one hand Monkey still keeps at a considerable distance from them. He is restricted by the fillet clamped on his head by the magic of the gods, yet he adopts a completely independent, even insolent attitude towards them. On the other hand many of the monsters are secretly in league with the gods and saints, while not a few actually come from them, as does most of their magic power. This mythical presentation in the feudal period was not without significance in that it exposed and ridiculed actual politics and reality. All the local evil forces, who oppressed the people directly during that period, received their authority from the court. During the Ming Dynasty the imperial guardsmen and eunuchs stationed in various localities were the greatest scourge of the people, while the landlords and local despots all had their connections with the government. It is Monkey, therefore, not the gods and saints, who is against the monsters. Monkey is actively engaged in wiping out monsters, while the gods and saints remain passive until forced to help. In fact, then, Monkey's attack on monsters in a world wholly dominated by the gods is an indirect struggle against the hierarchy of Heaven.

Thirdly, though Monkey considers Tripitaka as his master and strives to protect the monk on his pilgrimage, there is a sharp contradiction between them. Tripitaka is a weak and soft-hearted "elder". Though he is often endangered by the monsters, who want to eat his flesh, heart and liver, he insists on treating them kindly and will not let Monkey kill them. Monkey is the very reverse. He resolutely determines to kill the monsters and exterminate all the forces of evil. Thus irreconcilable conflicts flare up between master and disciple. Time and again Tripitaka drives Monkey away because he has killed some monster or evil spirit, reproaching him for indulging in evil ways and refusing to practise virtue; yet once Monkey leaves, Tripitaka finds himself in trouble. This portrayal of Monkey as a resolute fighter, upholder of justice and deadly enemy of the powers of evil is a forceful criticism of the character of Tripitaka, who represents the orthodox thought of the ruling class. Fourthly, the relationship between Monkey and his comrade-in-arms Pigsy is highly significant too. Pigsy has many of the characteristics of a property owner of the small peasantry. During the pilgrimage he constantly wavers, displaying a lack of confidence and resolution. When a woman entices him, he wants to stay with her and will not continue his journey. He is gluttonous and lazy, fond of petty gains, and these shortcomings always involve him in difficulties. In a fierce fight he holds back like a coward, letting Monkey bear the brunt; but when he sees that a monster is being defeated, in order to share the credit he runs forward brandishing his rake. However, he is simple and goodhearted. Despite his many serious faults, he consistently opposes the monsters and never gives in to the forces of evil. Of the four pilgrims, he is the one to undertake the hardest and humblest tasks, carrying the luggage, opening a way through the brambles, clearing away filth or rotten persimmons. He is not stubborn either but willing to admit his mistakes; thus he contributes an indispensable share on the pilgrimage. Pigsy makes a strong impression on readers, who find him contemptible and ridiculous yet cannot help liking him at the same time. Obviously this impression is inseparable from the writer's treatment of Pigsy, whose character is affirmed while his defects are sharply criticized.

3

The story of Monkey's three attempts to get the palm-leaf fan to cross the Flaming Mountain occupies three entire chapters, 59 to 61. The pilgrims are in the middle of their journey, and struggles against monsters and perils come thick and fast. This episode follows on from the earlier of their 81 perils and leads up to the later ones. It is an important and enthralling story, one of the chief adventures in the book, which has always compelled readers' interest. It has formed the theme of many operas, puppet-plays, picture books and decorative paintings.

The Ox Demon King and his wife Princess Iron Fan are unlike all the other monsters. They do not come from the gods and saints, nor are they out to injure the pilgrims (except that the Ox Demon King's son Red Boy has carried Tripitaka off several times by magic, meaning to take out his heart and eat his flesh to gain immortality, and wanting his father to join him in this). Of all the monsters they are two of the most sympathetic. This has something to do with Monkey's relationship with the Ox Demon King; for when Monkey was king of the monkeys in the Water Curtain Cave on the

Mountain of Fruit and Flowers these two were sworn brothers, as is told at the beginning of the novel. Owing to this special connection, Monkey does not treat them at first as ordinary monsters and when trying to borrow the fan he addresses them cordially as "sister-in-law" and "brother", showing great politeness for the sake of their former friendship. The Chinese people of the feudal period considered loyalty to friends as a great virtue. But this was a personal bond, a minor good; once it came into conflict with justice and major issues, friendship had to be sacrificed for the greater good. So this episode Monkey first speaks of friendship to his former sworn brother, but when the Ox resenting his treatment of Red Boy refuses to help him out by lending him the fan, Monkey gives up his personal friendship and treats the Ox as his enemy, starting a fierce battle. Thus Monkey's relationship with the Ox Demon King is significant. The Ox King is very aptly typified here as an ordinary feudal landlord in the actual society of feudal China. Descriptions of his relations with his wife and concubine and his fights with Monkey are full of interesting episodes and scenes, in which the author keeps poking fun at the social customs of that period.

In connection with the artistic achievement of this adventure of the Flaming Mountain, to my mind, there are three points which deserve attention. One is the penetrating and powerful manner in which Monkey's fearless fighting spirit and positive optimism in face of perils and obstacles are expressed through a wealth of detailed description. Another is the wisdom of Monkey's tactics against Princess Iron Fan and the Ox Demon King, for he does not merely rely on strength of arms and magic. This is especially true of his tactics against Princess Iron Fan, when he changes into a gnat, slips into her belly and so terrifies her by jumping up and down that she lends him the fan. Shrewd tactics like these are not simply interesting flights of fancy, but also full of meaning. Monkey did not adopt such ruses in his earlier fights. The third point is that Monkey had not yet attained his full stature as a hero, and he still reveals a number of weaknesses. He trusts too much in his own might and is also easily deceived by the enemy. In his first attempt to get the fan, after defeating Rakshasa by getting inside her, he takes the fan and walks off without any suspicion; but it turns out that he has been tricked into accepting a fake. In his second attempt, after using his wisdom and some hard fighting he gets the true fan but is so drunk with victory, so lacking in vigilance, that the Ox Demon King in the guise of Pigsy gets the fan back by a ruse. So Monkey is deceived again. There is a most amusing picture here of a small Monkey gloating conceitedly as he carries a huge fan which he does not know how to shrink back to its original size. This is Wu Cheng'en's kindly criticism of the shortcomings of his favourite character.

All Monkey's battles against the Ox King and his wife during his three attempts to get the palm-leaf fan are presented with great verve and gusto.

Li Ruzhen

A Journey into Strange Lands

(Excerpts from *Flowers in the Mirror*)

A Journey into Strange Lands

... NOW there was a licentiate* named Tang Ao of the county of Heyuan in Lingnan, who had lost his first wife and married another from the Lin family. Though he was eager to pass the higher examinations and become an official, Tang liked nothing better than roaming the country. And since he spent the better part of each year in travel, giving only half his mind to his studies, often as he took the provincial examination he never succeeded in passing.

One year he tried again, though, and this time passed the provincial examinations and came second in the palace test. But one of the censors slandered him to the empress, saying that Tang Ao had been in league with traitors and was not a loyal subject, that if he was given an appointment he would certainly form a faction, and that it would be better to degrade him to the status of a common citizen as a warning to all those in league with evil men. As a result of this report, Tang was demoted to his old rank of licentiate.

This threw him into such a frenzy that he could think of nothing else, and he determined to leave the dusty world. Sending his man home and travelling light, he

---

* A scholar who had passed the prefectural examination, one of the lowest examinations taken by those who wanted to enter the civil service.

roamed the country trying to forget his sorrows. He climbed all the mountains in his way and boated on all the lakes and rivers, until six months had passed and spring was at hand.

At last he reached that part of Lingnan where his wife's brother Lin Zhiyang lived. This was less than thirty *li* from his own home, yet close as it was he did not want to go back to face his brother and wife. He decided to make another trip instead, but could not think where to go. In low spirits, he ordered his boat to be moored and went ashore. He had not taken many steps when he saw an old building in the distance, and upon going nearer discovered that it was a temple to the God of Dreams.

"I have turned fifty," reflected Tang with a sigh. "If I think back, the past is just like a dream. Good dreams and bad — I've had both. Now that I have seen through worldly vanities, I had better find some immortal to teach me the Truth. I have not consulted any oracle yet — why not ask this god for guidance?"

Going into the shrine he offered a silent prayer, bowed before the image and sat down beside it. Then he saw a boy with cropped hair approach.

"My master invites you in, sir," said this lad. "He has something to say to you."

Tang followed the boy into the inner hall, where an old man came out to greet him. He promptly stepped forward and bowed, and they sat down in the places of host and guest.

"May I know your illustrious name?" inquired Tang. "What may I have the honour of doing for you?"

"My name is Meng, and I have been living in Rushi Temple," replied the old man. "I took the liberty of asking you here because you were thinking of finding an immortal and seeking for the Truth. May I ask you, sir, what grounds you have for making such a request? What arts can you command? How do you mean to go about this business?"

"I have no special grounds," answered Tang. "I am looking for an immortal because I want to leave the dusty world, renouncing the seven passions and six desires. As my whole mind is set on a life contemplation, I shall surely be able to gain immortality."

"You make it sound easy, sir!" The old man laughed. "But when you speak of purifying your heart and doing away with desire, this is simply an attempt to prolong your life and rid yourself of illness. Ge Xian the saint was right when he said: 'A man who would become an immortal must start with the virtues of loyalty, filial piety, benevolence and faithfulness. Unless he has led a virtuous life, it is no use his seeking the Truth. To become an earthly immortal he must do three hundred good deeds, to become a heavenly immortal one thousand three hundred.' Now you, sir, have no great achievements, no writings and no good deeds to your credit. You are wasting your time seeking for immortality when you have nothing to build on. That is like trying to catch fish up a tree."

"I am a poor simpleton," rejoined Tang. "Now that I have had the benefit of your instructions I shall do good deeds in the hope of finding the Truth. I used to long for advancement to restore the imperial house of Tang and deliver the people from their sorrows by good government. But as soon as I passed the examinations I met with unexpected misfortune, and did not know what I could do. What is your advice, father?"

"I am sorry you had this disappointment, sir. But it may prove a blessing in disguise. If you abandon all vanities and make a search elsewhere, you will win the Fairy Isles and the ranks of the immortals. You are destined for such a fate, sir. Go boldly ahead, and your desire may be granted when least you expect it. Since you condescended to consult me, I have told you what is needed — the rest is up to you."

Before Tang could ask further questions the old man disappeared. Hastily rubbing his eyes and staring around, he found himself still sitting beside the shrine, and realized he had been dreaming. When he stood up and looked at the image, he recognized the old man of his dream. He kowtowed again before returning to his boat and embarking.

Soon his junk moored before the house of his brother-in-law, Lin Zhiyang. Loads of merchandise were being carried out and, judging by the commotion, they were about to set out on a long journey. Lin came from the province of Hebei, but had spent most of his life in Lingnan and was a sea-trader. He had lost his parents many years before this, and his wife, a daughter of the Lu family, generally accompanied him on his voyages. He had now prepared for another trip, entrusting his household to his mother-in-law, and was just on the point of leaving when Tang arrived. After greeting him, Lin took his brother-in-law in to see his wife.

"We have not met for many years, brother," said Tang. "I was hoping to have a good talk with you, but I find your household in a rare commotion. Am I right in thinking you are just off on a voyage?"

"I have not been abroad for several years on account of illness," replied Lin. "Now I am glad to say my health is better, and I mean to venture abroad taking a few trifles overseas. That is better than sitting at home eating up my estate. It is my old trade, and I must resign myself to its hardships again."

Here was the very chance Tang was looking for.

"I have travelled every year till now I have seen nearly all there is to be seen," he said. "And since last leaving the capital I have felt out of sorts and depressed. I was just wishing I could make an ocean voyage to forget my troubles by exploring the islands. And here you are setting out — what a happy coincidence! Will you take me with you? I have several hundred taels of silver with me as travelling expenses, so I can promise not to be a burden to you. And I shall fall in with any wishes you may have regarding payment for my board and passage."

"Why, brother, we are close kinsmen," protested Lin. "How can you speak of paying for your board and passage? Wife!" He turned to her. "Did you hear what your brother-in-law said?"

"Ours is a large, sea-worthy junk," she told him. "One extra passenger will make no difference, and your board is not worth mentioning. But the ocean is not like our inland rivers and lakes. We are used to it and think nothing of it, but a faint-hearted traveller is terrified by his first taste of the wind and waves at sea. You scholars like to sip tea from morning till night, and must wash and bathe every day. Once on board, though, a bath is out of the question — everything is rough and ready. There's barely enough fresh water to wet your gullet, let alone drink your fill. You're used to comfort, brother. You could never put up with such hardships."

"Out at sea we are at the mercy of the wind," continued Lin. "I'd think twice about it, brother, if I were you. If you ruin your career because of a passing whim, won't you hold it against us later?"

"Your sister has often told me that because sea water is too salty you take a supply of fresh water and have to eke it out," said Tang. "But luckily I don't care for tea at all. I can do without baths too. As for the danger of storms at sea, I have travelled enough on the Yangzi and the great lakes not to worry about them. You say there is no knowing when we may be back, and you are afraid of holding up my advancement by making me miss the next examination. But I've given up all thought of an official career. The longer we are away, the better I shall like it. What could I hold against you?"

"If you are sure, I won't try to stop you," said Lin. "But when you left home, did you tell my sister your plans?"

"More or less. But to set your mind at rest I will write another letter home and tell her the date on which we shall be leaving. How about that?"

When Lin saw that Tang's mind was made up and that there was no gainsaying him, he had to agree.

Soon all was ready, and they went by skiffs to the harbour. When the sailors had loaded the cargo they took sampans to the junk, and set sail at once as the wind lay in the right quarter.

It was now the middle of the first month, and the weather was fine and clear. After sailing for several days they reached the open sea, and Tang gazed about him with exhilaration. Well does the proverb say: One who has seen the ocean thinks nothing of inland waters. He was in raptures. After sailing for many days they rounded Mount Portal and scudded before a following wind, uncertain how far they had gone.

Very soon a mountain range came into sight.

"That is the most imposing island we have seen," remarked Tang. "May I ask you its name, brother?"

"It is called East Gate Mountain, and is the first great range of the eastern sea," Lin told him. "The scenery is said to be magnificent, but though I have passed this way several times I have never been ashore. If you care to, we can anchor here awhile and explore the place together."

The name East Gate sounded familiar to Tang.

"If this is East Gate Mountain," he observed, "aren't we near the Land of Courtesy and the Kingdom of the Great?"

"We are," replied Lin. "East of this mountain lies the Land of Courtesy, the north border of which adjoins the Kingdom of the Great. How did you know that, brother?"

"I heard that beyond the sea lay East Gate Mountain and the Land of Courtesy, where all men dress most decorously and defer to one another. To its north, I was told, lay the Kingdom of the Great, where men cannot walk but travel about on clouds. Is that a fact?"

"I have been to the Kingdom of the Great," answered Lin. "All the people there have clouds attached to their feet and float comfortably along. Every soul without exception in the Land of Courtesy is a paragon of politeness. Beyond these two countries lies Black Tooth Kingdom, whose inhabitants are black from head to foot. There are weird-shaped creatures too in the lands of the Restless and the Childless, as you shall see for yourself when we get there, brother."

By now the junk had moored at the foot of the mountain, and the two of them landed and began to climb, Lin armed with a musket, Tang with a sword. They made their way up by a zigzag path across the foremost crag, and found a magnificent view stretching to the far horizon.

On a distant peak appeared a strange beast something like a boar. It was six feet long and four feet high, dark grey in colour, with two great ears and four long tusks like an elephant's.

"You seldom see a beast with such long tusks," marvelled Tang. "Do you know what it is, brother?"

"I'm afraid I don't. I should have asked our helmsman to come with us. He has sailed the high seas for years, and knows these parts like the back of his hand. He knows every single strange plant, wild beast or bird. Next time we come out on a jaunt I shall ask him too."

"If you have such a useful man aboard, we must certainly take him along. What is his name? Is he a scholar?"

"His name is Duo and he is the ninth of his generation. Because he is old, we call him Ninth Uncle Duo, and he considers that his name. As he is by way of being a Mr. Know-All, the seamen call him Mr. Know-Nothing to tease him. He studied when he was young, but never passed the examinations, so he gave up book learning for overseas trading. Later on he lost his money, and took to being a helmsman. He hasn't worn a scholar's cap for years. He's an honest, thoroughly knowledgeable fellow. Though he's over eighty this year he's still very spry, and walks like the wind. He and I get on well together, and as he happens to be a kinsman of my wife, I asked him specially to come on this trip."

Just then who should come down the hillside but Duo himself. Lin made haste to greet him, and Tang stepped forward with clasped hands to bow.

"We have met before, uncle, but never had a good talk," said Tang. "My brother has just informed me that you are my kinsman and my senior in learning. I should have paid my respects long before this — please excuse my remissness."

Duo made a modest rejoinder.

"I expect you have come here to stretch your legs after being confined on the boat, uncle," said Lin. "We were just talking about you. You're the very man we want." He pointed to the distance. "Can you tell us the name of that strange beast with the tusks?"

"That's a *dang-kang*," Duo told them. "It is called after its cry. As it only shows itself when times are good, this sudden appearance must mean the world is at peace."

Before he had finished, the creature brayed: "Dang-kang!" After a few cries it left the hillside, dancing.

*   *   *

"Do you see that forest in front, uncle?" asked Lin. "What are those tall, stout trees? Let us go and have a look. They may have some fruit we can pick."

They made their way at once to the noble forest, and soon came to a great tree fifty feet high, and so huge that five men would be needed to encircle it. Instead of branches it bore countless tufts like the beards of an ear of corn, each over ten feet long.

"The ancients spoke of Corn Trees," commented Tang. "That is what this looks like."

"What pity the corn isn't ripe yet," said Duo, nodding. "If you took a few grains back, they would be real curiosities."

"All the grain from last year must have been eaten by the beasts," said Tang. "There isn't one on the ground."

"However greedy the wild creatures are, they could hardly eat every grain," protested Lin. "Let's search the undergrowth. If we can find one that will be something new."

Each made a search, and before long Lin held up a huge grain.

"I've found one!" he shouted.

The two others came up, and saw that the grain was three inches wide and five long.

"If this were cooked, it would measure at least a foot!" remarked Tang.

"This is nothing special," Duo assured him. "Once when I was abroad I ate a huge grain of rice which kept me satisfied for a whole year."

"It must have been twenty feet long!" exclaimed Lin. "How did you cook it? That sounds like a tall story."

"It was five inches by a foot, and less than twenty feet when cooked," replied Duo. "But after eating it your mouth felt fresh and your spirits suddenly lifted; you had no desire for food for another year. You're not the only one to doubt that story, Brother Lin — I didn't believe it myself at first. But then I heard that during the reign of Emperor Xuan a part of the tribute sent by the Land of Beiyin was Refreshing Rice — one grain of which could satisfy a man for a year — and I realized that was probably what I had eaten."

"No wonder archers who miss a pigeon by a couple of feet complain that they just missed by one grain," interjected Lin. "I used to be very sceptical, and couldn't believe there were such big grains in the world. Now, uncle, I know that by one grain they meant a grain of this Refreshing Rice — cooked."

"It's too bad of you to say cooked." Tang laughed. "If poor marksmen heard you, brother, they might smash your jaw."

Suddenly a dwarf appeared in the distance on a tiny horse no more than eight inches long. Duo immediately darted after it. Lin was too busy looking for grain to have eyes for anything else, but there was no holding back Tang, who rushed in pursuit of the dwarf as it hurried forward. Spry as Duo was, he was not quite quick enough, and having tripped over a stone on the rugged path as he was overtaking the dwarf, he could only hobble along. This gave Tang a chance to pass him, and after half a *li*'s chase he finally seized the dwarf and swallowed it.

Presently Duo came up, panting, on Lin's arm. He looked at Tang and sighed enviously.

" 'Each bite and sup is predestined,' " he quoted. "How much more so in an important matter like this! You were born lucky, Brother Tang, to get such a thing without any effort on your part."

"Uncle Duo tells me you caught a dwarf riding a small horse," said Lin. "From a distance you seemed to be putting it in your mouth. Did you eat horse, rider and all? And what is this talk of luck?"

"This dwarf horse and rider are Live Fungus," Tang told him. "I did not know about it until I left the capital this time, disappointed of becoming an official, and took to reading about the diets the ancients followed to attain long life. Then among other things I read that if you meet a dwarf riding a cart or horse five or six inches long in the mountains, that is Live Fungus, which gives long life to whoever eats it and enables him to find the Truth and become an immortal. I do not know how much there is in this; but on the assumption that it could hardly hurt me, I caught it and ate it without offering you any."

"If that's true, you are now an immortal, brother!" Lin chuckled. "After eating Live Fungus you will never be hungry again, but can wander about as the fancy takes you. I am hungry though. You didn't by any chance leave a leg of that dwarf horse and rider to take the edge off my appetite, did you?"

"If you're hungry, Brother Lin, there's something here you can eat," suggested Duo. He plucked a dark plant that was growing in the green grass. "This will not only stop your hunger but clear your head."

Lin took the plant which tapered like a leek, with green flowers on a tender stem. He put it in his mouth and nodded his approval.

"Very fragrant and tasty, uncle. What is its name? If ever I am hungry when climbing in future, I shall eat some."

"I once read that in Magpie Mountain across the ocean grows a dark green flower like a leek, which serves as a food. This must be it," said Tang.

Duo nodded his head several times, and they went on.

"Amazing!" cried Lin. "I don't feel hungry any more. This is a wonderful plant — I must take two loads of it to the boat so that I shall have something to eat if we run out of food. Isn't this simpler, brother, than the old method of concocting elixirs?"

"This plant is quite rare overseas," Duo warned him. "You will never find so much. In any case, once plucked it starts to wither, while to stay your hunger you have to eat it fresh — dried, it is no use at all."

At that moment Tang plucked a green plant from the roadside. It had a leaf like a pine-needle but was emerald green, and on it was a seed the size of a grain of mustard. Removing this seed and pointing at the leaf, he said:

"As you have just eaten one plant, brother, let me eat this to keep you company."

With that he swallowed the leaf, laid the seed in his palm and blew on it. At once there sprouted another green leaf like a pine-needle, about a foot in length. He blew again, and it grew another foot. He blew three times till it was three feet long, whereupon he ate it.

"If you go on munching at this rate, brother, you'll soon have eaten all the plants here!" laughed Lin. "How does this seed change into a plant like that?"

"This is the herb called Soaring, otherwise known as Mustard-in-the-palm," was Duo's answer. "When you hold the seed in your palm and blow on it, it grows a foot each time until it is three feet long. Anyone who eats it can soar aloft, hence its name."

"If it can do that, let me eat some too!" cried Lin. "Then when I go home and thieves climb the roof of my house, I can soar through the air to catch them. Very useful, to be sure!"

But though they searched high and low, they could find no more.

"It's no use your looking, Brother Lin," rejoined old Duo. "This plant grows only when blown on, and who is there on this bare mountainside to do that? What Brother Tang ate just now was probably some stray seed blown on by a bird in search of food, which fell to earth and took root. It is not a common herb — you can't possibly hope to find it. In all my years of travel overseas this is the first time I've seen it, and if our friend here hadn't blown on it I shouldn't have known that this was Soaring."

"So after eating this you can stand in mid-air," marvelled Lin. "Amazing! Do have a try, brother. I shan't believe it till I've seen it."

"I have barely finished eating the plant," protested Tang. "It can hardly take effect so quickly — never mind, I'll have a try."

He leapt up and soared aloft, dancing, to a height of nearly sixty feet, and then stood in mid-air as firmly as if he had both feet planted on the ground. There he stayed without moving.

Lin clapped his hands.

"So you can walk on clouds now, brother!" He laughed. "This plant really makes you soar through the air — what a joke! Why not go a little further? If you find this way of travelling easy, you can sail through the sky in future without touching the ground at all. What a saving of shoes and socks!"

Then Tang made an attempt to walk through the air, but no sooner raised one foot than down he toppled.

"There's a date tree there with some big dates right at the top." Lin pointed it out. "Why not pick a few, brother, as you can soar like this? They'll help to quench our thirst."

But when they reached the tree and looked at it carefully, it was not a date at all.

"This is called Knife-flavour-nut because its flavour changes when cut," Duo informed them. "Those who eat it become earthly immortals. If we can lay hands on this, even if we don't become immortals we shall prolong our lives. Unfortunately these nuts only grow at the top of the tree, over a hundred feet high. Not even Brother Tang can reach them."

"Keep jumping, brother," urged Lin. "You may be able to make it."

"I can only rise fifty to sixty feet," replied Tang. "This tree is so high, how can I reach its top? You're like the frog who wanted to eat a swan."

But Lin would not take no for an answer, and lowered his head in thought.

"I have it!" His face cleared. "After leaping into the air, brother, rest for a while and then take another leap. That way you'll mount step by step as if you were on a ladder, and you're bound to get the nuts."

Still Tang was reluctant to try, and Lin had to urge him repeatedly before he took off again. After stopping in the air to take a firm stand, he leapt up vigorously once more; but this time he flapped wildly like a cicada's wings, and very soon — like a kite with a snapped string — he fluttered down to the earth.

"Why didn't you jump *up*, brother?" Lin stamped impatiently. "What was the point of jumping down like that?"

"I did try to go up," retorted Tang. "But I couldn't help myself. Don't think I came down on purpose."

"To go up, you must thrust hard with both feet," explained Duo. "As you weren't on firm land, of course you came down. If you could soar up step by step the way Brother Lin says, several thousand leaps would take you to Heaven, wouldn't they? It's not as simple as that."

"I smell something very sweet," interjected Tang. "Are these nuts fragrant too?"

"If you sniff carefully, the fragrance seems to be carried here by the breeze," said Duo. "Suppose we look around and try to track it down?"

They set out in different directions.

When Tang had crossed a wood and a precipice and hunted high and low, he saw growing from a crevice in a roadside boulder a red grass about two feet high, bright as vermilion and very pretty indeed. After examining it carefully, he realized what it was.

"The books on the diet for immortals speak of Vermilion Grass shaped like a small mulberry, with a coral stem and blood-red juice," he thought. "If you dip gold or jade in it they turn to mud, so mixed with gold it is called Gold Sauce and mixed with jade Jade Sauce. All who eat it become saints or supermen. I am glad Duo and Lin are not with me, for this shows I was fated to find fairy herbs today. I have nc gold with me, though — what can I do?"

Then he remembered a jade emblem on his cap, and decided to use that. He unfastened the emblem and plucked the grass at its root, crushed it in his hand and rubbed it on the jade, which sure enough changed into bright red mud. When he put this in his mouth, he was struck by its penetrating aroma. And as soon as he swallowed it, his energy increased a hundredfold.

"This Vermilion Grass refreshes at once!" he gloated. "It shows the miraculous power of these fairy herbs. Once I can do without mortal food, the rest should be easy. I wonder if all these fairy plants I have eaten today have increased my strength or not."

By the roadside he caught sight of a fallen tombstone, which must have weighed at least six hundred pounds. Walking over, he bent down and lifted it without the slightest effort. Then, thanks to Soaring, he launched himself up and hovered in the air for an instant before descending slowly. After one or two steps he set the stone down again.

"Since eating Vermilion Grass my senses seem strangely acute," he marvelled. "I can remember all the classics I read as a boy, and see in my mind's eye all the essays and poems I ever wrote. What a wonderful plant!"

At this point up came old Duo leading Lin.

"Why is your mouth so red, Brother Tang?" he asked.

"I'll tell you frankly, uncle," answered Tang. "Just now I found some Vermilion Grass, and took the liberty of eating it without waiting for you."

"What has it done for you, brother?" asked Lin.

"This plant grows from the congealed essence of heaven and earth," replied Duo. "Those who are inclined that way become earthly immortals after eating it. In all my travels, search as I might, I never found it; but today Brother Tang has been the one to discover it again — he is destined to be a saint. We can be sure that he will wander beyond the confines of this world and rank as an immortal in future. Well, well — who could have guessed that this scent would help him to attain immortality?"

"Why are you frowning, brother, if you're soon to become an immortal?" demanded Lin. "Are you homesick, or afraid of being a fairy?"

"I'm puzzled by the pain in my stomach since I ate that Vermilion Grass," responded Tang.

Just then they heard a rumble in his belly, and there was a bad smell. Lin put his hand to his nose.

"Good!" he cried. "You must feel better now that this grass has driven out that bad odour, brother. Do you feel empty, or have you still a bellyful of all the poems and essays you ever wrote?"

Tang looked down thoughtfully, and exclaimed in surprise.

"Just after eating that grass," he told old Duo, "I remembered all my youthful compositions word for word, from beginning to end. But since this belly-ache I can only remember about one-tenth — somehow or other I have forgotten the rest."

"That is strange," agreed old Duo.

"What's strange about it?" asked Lin. "My guess is that the nine-tenths he can't remember came out with that bad smell just now. The Vermilion Grass found them unsavoury and got rid of them, showing them up, incidentally, in their true colours — I got a good whiff of them. It's no use trying to recall them. The tenth that's left is all right, so the Vermilion Grass lets you keep that safe in your belly, where of course you can remember it any time. What worries me, though, is whether the grass took pity on that paper with which you came second in the palace test. If you want to publish your essays, brother, take my advice and don't ask anyone to make a selection — just cut out the nine-tenths you've forgotten today and print the remaining tenth, which is bound to be good. If you print good and bad alike, the Vermilion Grass may take exception to something you think highly of. What a pity this grass is so rare! If we could take some back, think of all the work it would save the printers! As it's so efficacious, why don't you eat a couple of blades too, uncle? Don't you intend to publish anything?"

"I've written a few things in my time," replied the old man with a chuckle. "But after eating this grass I'm afraid I wouldn't remember a single piece. Why don't you eat some, Brother Lin, to get rid of your bad gas?"

"What use would it be to me? I'm not printing a collection of drinks or cookery recipes."

"What do you mean?" asked Tang.

"My belly is just a hold for food and drinks: I can't compare with you two. If I were to print a book, it would be on gastronomy. But I don't wonder now at your love of travel, brother, for all these strange birds and beasts and these rare plants and fairy herbs we've seen today are most diverting!"

*　　　　*　　　　*

They were not far from the boat when a huge bird flew out from a copse beside the road. It had boar's tusks and long feathers, but was shaped like a man with human limbs and face. It had two fleshy wings which sprouted from under its ribs, as well as two human heads, one male and one female. And if you looked carefully, their foreheads were branded with the word "unfilial".

"So this is an Unfilial Bird," observed Duo.

At the word "unfilial", Lin raised his musket and fired, bringing the bird to the ground. And as it tried to take flight again, he hurried over and felled it with a few blows. A closer examination revealed that in addition to the brand "unfilial" on its foreheads, it had "heartless" on its mouths, "immoral" on its shoulders, "philanderer" on the right of its breast and "uxorious" on the left.

"I read of this in an old tale but never believed it," said Tang. "Now I have seen with my own eyes. There are more things in heaven and earth than we imagine. Because the unfilial are so close to beasts, I suppose in their next existence their spirits cannot inhabit human bodies, but their evil humours take the form of this bird."

"Brother Tang has given an apt explanation." Duo nodded his approval. "I saw such a bird once before, but it had two male heads and was not branded 'philanderer'. There is no such thing as an unfilial woman, so both heads are usually men's; but as these heads keep changing, sometimes both are female. I am told this bird has divine intelligence, and can do good deeds to expiate its crimes. After each good deed one of its brands disappears until finally all have gone, and after a few more years of a virtuous life its feathers drop out and it becomes an immortal."

"This is like the case of the butcher who became an immortal as soon as he put down his knife," observed

Tang. "Heaven gives all living creatures a second chance."

Now the sailors who had been to the spring for water came to have a look and asked what had happened.

"If it was unfilial, we need not stand on ceremony!" they shouted. "This fine plumage will make good feather dusters when we get home."

They grabbed a handful each, till feathers were whirling in all directions.

"Though it has that brand on its forehead it was begotten of someone else's evil humours," said Tang. "The bird is not to blame."

"We're plucking out its evil for it," retorted the seamen. "Then it will have to keep to the path of virtue. See how thick its plumage is! It must have been too miserly to part with one feather in its lifetime, but now we shall pluck it properly!"

They had plucked the bird and were starting back to the boat when a stream of foul-smelling glue gushed out of the copse. As they took to their heels a strange, rat-shaped fowl flew out. It was five feet long, with one crimson claw and two great wings. Swooping down on the Unfilial Bird, it bore it off into the air. Lin hastily loaded his musket and took aim, but his fuse was wet and the bird was gone in a flash.

"In all our travels abroad we have never seen a bird like that," remarked the seamen. "Even Ninth Uncle with his great stock of ocean lore, old and new, must be at a loss today."

"That was Flying Saliva," Duo told them. "That fowl's saliva is like glue. When it is hungry it spits on a tree so that other birds flying past are caught and held there. It probably had not eaten today, that was why the saliva streamed from its beak; but now it should make a good meal of the Unfilial Bird. See how universal the hatred of evil is — men pluck out the Unfilial Bird's feathers and wild creatures devour its flesh!"

This said, they went back together to the junk, and hoisted sail without further delay.

*   *   *

In a few days they moored at the Land of Courtesy, where Lin disembarked to do business. Tang, who knew this land's reputation for politeness and guessed that it must be a place of great refinement, asked Duo to go ashore with him to see the sights. A walk of several *li* brought them to the city wall, over the gate of which were inscribed the words: "Goodness Alone Is a Treasure."

Having read this they entered the city, where they found many buildings and many folk buying and selling. The citizens' dress and speech were like those of the Middle Kingdom,* and when Tang knew he could communicate with them he asked an old man the reason for their courtesy. But the old man could not understand him, nor tell him how their land came by its name. Not one of Tang's questions could he answer.

"My guess is that they received this name from their neighbours, as well as their reputation for politeness," said Duo. "That must be why this old man does not know. We saw examples of their courtesy just now when those farmers let passers-by through their fields

---

* A conventional name for China.

and travellers ceded right of way. And look how polite they all are, gentry and common folk, rich and poor alike. They deserve their reputation."

"True," replied Tang. "But we must look round carefully to get a better picture of the country."

By now they had come to the busy market-place, where they saw a serving-man fingering some wares.

"Brother," he said to the vendor, "how can I buy such excellent goods for so little? You must raise the price before I can agree. If not, I shall know you don't really want to sell."

"It's the shopman who usually asks a stiff price while the customer haggles," whispered Tang to Duo. "Now this shopman has stated his price, but instead of bargaining the customer wants to raise it. Whoever heard of such a thing? No wonder they are known for their deference to each other!"

Then they heard the shopman reply:

"I appreciate your concern, but though I am blushing already to have asked so much, you want to shame me further by calling it too little. It is not as if my goods have a fixed price that leaves no margin for profit. As the proverb says: 'The price asked is as high as Heaven, that offered as low as the earth.' Yet instead of lowering it you want to raise it. If you refuse to show any consideration, I shall have to ask you to carry your custom elsewhere — I really cannot agree."

"With us it is always the customer who says 'The price is as high as Heaven'," Tang pointed out. "That applies to the other saying too. But here the shopman quotes them — how amusing!"

Then the serving-man went on: "It's hardly honest, is it, brother, to ask a low price for such good wares yet accuse me of being inconsiderate? Honesty is the best policy, and everyone has a sense of values. You can't make a fool of me."

Though they bargained for some time, the shopman refused to raise his price. Then the other sulkily paid what was asked, but took only half of the goods. As he turned to go, however, the shopman barred his way, saying he had paid too much and taken too little. Two old men who came by acted as arbiters, and made the customer take four-fifths of the goods at the price agreed on. So a compromise was reached, and the serving-man left.

Meanwhile Tang and Duo were nodding quietly. After walking a little further, they came upon a soldier who was also making a purchase.

"When I asked the price of your honourable wares, you told me to give what I thought fit," said the soldier. "But when I did, you complained it was too much, though I'd already come down a good deal. To insist shows not only prejudice but unfairness."

"I dared not fix a price, sir," replied the stall-holder. "I wanted you to decide because my poor goods are neither fresh nor anything special — much inferior to what you'd find elsewhere. As they are not worth half the sum you've offered, I can't possibly take so much!"

"It's usually the customer who claims that the goods are nothing special," commented Tang, "while it's the shopman who says he has come down drastically. Here it's the other way round, though. They have different customs."

"How can you say such a thing?" protested the soldier meanwhile. "I may not be an expert trader, but I know good wares from bad. I'm not such a fool as to take one for the other. When you charge only half what first-class goods are worth, you are cheating people and going in for sharp practice."

"If you really want to help me," retorted the other, "the fairest thing would be to halve your first price. If you think that's too little, I won't presume to argue but will ask you to go and find out the prices elsewhere. Then you'll know I'm not cheating you."

Long as the soldier argued, the other refused to sell till he took a few goods at half the price first offered. Then the customer picked some out and was making off when the stall-holder stopped him, protesting:

"Why just choose the worst and leave the best for me, brother? A man who drives such a hard bargain must seldom succeed in buying anything."

"I let you take an advantage because you insisted." The soldier was indignant. "I took some goods which are not quite your best, for my own peace of mind, not expecting you to start finding fault again. Besides, it's your second-best goods that I want — the best are no use to me, much as I appreciate your kind intentions."

"If you want a cheap line, that's up to you. But seconds are seconds. How can you pay a top price for inferior quality?"

The soldier made no answer, but took his purchases and prepared to go. When the bystanders accused him of underhand treatment, however, he was unable to gainsay them and had to take as much good merchandise as bad.

Having watched this, Tang and Duo went on till they came upon a farmer buying from a pedlar. The price had been settled, the money paid, and the customer was going off when the pedlar examined the silver carefully and weighed it in his balance.

"Come back, brother!" He hurried after the farmer. "You've given me too much silver and the quality is too good. We always use the second-grade silver here, so as you have paid in the best quality you ought to make a reduction in the amount, yet instead I find you have given me overweight too. A substantial citizen like you shouldn't haggle over such trifles, but there's no reason why I should suffer either. Please make the usual reduction."

"Don't be so niggardly," retorted the farmer. "If there is too much, just deduct it next time I buy your excellent goods."

He tried to make off, but the pedlar barred the way.

"Now, none of that!" he cried. "Another of my worthy customers left some silver with me last year, saying he would settle next time; but I've not set eyes on him since. As I can find no trace of him anywhere, I shall be in his debt during my next existence. Now that you want to do the same, sir, what will happen if you disappear? In my next life I shall have to toil as a donkey or horse to repay the first gentleman, which will keep me too busy to repay you. That means I shall have to be a donkey or horse in the existence *after* that to settle with you. In my humble opinion, rather than wait till next time you honour me with your custom, you had better settle today. It is simpler that way, because as time goes on you may forget the exact sum."

After much deferring to each other, the farmer took two additional knick-knacks in lieu of his extra silver. Still the pedlar complained that this was too hard a bargain, but as the farmer was now well away there was nothing he could do. Just then a beggar passed by, and the pedlar muttered to himself:

"In his last life this fellow must have cheated someone — that is why he is a beggar now."

Saying this, he weighed the silver again, handed the surplus to the beggar, and moved on.

"The transactions we have seen certainly give a picture of gentlemanly conduct," observed Tang. "No further inquiries are needed. But let us stroll on a little. This is such beautiful country, we may as well see more of its fine scenery."

After rambling for a while they returned to the boat and found Lin already there, having sold all his goods. They set sail without delay.

*   *   *

They voyaged for several days till they came to the Kingdom of the Great. As this country lay next to the Land of Courtesy, its customs, language and products were much the same; and there was so much commerce between both kingdoms each year on account of their proximity that Lin did not think he could make a profit here, and decided not to trade. But because Tang wished to look round, they went ashore with old Duo.

"I have always wanted to come here," confided Tang, "ever since I heard of the Kingdom of the Great where instead of walking men ride about on clouds. Today Heaven has granted my wish."

"We are still over twenty li from where they live," Duo told him. "We must put our best foot forward, for this is a bad road to travel at night. A steep mountain lies ahead, intersected by paths which lead in all directions, and the people here have made this their capital. The mountain is surrounded by paddy fields, but everyone lives up above."

After some hours they approached the mountain, and began to see people in the open country. Two or three feet taller than the men elsewhere, they sailed about on clouds half a foot or so from the ground, and when they wished to stop the clouds would halt. Our three travellers climbed the mountain and threaded their way over two peaks, till a maze of paths lay before them intersecting the summit but not extending outside.

"We seem to have lost our way," said Duo. "But I see a thatched temple in front. We can ask the way from the monk there."

They walked up to the temple, and were about to knock when an old man arrived carrying a pot of wine and a pig's head. He opened the gate and started in.

"Excuse me, sir," Tang accosted him, "can you tell us the name of this temple? And is there a monk here?"

With a word of apology, the old man hurried in to put down the wine and pork. He returned at once to greet them formally.

"This is a temple to Guanyin, the Goddess of Mercy," he told them. "I am the monk here, gentlemen."

"If you are a monk, why is your head unshaved?" asked Lin curiously. "As you drink wine and eat pork, no doubt you keep a nun too?"

"The only nun here is my wife. There are just the two of us, and we have looked after this temple since we were young. In our country we never used to speak of monks; but when we heard that in the Celestial Empire all temple attendants since the Han Dynasty have shaved their heads and called themselves monks or nuns we decided to follow suit, though we do not fast or shave our heads. So I am a monk and my wife is a nun. May I ask where you three gentlemen are from?"

When Duo had told him, the old fellow bowed.

"So you are three worthy citizens of the Celestial Empire!" he exclaimed. "Excuse me for not recognizing you. Please come in and have some tea."

"We have yet to cross the mountain, so we must not delay," said Tang.

"What do you call the offspring of monks and nuns?" inquired Lin. "They can hardly be the same as other children."

"My wife and I are the caretakers here," replied the old man with a smile. "As I like other good citizens break no laws and neither steal nor whore, why should my children have a special name? Just tell me what the children of caretakers of Confucian halls are called in your honourable country, and we will call ours the same."

"We have noticed that all your worthy countrymen have clouds under their feet," put in Tang. "Are you born with these?"

"They spring from the feet," replied the old man. "You cannot force them to grow. The most honourable are the many-coloured, and after that the yellow. No distinction is made between the rest, except that the black are the lowest."

"We are a long way from our boat," said Duo. "May we trouble you, father, to set us on the right road? We must be on our way."

Then the monk pointed out their path.

They threaded their way through the hills to the populous centre of the city, where everything reminded them of the Land of Courtesy, except that the people had clouds of different shapes and colours under their feet. As a beggar passed on clouds of many colours, Tang turned to Duo.

"How is it, uncle, if many coloured clouds are noble while black are despised, that this beggar has coloured clouds?"

"That monk we met eats meat, drinks wine, and has a wife," pointed out Lin. "He is obviously a time-serving glutton, yet he had multi-coloured clouds too. There can hardly be anything good about this beggar or that monk."

"When I was here before, I asked the same question," said Duo. "Though some colours are better than others, they depend entirely on a man's character and behaviour, not on his wealth and position. If a man is true and honest, coloured clouds will appear at his feet. If he is evil and vicious, his clouds will be black. These clouds spring from his feet, and their colour is determined by his heart — he has no choice in the matter. That is why the rich and great often have black clouds, while the poor have coloured ones. Still, the general morality here is good, and you find only one or two black clouds out of a hundred. Perhaps because they would be ashamed of the black, they shrink from evil and do as much good as they can. And as there is nothing petty-minded about them, neighbouring peoples call this the Land of the Great. Men far away who do not know the facts assume that all the inhabitants are giants, but this is the real meaning of the name."

"That was puzzling me," agreed Tang. "I had heard

that the people here were several dozen feet high, yet they are no taller than we are. So that was simply a rumour."

"It is in the Land of Giants that they are so tall," Duo informed him. "You will see what real giants are like there."

Just then the passers-by scattered to make way for an official. With a black gauze hat and round collar, a red sunshade carried above him, and a retinue of runners and attendants, he was an imposing sight. But the colour of the clouds at his feet was hidden by a red silk veil.

"No doubt it is so easy for the officials here to move about on clouds that they dispense with carriages," commented Tang. "But why do they wear these footveils?"

"Ugly clouds, of a grey-black colour, often spring from their feet, and they are considered unlucky," Duo explained. "All men with such clouds must have done evil in secret. But though they can deceive their fellows, these clouds are quite pitiless — they turn this unlucky colour and make their owners ashamed to face the world. So they veil their feet from the public eye, like the robber who stopped his own ears to steal a bell. Fortunately these clouds change as a man's heart changes. If he sincerely repents and seeks to do good, his clouds' colour will change accordingly. If he sports an ugly cloud a long time, the king will look into his case and punish him; and his countrymen will shun him because he refuses to mend his ways but takes delight in evil."

"Heaven is most unfair," was Lin's comment.

"Why do you say that?" asked Tang.

"Isn't it unfair to provide these clouds only for the Land of the Great? If everyone in the world had a label like this, and a black cloud grew from the feet of all skulking rascals to shame them publicly, then every man seeing them would be on his guard, and a very good thing too."

"Not all bad men have black clouds under their feet," said Duo. "But the black vapour over their heads reaches to Heaven, and that is much worse for them!"

"Why don't I see that black vapour?" demanded Lin.

"You don't see it, but Heaven does, and so it distinguishes between good and bad. It appoints a good end for the good, and an evil end for the evil — all are judged according to fixed principles."

"In that case I won't accuse Heaven of unfairness," conceded Lin.

After wandering for a while they started back to the junk, afraid of being late.

*   *   *

Some time later they reached the Land of the Restless, where they put in to port and went ashore. All the people on the streets had coal-black faces, and walked with a jerky gait. The travellers' first impression was that this agitation was due to haste, but a closer look revealed that even those sitting or standing kept rocking and rolling without a second's rest.

"The name 'restless' is an apt one," remarked Tang. "No wonder the ancients described them as unable to keep still. They fidget too much to sit or stand quietly."

"They look as if they all had convulsion," declared Lin. "How can they sleep at night with this wiggling and waggling? Thank Heaven I was born in the Middle

Kingdom. If I were a native here and had to carry on like this, in less than two days I'd have shaken myself to pieces."

"How long do you suppose they live," asked Tang, "in view of their busy life and the way they keep on the go every second of the day?"

"Men abroad have a saying about this land," Duo told them. " 'The Restless live long.' Though they are always on the go here, their limbs are exercised but not their minds. And as no grain is produced here and they eat only berries and fruit — no cooked food — this helps them all to live to a ripe old age. But I am subject to spells of giddiness, and it makes me dizzy to see all this rocking and wriggling, so if you'll excuse me, I'll go back first. Take your time about looking round."

"This town is a small one with nothing worth seeing," rejoined Tang. "If Ninth Uncle is giddy, let us all go back together."

With that they returned to the boat.

*　　　　*　　　　*

Aboard they went on talking, and Tang said to Lin:

"At East Gate Mountain, brother, you told me that after the Land of Courtesy and the Kingdom of the Great we would find the Black Teeth — why haven't we seen them yet?"

"Brother Lin was right in saying the Black Teeth are close to the Land of Courtesy," said Duo. "But they are close by land, not by water. We shan't get there till we have passed the Land of the Childless."

"I assume that is the country otherwise known as Barren," rejoined Tang. "They say the people there never give birth and therefore have no descendants. Is this true?"

"As far as I know," replied Duo, "I was puzzled to hear that there is no difference between the sexes there. And when I visited the place, the men and women did look pretty much alike."

"Without sex they can hardly have children," said Tang. "But in that case, after one generation dies they should become extinct. How has their race continued since ancient times?"

"Though they cannot give birth, their bodies do not decompose after death," explained Duo. "After one hundred and twenty years they come to life again. This is what the ancients meant by resurrection after a century. As they live, die and live again in an endless cycle, their number never grows less. Knowing that they will come to life again, they are not very greedy for fame or profit. The fact of man's mortality makes them realize that all fame and profit — even the greatest honour and magnificence — will come to nothing after death, but fade away like a dream. And by their next life the world will have changed, and they will have to struggle all over again if they are ambitious; while before they know where they are, old age will overtake them and the envoy from the underworld will come to fetch them. Seen like this, life is nothing but a dream. So when one of their countrymen dies they say he is asleep, and the living are said to be dreaming. Having seen through life and death, they have little desire for rank and riches, while our blind pursuit of these things is quite unknown."

"If this is true, what fools we are!" exclaimed Lin. "They live again, yet see through riches and rank; while we who have no chance of another life struggle tooth and nail for such things. If the men there knew this, how they would laugh at us!"

"If you are afraid of their laughter, brother, why not overcome your ambitions?" asked Tang.

"Life is only a dream, fame and riches are vanity — if you tell me that, I agree," admitted Lin. "But show me a chance to seize some fame or profit, and like a fool I imagine I am immortal and risk my neck for it. I wish next time that happens someone would punch my head to point out my stupidity, or give me a warning."

"Once you are carried away, I'm afraid you wouldn't listen if I put in a word," said Duo. "Or, more likely, you would call me a fool."

"Ninth Uncle is right," agreed Tang. "Ambition is a snare and a delusion. While you are preening yourself on your achievements, how can anyone disillusion you? You will persist until it is time to sleep. And only when your eyes close will you realize you have been wasting your time, for life is simply a dream. If men would only see this, even if they could not overcome their ambition once and for all, a better understanding of the matter would make them think twice and show more tolerance, in which case they could save themselves a great deal of trouble. This is not only a good philosophy of life, but a splendid recipe for happiness. The men of the Land of the Childless could do no more than this."

*   *   *

One day they reached the Kingdom of Black Teeth, where the people were jet-black from head to foot, and had black teeth as well. Their red lips, red eyebrows and red clothes only emphasized their general murkiness. Tang assumed that being black they must be ugly, but unable to see them clearly from the boat he asked old Duo to go ashore with him.

When Lin knew that they meant to take a stroll, he went ashore first to sell cosmetics, and the other two presently followed.

"Do you think their behaviour matches their appearance?" asked Tang.

"They're a long way by sea from the Land of Courtesy, but its neighbour by land," replied Duo. "I doubt if they can be too barbarous. I have passed this way many times but never come ashore, for they look so repulsive they can hardly be worth talking to. Thanks to you, brother, this is my first chance to observe them. We shall probably just find this an opportunity to stretch our legs, and must not expect very much. One look at them and you can imagine the rest."

Tang nodded several times, and they entered the city. Brisk business was being done, and the language was fairly easy to understand. The women in the streets did not mix with the men, for in the large main highway the men kept to the right and the women to the left — a fair distance from each other. Unaware of this, Tang headed towards the left until someone called out:

"Will the honourable visitors kindly keep to this side!"

They hurriedly crossed the road, and found that they had been on the women's side.

"I never noticed!" Tang smiled. "Black as they are, they observe the due distinctions between the sexes. See, uncle, the men and women in the street don't talk to each other but walk by with lowered heads and no lewd glances. I never expected them to be so correct. They are obviously influenced by the Land of Courtesy."

"When we were there, they told us that all their customs and civilization came from the Middle Kingdom. Now the Black Teeth have learned from the Land of Courtesy; so as a centre of influence our country is a mother to all the others."

As they were talking they heard a cry:

"Who'll buy my rouge and powder?"

And there was Lin with a bundle in his hand.

"Why have you been so long, brother?" asked Duo.

"When I heard you were coming ashore to see the sights I decided to do some trading," answered Lin. "But not having dealt here before, I didn't know what would sell best and brought cosmetics, because these people are blacker than charcoal. Who could have guessed that the women here think it vulgar to paint and powder, and not one of them would buy — they all wanted books instead. I couldn't understand why till I made inquiries and learned that their social standing is based entirely on book learning."

"How is that?" inquired Tang.

"The custom here is to honour men for their learning, no matter whether they are rich or poor. The same thing goes for women. When girls grow up, if they are good scholars their hands are asked in marriage; but if they are dunces, even daughters of great houses have no suitors. So all the boys and girls in this country study. Next year, apparently, the queen has arranged for another general examination for women, and since word of this spread they all want to become licentiates and are more eager than ever to buy books. When I found this out, I knew I couldn't get rid of my goods but went on trying till I met you."

They had now reached a crowded part of the town.

"These people are so dark that at first I rather averted my eyes from them," confessed Tang. "But now I see everybody on the road is extraordinarily handsome, while men and women alike have a most scholarly air. An elegant refinement seems to radiate from their blackness. Indeed, if you look closely, you realize that dark glossiness is just the thing, and the very thought of powder and paint disgusts you. They make me blush for my own ugliness. Here, among all this scholarly refinement, I realize how disgustingly vulgar we must look. Rather than stay to be laughed at, let us leave as fast as we can!"

The three of them slunk furtively back, comparing the Black Teeth's dignity and distinction with the very sorry figures they cut themselves. The result was that they found it equally hard to keep moving or to stand still, to walk briskly, slowly or at a moderate speed. Thoroughly out of countenance, they braced themselves to proceed at a steady pace, with arched backs, expanded chests and stiff necks, their eyes fixed straight ahead as they plodded on step by step — the traditional scholar's gait. So at last they got out of the city, pleased to find the district outside almost deserted. Then they stretched themselves, shook their heads once or twice, and relaxed with deep sighs of relief.

"You hit the nail on the head just now, brother," said Lin. "Close up, they certainly are magnificent. I don't wonder you want to walk properly after seeing them. You made even me, for all my easy-going ways, try to put on scholarly airs and pass myself off as one of the literati. In fact, I threw myself into the part so thoroughly that now I have a back-ache, stiff legs, a sore neck, and pins and needles in my feet. My head is reeling, everything is dancing in front of my eyes, my tongue is parched and my throat is dry — I couldn't have kept it up one moment longer. Another second and I should have collapsed. Let's get out of here quick!"

During this speech they had reached the boat, where Lin ordered his men to weigh anchor and set sail.

*　　　　　*　　　　　*

A few days later they came to the Land of Dwarfs.

"I take it this is the Kingdom of Pygmies mentioned by the ancients, where the people are eight or nine inches tall," said Tang. "What are the customs here, uncle?"

"They are a mean, completely heartless lot. And all they say runs counter to common sense. If a thing is sweet, for instance, they say it is bitter; if it is salty, they swear that it is tasteless. You simply don't know where you are with them. But this is nothing to marvel at — this has always been their way."

The two of them landed and walked to the city wall, stooping to pass through the low gate. The streets were so mean and narrow that they could not walk abreast. Once inside the city they saw that the dwarfs were less than one foot high, and the children a mere four inches. They went about in small groups, armed, for fear lest large birds carry them away. They were always making contradictory statements, and showed themselves cunning and crafty.

"I never thought there were such petty creatures in the world," said Tang.

After roving for a while they met Lin returning from selling his goods, and went back to the junk together.

*   *   *

One day they reached a far-stretching territory and saw a great city towering like a mountain in the distance. This was the Land of Giants. While Lin set off alone to trade, Tang went ashore with Duo. But his first sight of the giants made him turn tail and run.

"This is simply terrifying, uncle!" he cried. "I never believed old accounts I read of giants between a hundred and two hundred feet tall; but these must be pretty well eighty feet, they stride so high above us. Why, one of their feet reaches above my chest! The sight is enough to terrify anyone. Well, we were wise to leave while the going was good. If they had seen us and picked us up for a better look, we'd have dangled tens of feet above the ground!"

"These giants are not the largest," responded Duo. "They reach only to the ankles of really big ones. I talked once with some old fellows abroad who described the ogres they had seen. One said: 'I remember seeing a giant in foreign parts who was over a thousand _li_ tall and more than a hundred _li_ across. He had a liking for wine, and used to drink five hundred gallons at a time. Though he gave me quite a turn, I read later in some old book that this was a Wulu.'

"Another said: 'North of Dingling I once saw a sleeping giant who was as tall as a mountain. His footprints made valleys, and by lying crosswise he could dam a river — he was over ten thousand *li* long.'

"Yet another said: 'I've seen a still bigger one. The Wulu would only measure up to his ankles. Think how much material he needed for his gown — all the cloth on earth was bought up for it, and making it kept all the tailors busy for years. It sent up both the price of cloth and the cost of tailoring — everyone in either business made his fortune. In fact all the drapers and tailors today are praying for that giant to make another gown so that business will boom again. One tailor at the time stole some material from the lapel on which he was working, and opened a big cloth shop with it, changing his trade. Do you know the size of this giant? 193,500 *li* from head to foot!'

" 'How do you know so exactly?' the others asked.

"He told them: 'We read in the classics that this is the distance between heaven and earth, and this giant's head just reaches heaven when he stands on the earth. Not only is he huge, he likes to talk big too — his tongue matches his size.'

"The others objected: 'We hear there is such a strong wind in heaven that birds flying too high are torn into shreds. If this giant's head reaches the sky, how is it his face isn't blown to bits by the wind?'

" 'Because he's so thick-skinned.'

" 'How do you know?'

" 'If he weren't, he wouldn't talk big all the time, not caring what a fool he makes of himself.' "

*　　　*　　　*

Next they came to White Land, and Lin took silks,

brocades and seafood to sell there while Tang asked Duo to go ashore with him.

"This is a populous country and a wealthy one," said Duo. "Their language is intelligible too, but the place doesn't seem to suit me. Whenever I come here, some trouble happens or I fall ill. I'm glad you've given me another chance today to have a look round."

Having disembarked and walked for several *li*, they saw white ridges on every side, with limestone hills in the distance. The fields were planted with millet and the ground was covered with white flowers. Being some distance from the farmers, Tang and Duo could not see their faces clearly, but observed that they wore white.

Soon they entered a jade city and crossed a silver bridge. Shops and houses stretched in all directions, each with high, white-washed walls. All was noise and bustle, with much traffic and trading. Old and young alike in that country were strikingly handsome, with faces white as jade, vermilion lips, arched eyebrows and sparkling eyes. Moreover they wore white clothes and caps of spotless silk, had gold bracelets on their wrists, fragrant beads in their hands, a great crimson tassel three feet long on their caps, handkerchiefs printed with two flying swallows pinned to their gowns, and ornaments of emerald and agate. Their garments must have been scented with some rare perfume, for its fragrance was wafted to you from a distance.

Tang devoured these people with his eyes, exclaiming repeatedly in admiration.

"Such beauty set off by such a dress — how exquisite!" he cried. "This must be the finest of all foreign lands!"

Lining both sides of the streets were taverns, eating-houses, perfumers and silversmiths. They also saw great heaps of silks and brocades, and countless clothiers, hatters, shoe-makers and hosiers, to say nothing of stalls selling beef, mutton, pork, chicken, duck, fish, shrimps and seafood, as well as every kind of confectionery. All was there in abundance and all was of the best — food, drinks, apparel and jewellery. The aroma of wine and good victuals rising from each street and lane must surely have reached up to heaven!

Soon Lin and one of his seamen emerged from a silk shop, and Duo stepped up to him.

"Have you done good business, brother?" he inquired.

"You two have brought me luck," replied Lin, beaming. "I've sold a great deal, and all at a handsome profit. When I go back I mean to buy plenty of wine and meat to feast you. But I still have some handkerchiefs, purses and other knick-knacks which I want to sell to well-to-do families in that lane in front. Would you care to come with me?"

"Certainly," answered Tang.

Lin sent the sailor back first with the money he had made, telling him what meat and wine to buy on the way. Then, carrying his wares himself, he went with Tang and Duo into the lane.

"This will do," he told them presently. "That impressive gate-house in front must belong to some substantial citizen."

As they reached the gate, out walked an exquisite youth, to whom Lin explained his errand.

"Please come in if you have rare goods," said the young man. "Our master will be glad to buy them."

While stepping over the threshold, they saw a white paper notice pasted by the gate. On it was the word "Academy".

Tang started at the sight, and said to Duo:

"This is a school we've come to, uncle!"

Duo also was taken aback, but it was too late to retreat, for now they were in and the young man had gone to announce them.

"These people have such refined and handsome features that one can imagine how great their natural endowments and erudition must be," remarked Tang to Duo. "We must be twice as careful as we were in the Land of Black Teeth."

"Why?" inquired Lin. "If they ask any questions, you can always say you don't know."

The three of them entered a reception room, where a man of about forty wearing tortoise-shell glasses was sitting. There were four or five students too in their late teens or early twenties, all handsome and smartly dressed. Their tutor also was a good-looking man. In this room were shelves lined with books, and stands filled with writing-brushes. A jade placard in the centre of one wall bore the gilded inscription "A Sea of Learning and a Forest of Literature", and this was flanked with a couplet on white paper:

Study the Six Classics to instruct the world,
Master the Myriad Arts to educate men.

Impressed by this display, Tang and Duo walked on tiptoe and hardly dared to breathe.

"These are men of a superior state," whispered Tang. "Their whole bearing marks them off from the common herd. They show us up as somewhat vulgar again."

Not presuming to make any salutation, they stood respectfully at one side of the room. The tutor, seated opposite the door, had fragrant beads in his hands. After scanning the three of them, he beckoned to Tang:

"Come here! Let the scholar come here!"

Alarmed by this form of address, Tang made haste to step forward and bow.

"Your student is no scholar but a merchant," he disclaimed.

"May I ask where you are from?" inquired the tutor.

"From the Middle Kingdom." Tang bowed again. "I have come here to do business."

"Wearing the cap of the literati and coming from the Middle Kingdom, how can you deny being a scholar? Are you afraid I may test you?"

"I did study as a youth, sir," admitted Tang, now that his cap had given him away. "But all these years of trading have made me forget the few books I ever read."

"So you say, but surely you can still write poems?"

"I have never written a poem in my life." Tang felt more nervous than ever. "I never even read them."

"What! From the Middle Kingdom and you can't write poems? Impossible! Don't try to throw dust in my eyes. Admit the truth!"

"It is the truth," Tang protested desperately. "How dare your student lie to you?"

"Your cap is obviously the badge of a scholar, so of course you can write poems. If you have no pretensions to learning, why should you pose as one of the literati and hide your true profession? I am beginning to suspect you wear this cap to take people in, or in the hope of securing a teaching post. Ambition has corrupted you! Never mind, let me set you a subject and see what you make of it. If you do well, I shall find you a good position as a tutor."

This said, he picked up the rhyme book.

Tang was quite frantic by now.

"Your student did study a little at one time," he blurted out. "How fortunate I am today to have met a great scholar like yourself! If I could scribble at all, I should certainly seize this chance to profit by your instruction — I am not so blind to the favour you are doing me. In any case, I would do my best for the sake of advancement. The fact is I am too unversed in literature to carry out your respected orders. If you question my companions, they will confirm that this is no empty excuse."

"Is this scholar really unlettered?" the tutor asked Duo and Lin.

"Not a bit of it," answered Lin. "He has studied since he was a boy, and came second in the palace test."

Tang quietly stamped and fumed to himself: "You will be the death of me, brother!"

"I'll tell you the truth, sir," Lin went on. "Though my friend here has plenty of learning, after passing the examinations he threw all his books away. If you like to test him now on trade regulations and the abacus, you'll find he answers all right. But please give that job you mentioned just now to me!"

"So it seems he has given up his studies," said the tutor. "Can you or your old friend write poems?"

"We are two plain merchants who have never studied," replied Duo. "How can we write poems?"

"Evidently you are all boors," said the tutor to Lin. "But in that case, why ask for a post? It is a pity you have wasted your good looks by not acquiring any learning, though as a merchant you should know a few characters. You must be teachable, of course, but you are all travellers who will not be here long. If you would stay a couple of years, I could undertake to coach you. I do not want to boast, but a little of my instruction would give you enough of my learning to last you all your lives. Once home again, if you kept up your studies, you would win such a reputation for scholarship that not only would friends from nearby flock to you, but even those from far off. As you know nothing of literature and cannot write poems, however, we have no common topic of conversation, and standing there you look unendurably vulgar. Will you kindly wait outside till this class is over, when I will examine your goods. You would not understand our literary talk, and if you stand there much longer I am afraid you will infect us with your coarseness. Though I am not to be shaken, my students are young; and were they to be contaminated by you it would cost me great efforts to refine them again."

Assenting meekly, the three men walked slowly out to the corridor. Tang's heart was still thumping wildly for fear the tutor might speak of literature again, and he was just thinking of leaving first with Duo when a student came out and beckoned to them.

"Our master will see your goods now," he said.

Lin hastily picked up his bundle and carried it in, and the other two waited for him for some time while the tutor, who wanted to buy his entire stock, was haggling over the price.

Tang seized this chance to tiptoe into the study to

look at their books. After skimming through two essays, he hurried out.

"Why are you so red in the face, brother, after looking at their books?" asked Duo.

Before Tang could answer, Lin came back, having completed his sale, and the three of them went out into the lane together.

"I've been made a proper fool of today!" swore Tang. "I took it for granted he was a first-rate scholar. That's why I treated him with such respect and called myself his student. The fact is the man is nothing but a fraud! I never saw anything like it!"

"How did you find their compositions?" asked Duo. "Can you remember any of them, brother?"

"I saw the way they broached a theme,* and that was quite enough. The subject was: 'Having heard a beast cry, he cannot bear to eat it.' This was broached as 'A man who has heard a beast cry cannot bear to eat it.' "

"Well, that shows a good memory at least," said Lin.

"What do you mean?" asked Duo.

"He repeated the whole title without forgetting one word — doesn't that show a good memory?"

Tang continued: "Another subject was: 'If you do not miss the right season to work on a hundred *mu*, it can keep a family of eight from hunger.' The student wrote 'If you work hard on a hundred *mu*, four couples will have enough to eat.' "

"So he gave us 'four couples' for the 'family of

---

* The prescribed form of essay for the civil service examinations in the Qing Dynasty was divided into eight parts. The subjects were isolated quotations from the Confucian classics. The first part of the essay, "broaching the theme", had to present the subject briefly.

eight'," commented Lin. "Well, four couples is an exact equivalent — no straying off to seven or nine for him."

"I can't remember all the rest," said Tang. "But to think I bowed and stood in the presence of such dolts, interlarding all I said with 'Your student'! I could die of shame!"

"Never mind!" said Lin. "We may have been fooled, but we didn't sweat for them or put ourselves out in any way. Forget it."

Just then they saw a boy lead past a strange beast something like a buffalo, which was wearing a hat and clothes.

"Tell me, uncle, is this the Medicine Beast they say the Plain Folk had in the days of Shen Nong?" asked Tang.

"The same," replied Duo. "It has a gift for curing diseases. If a man is ill and tells this beast his symptoms, it will go to the country and bring back an herb; and when the patient extracts the juice and takes it, boiled, he invariably feels better. If his illness is so bad that one dose is not enough, the next day he must describe his symptoms again and the beast will go out once more and bring back the same herb or some others. When these are prepared in the same way, the patient is always cured. This has gone on right up to the present. In fact, I hear there are more of these beasts than before, as they are multiplying by degrees. You now find them elsewhere as well."

"No wonder it wears clothes if it can cure illness!" said Lin. "Can it take a pulse, uncle? Does it read medical books?"

"No, neither," was Duo's reply. "It probably just knows the taste of a few herbs."

"You brazen-faced beast!" Lin wagged a finger at it. "You have studied no medical books and can't take pulses, yet you have the impudence to come and treat patients! You are playing with human lives!"

"If it hears you swearing at it, it may prepare a dose for you," warned Duo.

"I'm not ill, why should I take medicine?" demanded Lin.

"You are not ill now," retorted Duo, "but after taking its medicine you will be."

Talking and laughing they had reached the boat, and going aboard they feasted merrily.

*   *   *

As they sailed on at a good speed with the wind behind them, Tang and Lin were standing in the helm to watch Duo direct the seamen working the rudder, when in front they saw long columns of green vapour rising straight up to heaven. This seemed something like mist or smoke, and dimly through it they could make out a city.

"That's a fair-sized place," said Lin. "What is it called?"

Old Duo consulted his compass and looked out.

"I should say that's the Land of Virtuous Scholars in front," he answered.

"That green vapour seems to have a strange smell," remarked Tang. "What causes that, uncle?"

"I have passed this place only at some distance before. I don't know the reason for that smell."

"Surely it's written in books what odour goes with green," put in Lin.

"Judging by the Five Elements and Five Flavours, the east belongs to the element of wood," replied Tang. "Its colour is green and its flavour sour. But I don't know if that applies here."

Lin gazed ahead and sniffed hard.

"I think you're right, brother." He nodded twice.

They were now fairly near the shore, and could see thousands of plum trees, each over a hundred feet high, virtually surrounding the city.

Before long they put into harbour. Lin knew that no merchants ever came to this place and no trading was done here; but fearing Tang must be finding it dull on board, he ordered the crew to moor here and offered to accompany Tang and Duo ashore.

"Why not take a few goods, Brother Lin?" suggested Duo. "You may find some customers."

"I never heard of anyone trading here. What shall I take?"

"As this is the Land of Virtuous Scholars there should be many literati here; so lines like ink and brushes would be best. They're easy to carry too."

Lin nodded and made up a bundle of stationery. Then the three of them got into a sampan, and some seamen rowed them ashore. As they landed and plunged into the plum orchard, a penetrating, sour odour made them hold their noses. Old Duo remarked:

"I once heard that this land has leeks all the year round as well as evergreen plums. I don't know about the leeks, but it seems to be true about the plums."

As far as the eye could see beyond the fruit trees, there were vegetable gardens tended by men dressed like scholars. After walking for some time they approached the city gate, and saw a couplet engraved on the stone wall in letters of gold as large as a man's head, which could be seen sparkling and glittering in the distance.

> To raise your social standing, do virtuous deeds.
> To have good descendants, make them study hard.

"This couplet throws light on the country's name," said Duo. "What an apt motto for the Land of Virtuous Scholars! No wonder this is inscribed over the city gate."

"Tradition has it that their king is descended from Zhuan Xu,"* observed Tang. "This must be a place of genuine refinement, not like White Land."

As they reached the gate, guards stepped up to ask their business and search them before letting them proceed.

"Do they take us for thieves to search us like that?" asked Lin. "I'm sorry I didn't find any of that Soaring Grass. If I'd eaten that, I would have sailed over the wall, and none of them could have stopped me!"

In the main street they noticed that all the men were wearing scholars' caps and dark or blue gowns. The tradesmen, too, were dressed like literati, and had more of a cultured than a commercial air. Apart from daily necessities, they sold mostly plums and leeks, stationery, spectacles, toothpicks, books and wine.

"Rich and poor alike all dress like scholars here," commented Tang. "How strange! Let us try to find

---

* A legendary sage king of China.

out something about their customs, as their language is fairly easy to understand."

Once out of the hubbub of the market-place, from house after house they heard the clear chanting of students reading aloud. And over almost every door were tablets bearing gilded inscriptions such as: "Worthy and Upright", "Filial, Brotherly and Industrious", "Intelligent and Just", "Virtuous and Wise", "Well Versed in the Classics", "Never Weary of Doing Good". There were shorter inscriptions too: "Benevolence", "Justice", "Propriety", "Faith", and many others. To all these were appended names and dates. On a nearby gate they saw a piece of red paper bearing the words the Academy. A couplet over the gateway read:

> Browse in the fields of morality.
> Rest in the garden of literature.

Between this hung a tablet with dragon designs inscribed in letters of gold: "Trainer of Talent". A deafening chanting was going on inside.

Lin pointed at his bundle.

"I'm going in to try my luck," he said. "Would you two care to come with me?"

"You must excuse me this time, brother!" said Tang. "I don't want to use up all my stock of 'your student' today!"

"Well, have a stroll nearby. I'll join you presently."

So while Lin entered the academy the other two wandered on. Presently they saw two gateways with black inscriptions. One was "Repentance", the other "Restored to Virtue". These also bore names and dates.

"What do you make of these, uncle?" inquired Tang.

"It looks as if these men have committed crimes. See how many gilded inscriptions there are to only two of these black ones. Obviously most of the people here are good, with only a few bad men. They deserve the name Virtuous Scholars."

Sauntering back to the market, they enjoyed the sights for some time till Lin came up with an empty wrapper, grinning from ear to ear.

"So you've sold out," observed Tang.

"I've sold out — at a big loss."

"How was that?" asked Duo.

"I found the academy full of students, all eager to buy my goods. But the sour-faced, tight-fisted fellows couldn't bear to part with their money, and wouldn't offer me a proper price. Still they couldn't bear it either when I refused to sell, and wouldn't let me go. After endless haggling, they piled various things together and added one copper to their offer! It was pathetic. As I'm a soft-hearted fool, I decided to learn from the Land of Courtesy, and sold at a loss."

"If you made no profit, why are you smiling so broadly, brother?" asked Duo. "There must be a reason."

"I've never in my life talked of literature before," said Lin. "But I made a remark today that everyone applauded, and that has kept me chuckling all the way here. As I don't wear a scholar's cap, those students asked me if I had ever studied. I know Brother Tang says a man should always be modest, but I thought modesty on top of my ignorance would make them despise me too much. So I told them: 'I come from the Celestial Empire. As a boy I studied all the classics, as well as poetry, history and philosophy. And I've lost count of all the poems of our own Tang Dynasty I've read!'

"When they heard my boast, they tried to test me by asking me to write a poem. That made me break into a cold sweat, I tell you! I thought: 'Lin Zhiyang, you're no licentiate and you've never done a bad deed in your life — you don't deserve this torture of examination! Even if you have done some wrong, this punishment is too much!' Though I cudgelled my brains, all I could do was mumble some excuses and say I had no time to stay. But those niggardly devils refused to let me go until I had written something. While they were pestering me, I noticed two boys making couplets. Their tutor had given them as the first line: 'Wild geese in the clouds', and one paired this off with 'Seagulls on the waves', the other with 'Fish beneath the water'.

"I told them: 'Today I'm not in the mood for poetry, and I can't say when I'm likely to feel inspired, but I can make you a couplet. If you want a taste of my quality, I'll give you a couplet for "Wild geese in the clouds".'

" 'Fine!' said they. 'What is it?'

" 'Shot with a fowling-piece,' said I.

"They all gaped at me, not catching on, and asked for an explanation.

" 'You mean to say none of you understand a simple thing like that?' I said. 'All you can match with "Wild geese in the clouds" is "Seagulls on the waves" or "Fish beneath the water", which have nothing to do with the first line. My "Shot with a fowling-piece" follows from "Wild geese in the clouds".'

" 'What do you mean?' they asked. 'How does it follow?'

" 'When you look up and see wild geese in the clouds, you shoot at them with a fowling-piece,' said I. 'That's how it follows.'

"Then they caught on, and said: 'That certainly is an original approach.' "

"You were lucky in your students, brother!" Tang laughed. "Anyone else might have given you a punch on the jaw!"

"Though my jaw isn't punched, my throat is parched after all that literary talk. When I asked those students for some tea, they gave me a cup that had no tea-leaves in it, only two leaves from some tree. And drop by drop they poured me just half a cup. I swallowed it in one gulp, and am still thirsty. How about you?"

"I'm feeling dry too," said Duo. "But now our luck is in, because I see a tavern in front. Why not drink a few cups there, and ask about local customs at the same time?"

Lin's mouth began to water.

"Good old Ninth Uncle!" he cried. "He hits the nail on the head every single time!"

They went into the tavern, and found a table downstairs. The waiter who came up to them was also dressed like a scholar in cap and gown. With his spectacles and fan, he looked most refined. He bowed and asked with a smile:

"We are honoured by the patronage of three such worthy gentlemen. Do you desire wine? Will you perchance partake of some dishes also? Pray signify your wishes."

"You are a waiter," said Lin. "You look silly enough

wearing glasses. Why use all those high-faluting expressions too? The students I met just now didn't put on such airs, yet here is this waiter posing as a scholar! A half-empty bottle makes more of a splash than a full one. I'd have you know that I'm an impatient man, too thirsty right now to exchange compliments with you. Hurry up and bring wine and food!"

"Deign to inform me, sir, whether you desire one pot of wine or a pair? One side-dish, pray, or two?"

Lin banged the table and shouted:

"Cut out those 'deigns' and 'desires', and bring what I ordered! Any more of your gibberish and I'll punch your nose!"

"Certainly, sir! No offence meant, sir!"

The frightened waiter scuttled off to fetch a pot of wine and two dishes — some green plums and some leeks — as well as three cups. Having respectfully filled their cups, he withdrew.

Lin had a passion for wine, and at the sight of the pot his spirits rose.

"Your health!" he cried to the others, and drained his cup.

But the next second he was frowning and frothing at the mouth. Nursing his jaw, he shouted:

"Waiter! You fool! You brought us vinegar!"

There was an old hunchback sitting at the next table, elegant in scholar's dress and spectacles, holding a toothpick. As he drank alone, he rocked to and fro chanting scraps of literary jargon. Interrupted at the height of his enjoyment by Lin's roar to the waiter, he stopped chanting and waved a deprecating hand.

"If you have quaffed the contents of your cup, sir, how can you reveal what it was? If you speak, you will implicate me. In fear I implore you, brother, to keep silent!"

Dumbfounded by this nonsense, Tang and Duo started laughing to themselves.

"Another literary character!" exclaimed Lin. "What business is it of yours if I take the waiter to task for bringing us vinegar? How can it implicate you, I'd like to know?"

The old man rubbed his nose with the first and middle fingers of his right hand.

"Lend me your ears, sir," he said. "As pertaining to wine and vinegar, wine is inexpensive, while vinegar is costly. The flavour determines the price. Wine, being weak, is inexpensive; while vinegar, being strong, is costly. All customers apprehend this. That fellow must have laboured under a misapprehension. What pleasure equalled yours on receiving the potion? And having drunk it, how can you reveal the fact? Yet you not only speak of it but accuse him of negligence. If he hears you, he will surely increase the price. For you to pay more is your affair, and on your own head be it. But as you and I are drinking the same wine, we should be charged the same. If he asks you for more, he will ask more from me too. Therefore I say you are implicating me. Thus strictly speaking you should pay my score; but should you refuse, he would not let me off. Should I protest, he would not listen. A brawl would ensue, and I should have to fly. So what do you mean to do, sir?"

He went on in this strain till Tang and Duo were choking with suppressed laughter, and Lin could stand no more.

"Say what you like, I can't follow you," he said. "But this sour taste in my mouth is disgusting."

One look at the green plums and leeks — their only dishes — set his teeth even more on edge.

"Waiter!" he bawled. "Bring some different dishes, quick!"

"Coming, sir!" answered the waiter.

He brought four more dishes: salted beans, green beans, bean sprouts, and bean sauce.

"Not these! Something else!" said Lin.

The waiter brought another four dishes: dried bean-curd, beancurd skin, beancurd with soya sauce, and pickled beancurd.

"We're not vegetarians!" protested Lin. "Why bring nothing but beans? What else have you got? Look sharp now!"

"Though these dainties find no favour in your eyes, sir, in our humble realm this is the food of princes. You should not spurn them, sir. This is all we have — nought beside."

"We have enough dishes here," said Duo. "But is there no better wine?"

"Wine is of three varieties," explained the waiter. "The first grade is strong, the second weak, the third even weaker. May I take your question to signify that you prefer weak wine?"

"We are poor drinkers, and cannot take strong liquor," said Tang. "Bring us a pot of the weak wine instead."

This the waiter did at once.

They found this, although slightly sour, quite drinkable.

Soon in came another old man, dressed like a scholar

with a most dignified air, who also sat at a table downstairs.

"Bring half a pot of weak wine, waiter, and a dish of salted beans," he ordered.

Struck by his distinguished appearance, Tang stepped forward and greeted him.

"Good day, reverend sir. May I ask your honourable name?"

"My humble name is Ju." The old man returned his greeting. "Whom have I the honour to address?"

At this point Duo and Lin stepped forward too. They exchanged greetings, introduced themselves, and explained what brought them there.

"So you gentlemen are from the Celestial Empire," said the old man. "Excuse my lack of respect!"

"As you have come to drink, sir," suggested Tang, "won't you give us the pleasure of your company instead of drinking alone? We should count it a privilege."

"You are too good," responded the old man. "But how can I impose on you at our first meeting?"

"Don't stand on ceremony," urged Duo. "Let us move our things over."

They ordered the waiter to carry over the wine and beans, and offered the old man the seat of honour. But as he was a native there he refused, and finally they sat down as host and guests. They toasted each other and sampled the food.

"May I ask you, sir," said Tang, "why peasants, artisans and merchants here all dress like scholars? Do officials wear the same costume? Is no distinction made between high and low?"

"It has been the custom here since time immemorial for all to dress alike, from the king down to the common citizens," replied the old man. "The only difference is in colour and material. Yellow is the most honourable colour, then red and purple, then blue, while black is rather common. And the reason why peasants and merchants dress like scholars is that we have a rule that all who do not take the examinations are vagrants. They perform menial tasks and do not rank among the four classes of citizens. Even the few who farm for a living are jeered at, for vagrants should not have any fixed profession, and respectable citizens keep them at a distance. That is why from childhood all my countrymen study. Though not all can wear the blue gown of a successful candidate, if once you qualify to wear a black gown and scholar's cap, you count as a student and not as a vagrant. Then you may continue with your studies or, if that is impossible, work as a farmer or an artisan, as a member of some recognized profession."

"Judging by what you say, sir," rejoined Tang, "in your honourable country even the common citizens take the examinations. But in such a large kingdom, can everyone be literate?"

"The rules for the examinations vary. Some test your knowledge of the classics, others of history, poetry, statesmanship, letter-writing, music, phonology, law, mathematics, calligraphy and painting, medicine and fortune-telling. Proficiency in any of these subjects will win you a cap or a black gown. To advance in life you must be educated. And you cannot wear a blue gown without a good knowledge of literature. That is why the founder of our kingdom engraved that inscription above the city gate: 'To have good descendants, make them study hard.' That is an incentive to advancement."

"There is something I would like to know, sir," said Duo. "I take it those placards with gold inscriptions over so many gates here are rewards from the king when he has heard something to the credit of the inmate, and serve as an example to others. But what is the meaning of certain inscriptions in black, like 'Repentance'?"

"The student in such cases has behaved badly or broken the law, though he is not guilty of any great crime. The king orders him to put up such a placard to show his penitence. If he breaks the law again, his punishment is harsher. If he turns over a new leaf and starts to do good, his neighbours may report it or the authorities may learn of it and memorialize the throne, and then the placard will be taken down. If after this he leads a virtuous life and his good reputation spreads, it may be reported to the king, who will let him put up a gilt inscription. If a man with a gilded placard does wrong, he loses the placard and is severely punished too, because more is expected of a good man. This is how our ruler assists men to tread the path of virtue and discourages evil-doing. Fortunately most of us are educated, and learning can change a man's nature and enable him to observe the sages' precepts. So actually we have very few wrong-doers."

By now they had finished several pots. The old man questioned them about the Celestial Empire, and exclaimed in admiration at their replies. After much further talk, he told them he had drunk enough and must go home. And as it was growing late, Tang paid the bill and said they would leave too. The old man stood up, produced a large handkerchief and spread it on the table to wrap up all the salted beans left over, which he put in his pocket.

"You have paid for these, sir," he said. "I may as well take them home instead of leaving them to the waiter. I shall enjoy them tomorrow when I come back to drink."

Meanwhile he had picked up the winepot, lifted the lid, and looked inside. When he saw there were still two cups left, he handed it to the waiter, saying: "I shall leave this wine with you. If any is gone when I come back tomorrow, I shall fine you ten cups!"

He emptied all the beancurd into one dish, and handed this to the waiter too with instructions to keep it for him.

As the four men were walking out together, they saw a toothpick on a table at one side which someone had used. The old man picked this up, sniffed at it, wiped it and put it in his sleeve. So they left the tavern and he bid them goodbye. Tang, Duo and Lin left the city, boarded their boat and set sail.

*　　　　*　　　　*

A few days later they came to the land called Double-faced, and Tang expressed a wish to go ashore.

"This country is so far from the sea that I have never visited it," said Duo. "I would gladly go with you, brother, but I am so old and feeble that although the wound I made in my leg by falling over that stone while chasing the Live Fungus has healed, each time I exert myself it starts aching again. The last few days I have found it rather hard to keep up with you on your rambles. I will go ashore with you, but won't come the whole way if the journey proves too far."

"Let us start out anyway," urged Tang. "If you can make it, uncle, so much the better. If it is too tiring, you can turn back half-way."

So they went ashore with Lin, and walked for several *li* without seeing any sign of their destination.

"I can manage another twenty *li* or so," said Duo. "But I'm afraid the return journey would be a strain and set my legs aching. Excuse me if I go back now."

"I thought you had a marvellous cure for bruises which you were always giving other people, uncle," said Lin. "Now that you're suffering yourself, why don't you take a good dose?"

"I was fool enough to take too little to clear up the trouble at the time," explained Duo. "And now I've left it so long, I'm afraid those herbs would be useless."

"I came out in such a hurry today that I forgot to change," remarked Lin. "My old, ragged cotton gown wasn't so conspicuous when there were three of us, but now that you are going back, uncle, Brother Tang and I will look like a rich man and a pauper — he in his scholar's cap and silk, I in this old cap and cotton. Any snobs we meet will look down their noses at me."

Duo answered with a chuckle:

"In that case just tell them: 'I have a silk gown too, but I came out in too great a hurry to put it on.' Then they'll change their attitude."

"If they do, I shall put on airs and talk big."

"What will you say?"

"I'll tell them I not only have a silk gown, but my family once owned a pawnshop and one of my kinsmen was a high official. Then they ought to treat me to a feast."

So Lin went on with Tang.

When Duo got back to the boat his leg was so painful that he had to take some medicine and lie down, and soon he was asleep. By the time he woke the pain had disappeared, his legs were better and he felt quite cheerful. He was chatting in the fo'c's'le when Tang and Lin came back.

"Well, how did you find the Double-faced Kingdom?" asked Duo. "And why have you changed clothes?"

"After leaving you we covered another dozen *li* before we came to any inhabited district," Tang told him. "But we could not see what the people's double faces were like because they wear big caps which hide the back face and show only the front. I accosted one of them to ask about their customs, and when we entered into conversation I was absolutely charmed by his mildness and amiability, and his modest, respectful looks. I had never seen anything like it."

"While that fellow was talking and laughing with Brother Tang, I put in a word too," said Lin. "The Double-face turned and looked me up and down. Then his face changed and he gave me an icy glare. His smile disappeared and all his politeness too. In fact, he kept me waiting for quite a time before he threw me half a sentence."

"A man has to speak in whole sentences," said Duo. "What do you mean by half a sentence?"

"He did make a whole sentence," retorted Lin, "but he growled it out in such a surly way that half of it was lost by the time it reached me. Because of this cold treatment, when we walked away we decided to change clothes to see whether they would still be so haughty to me then. No sooner said than done — I put on Brother Tang's silk gown and he my cloth one, and we went up to them again. This time they were all smiles and politeness to me, but they cold-shouldered him."

"So that is the meaning of Double-faced!" Duo sighed.

"That's not all," went on Tang. "Later while Brother Lin was talking to one of them, I tiptoed up behind him and stealthily lifted his cap. Then I found a most vicious face — rat's eyes and a hawked nose with great fleshy jowls! The moment it saw me it twitched its shaggy eyebrows and opened its bloody mouth, shooting out a long tongue which puffed out poisonous fumes. Then a cold wind blew, a black mist swirled all around, and I could not help crying: 'Heaven help us!' And when I looked again, Brother Lin was on his knees."

"I can understand Brother Tang calling out in terror," said Duo. "But why did Brother Lin drop to his knees?"

"I was chatting pleasantly with the fellow when Brother Tang suddenly lifted its cap and discovered its secret," explained Lin. "At once it showed its true colours. Its face grew ghastly, with long fangs, and it shot out a tongue like a flickering sword. I was so afraid it would murder us that my knees gave way and I kowtowed to it several times before making off. Don't you think this extraordinary, uncle?"

"Such things happen all the time. It is not in the least extraordinary. I'm only a few years older than you, but I've seen a good deal in my time. My guess is that neither of you choose your company carefully enough, and this is the result. Luckily your eyes were opened in good time before anything could happen. You must be more careful in future what strangers you talk to, if you want to keep out of trouble."

*　　　*　　　*

Their junk cast off again, and moored a few days later at the Winged Men's Kingdom, where the three friends went ashore and walked several *li* without meeting a soul. Afraid to go too far, Lin wanted to go back; but Tang was set on seeing the men of this country, having heard that wings grew from their heads so that they could fly — though not high — and that they were hatched from eggs, not conceived in a womb. Unable to dissuade him, Lin had to go with them. After several more *li* they came upon some winged men, with bodies five feet long and heads the same length. They had a beak like a bird, red eyes, white hair and wings on their backs; and they were bright green all over, as if clothed in leaves. Some of them were walking while others were flying about twenty feet from the ground, flitting to and fro in a delightful manner.

"Both bodies and heads are about five feet long," said Lin. "Why are their heads so elongated?"

"I've heard that they are great flatterers here," answered Duo. "As the northerners say, 'They like to wear tall hats,' and wearing tall hats day in and day out makes your head grow longer and longer. That is what comes of flattery."

"Just look at them soaring and skimming through the air!" exclaimed Tang. "It's a great deal faster than walking. We're a long way from the boat, and I've just seen a few old fellows pay flying porters to carry them. Why don't we get ourselves carried back to the junk?"

As Lin's legs were already stiff, he forthwith hired three porters; and climbing on their backs they flew straight off. In a twinkling they reached the boat, where the porters folded their wings and alighted, and our three friends got down and paid their fare. Then they weighed anchor and set sail again.

* * *

The three friends were talking in the stern one day when old Duo suddenly turned to call to the crew:

"A storm-cloud is heading this way — that means a gale. Lower the sail to half mast and tighten the rigging, or we may not be able to make port. We shall have to run before the storm."

When Tang heard this, he stared about him. The sun was bright and there was no wind — he could see no sign of an impending storm. True, a dark cloud was sailing slowly up the sky, but it was barely ten feet long. He gave a laugh.

"I can't believe there'll be a storm on a fine, clear day like this. Do you mean to tell me that tiny black cloud hides a tempest? Never!"

"That's a storm-cloud all right," replied Lin. "But you couldn't be expected to know it, brother."

The words were still on his lips when a howling burst out all around, and the gale was on them. Waves were lashed up to the sky, and the boat was driven before the wind faster than a horse could gallop. The blast grew stronger and stronger till it was a veritable hurricane, and Tang, taking refuge in the cabin, began to appreciate old Duo's eagle eye. The tempest blew and blew. They swept past several ports because the wind was too fierce to let them put in. In fact their sail had billowed out so far in the gale that they could not lower it. This wind blew for three days before it abated a little. Then, by dint of tremendous efforts, they moored at the foot of a mountain.

Tang stood in the stern and watched them handle the rigging.

"I've sailed the high seas since I was a boy, and seen plenty of storms," Lin told him. "But this is the first that has blown without any let-up for three whole days and nights. I've lost my bearings completely, and have no idea where we are. If this squall had headed in the direction we came from, in another two days we'd probably have been home."

"A hurricane like that must be rare," agreed Tang. "How far did it carry us? Where are we now?"

"As far as I can tell, this is Salvation Bay," replied Duo. "There is a high mountain here which I have never climbed. As for the distance, in that wind we must have travelled between three and five thousand *li* a day. In three days we should have come over ten thousand *li*."

"You see now, brother, why I told you this spring that it's hard to tell how long a voyage will last," said Lin.

As the wind had dropped somewhat by now, Tang stood on the poop and looked around. The mountain here was much higher than East Gate Mountain. The distant sky seemed brilliant, and the mountain towered green to heaven. He gazed and gazed, and his mouth watered at the sight. As Lin could not go ashore on account of a cold, Tang landed with old Duo. Fortunately they were sheltered by the hill as they climbed from the force of the wind.

"We are at the extreme south of the ocean now," said Duo. "If not for the gale we would never have come so far. Though I touched here in my young days, I have never been up this mountain. But they say there is a Fairy Islet here. I wonder if this is it? Let us go on anyway. If we meet someone, we can ask."

They walked on some way till they came to a stone tablet inscribed with the words Fairy Islet.

"So you were right, uncle," said Tang.

Skirting a cliff and crossing a forest, they gazed around them. As far as eye could see stretched a lovely prospect — clear water and peaceful hills. The further they went the lovelier the view. They felt they were in fairyland.

They had wandered about for some hours when Tang said:

"When we climbed East Gate Mountain I fancied that was the most impressive mountain on earth; but this is a paradise. And look at the way these white cranes and deer stand still to let us stroke them — would they do that if there were no fairies here? Besides, here is an abundance of pine and juniper seeds, which immortals love to eat. There must be immortals in a place of such beauty. That storm was arranged for my benefit!"

"Lovely as it is, we must be getting back," said Duo. "It will soon be too late to follow these steep paths. Let us start down. If the wind is still too high to sail tomorrow, we can come back again. Brother Lin isn't well, so we ought to get back early."

Tang was so much under the spell of his surroundings that he could hardly tear himself away. Though he started back, he kept stopping to drink in the view.

"If you go at that pace, brother, we shall never get back to the boat," protested Duo. "How can we find our way down after dark?"

"I won't hide from you, uncle, that since I came up here, all ambition has left me, and I feel life on earth is vanity. The reason I walk so slowly is that I am loath to return to the dusty world."

"They say long study makes scholars lose their wits. It's not reading, though, but travelling that is making you lose yours! Go on, Brother Tang! This is no time for poetic fancies!"

Tang was still gazing round when a white monkey bounded towards them holding a fungus. The creature was barely two feet long, with crimson eyes and vermilion spots on its coat.

"Look at the plant it's holding, Brother Tang!" cried Duo. "That must be a fairy herb. Let's catch it and share the fungus!"

Tang nodded, and together they gave chase. He soon overtook the little beast and reached out to seize it, but the white monkey leapt aside and made off again. This happened several times. Luckily the path it took was the one they had come by. They pursued it till it ran into a cave by the pathway. Tang was hard upon it and, as the cave was a small one, he was easily able to catch it. He handed the herb to Duo who ate it.

The old man was delighted and carried the monkey in his arms as they hurried on down the mountain.

When they reached the junk Lin, still out of sorts, was asleep. After supper Tang sorted out his clothes and belongings.

The next day the wind veered to the right quarter for them, and the seamen made ready to weigh anchor. Tang had gone ashore, however, first thing in the morning, and by evening was still not back. Lin's wife began to be alarmed.

Though Lin was still in bed, this news worried him too; and the next day he asked Duo and the sailors to make a search. But Duo could not go because his stomach was upset after eating the fungus, and the crew searched all day in vain. Then Lin, who was slightly better, struggled ashore himself. They looked for several days, but found no trace of Tang.

Duo had recovered now, and he said to Lin: "Though Brother Tang said he wanted to see strange countries, I don't believe that was his real reason for joining us — he was thinking all the time of becoming a hermit and leaving the world of men. That day when you were unwell and I spent so many hours on the mountain with him, he was very unwilling to come back. I had to speak to him several times and it was thanks to our chase of the white monkey that he finally came down. But the next day he went ashore alone, without asking me to go with him. Don't you think he may have seen through the follies of this world and the vanity of wealth and fame? Remember he had eaten the herb of immortality as well as Vermilion Grass, so he had more than mortal perception. It wasn't an accident that when the three of us were out together he was the one to find Live Fungus and Vermilion Grass. In fact, back at East Gate Mountain he dropped a hint of what he was after.

Putting two and two together, the man must have become an immortal. Otherwise why should he stay away all these days? I advise you to stop looking for him, Brother Lin. You may search for another two months but still not find him."

Though Lin was partly convinced, Tang was a close relative and he would not give up hope, so day after day the search parties went out. The seamen urged him dozens of times to leave, but Lin and his wife refused to set sail without Tang.

One day the seamen lost patience, and came in a body to the cabin.

"Not a soul lives on this great mountain," they said to Lin. "But the place is swarming with wild beasts. Though we carry arms in the evening and take it in turns to stand watch, we still feel unsafe. How could Mr. Tang live there alone? He has been gone so many days now that even if the beasts haven't killed him he must have died of hunger. If we wait any longer this favourable wind may change, and in that case we may run out of rice and water. By waiting for one man, you are risking the lives of us all."

As they complained and protested, Lin scratched his head and did not know what to do.

"There's truth in what you all say," called his wife from the inner cabin. "But we are Mr. Tang's close relatives — how can we leave without knowing what's become of him? If he comes back and the junk has gone, won't we be his murderers? Still, as you all want to leave, we won't wait too long — just another two weeks from today. If there is no news by then, we can set sail."

So there was nothing the seamen could do but wait,

complaining bitterly. Lin turned a deaf ear to their protests, and went on searching the mountain every day till two weeks had slipped by and the sailors made ready to leave. But even then he would not give up hope, and asked old Duo to make one last trip with him. Duo had to agree, and together they climbed the mountain and wandered for hours till they were drenched in sweat and their legs ached. Only then did they start back. After several *li* they reached the stone tablet inscribed with the name Fairy Islet, and saw that a poem had been appended to it. The calligraphy was vigorous, the ink fresh and glistening. The poem read:

> For many autumns I followed the waves,
> Fortunate to escape a watery grave;
> Today I have reached the ocean's source —
> Why should I take the boat and go on roaming?

Beside this the date was written, and the signature "Tang Ao, who renounces the world and returns to the Fairy Islet".

"See that, Brother Lin!" cried Duo. "I told you he must have become an immortal, but you wouldn't believe me. Leaving his poem out of it, just the way he signs himself as one who renounces the world should tell you the rest. Let's go. It is no use worrying or searching any more."

Back on the junk, they copied out the poem for Lin's wife and the others. And Lin had no choice now, but with tears in his eyes had to allow the seamen to cast off. At once they set sail for Lingnan.

Some Notes on *Flowers in the Mirror*

Li Changzhi

ABOUT a century after Swift first diverted the English-speaking world with *Gulliver's Travels* (1726), his biting satire on courts, political parties and statesmen, there appeared in China in 1828 the novel *Flowers in the Mirror* (*Jing Hua Yuan*) by Li Ruzhen (c. 1763-1830). In this novel, Li Ruzhen, using a device similar to Swift, satirized the evils of his society, partly through the travels of his hero, the scholar Tang Ao, who like Gulliver visited many strange lands. This novel has 100 chapters. In chapters 1 to 50, we read how Empress Wu usurped the imperial power of the Tang Dynasty and made herself head of state (A.D. 684-705). One late winter day after drinking, she ordered all the flowers to blossom at once, and the 100 flowers promptly obeyed her order. Then the Heavenly emperor was angry with the Goddess of Flowers and banished her with all the flower fairies to earth. She became the daughter of the scholar Tang Ao. Tang passed the palace examination, but because he was slandered and demoted he decided to give up an official career. He went on an ocean voyage with his wife's brother Lin Zhiyang, who was a merchant. Accompanied by an old sailor, Ninth Uncle Duo, they travelled to many strange lands and had various adventures, until Tang Ao, who had eaten some herbs of immortality, disappeared on a fairy islet. When his daughter knew of this, she made a vain search for him with her uncle Lin. At the fairy islet she received a letter from her father, bidding her change her name and take the government examination for talented women. He promised that they would meet again. The girl also found a stone tablet inscribed with the names of the flower fairies together with their mortal names. Having copied these down, she returned home.

Chapters 51 to 100 deal with different themes. The empress held an examination for talented girls, and passed 100 candidates — the flower fairies and Tang's daughter. The girls held many parties to celebrate, at which they showed their skill in calligraphy, painting, lyre-playing, chess, medicine, fortune-telling, astrology, phonetics, mathematics . . . as well as all sorts of riddles and drinking games. Then Tang Ao's daughter went to look for her father again. Meanwhile some loyal supporters of the true imperial house rebelled against the empress, and stormed the four strongholds of Drunkenness, Lechery, Avarice and Wrath. The emperor was restored to the throne, though the empress was still highly respected. She held another examination for talented girls, and summoned all the successful candidates to a feast. With this the novel ends.

The contents of *Flowers in the Mirror* show the author's wide knowledge and interests. The names of the strange lands across the ocean in the first part of the novel are taken from the *Book of Mountains and Seas*, an ancient record of myths; but the details are all Li Ruzhen's own, introduced to express his views on social reform. The descriptions of scholarly accomplishments in the second part, as well as the riddles and puns, are taken from the author's personal experience. He was an eminent phonetician, the pupil of the celebrated historian and philologist Ling Tingkan (1755-1809). His ancestral home was Beijing, but for many years he lived in Haizhou in northern Jiangsu, where he stayed with his brother, who was a magistrate. There he married and settled down. He served as assistant magistrate in Henan during a flood of the Yellow River, and worked on water-conservancy and dyke-repairing. Like all honest intellectuals of that time, he disliked the civil service examinations, by means of which the ruling class restricted freedom of thought and chose its officials. As he was not too successful in these examinations, he spent most of his time on other studies, notably philology and phonetics. He compiled *Li's System of Phonetics* and made a thorough survey of the differences and similarity between northern and southern dialects. He began to compile a dictionary of dialects, to continue the work of the Han scholar Yang Xiong (53 B.C.-A.D. 18), but this was never finished. The book by which he is known today is *Flowers in the Mirror*.

Li Ruzhen had a good deal in common with Wu Cheng'en (c. 1500-1582), author of *Pilgrimage to the West*, and Wu Jingzi (1710-1754) who wrote *The Scholars*. These three novelists were all scholars, familiar with the life of the literati and with their weaknesses and foibles. *Pilgrimage to the West* now and again pokes fun at such men, while the whole of *The Scholars* is a satire on the literati. *Flowers in the Mirror* is a satire of the same sort, but presented in an allegorical form. Because Li Ruzhen specialized in language studies, there is more conscious erudition and pedantic wit, and an excessive number of puns and classical quotations, which sometimes are quite boring. This may be said to be the novel's main defect. Although *Flowers in the Mirror* cannot compare with *Pilgrimage to the West* or *The Scholars,* it expresses more modern ideas. Li Ruzhen was in touch with modern thought. This comes out most clearly in the first part of the book, that dealing with the voyage into strange lands.

This section, which describes the adventures overseas of the scholar Tang Ao, the merchant Lin Zhiyang and the sailor Ninth Uncle Duo, recalls to mind Chinese maritime trade, which developed during the 15th century. In the 17th and 18th centuries the Qing government prohibited such trading for fear it might introduce new ideas to the country and thereby strengthen the people's resistance to its rule. It is quite remarkable that Li Ruzhen chose this theme. Moreover, in these adventures we find some fairly modern democratic ideas. For instance, in the Kingdom of the Great all men are equal, whether nobles or commoners. All good men have coloured clouds under their feet, all bad men black clouds. This is a new concept of social relationships, which may have grown out of the author's awareness of the hypocrisy of arbitrary social distinctions in feudal society. His appreciation of working men is also noteworthy. His most sympathetic character is honest, well-read Ninth Uncle Duo. This shrewd old sailor has a rich fund of practical experience, a good knowledge of medicine, and a strong sense of humour.

Many of his ideas were remarkable for that time. In the Land of Virtuous Scholars, for instance, he makes an old man propose the reformation of the examination system. In the Kingdom of Black Teeth, he provides a new criterion of beauty, contending that beauty comes from simplicity, honesty and scholarship, and is not a question of powder and paint. In the Land of the Childless, he points out that if human beings could do away with selfishness, they would be happier. These were original and radical views for 19th-century China.

The same may be said of his criticisms of the evils of feudal society, which he has in mind when he ridicules the craftiness of the dwarfs, the sycophancy of the winged men, the boastfulness of the giants, and the viciousness of the double-faced, who smile at you but puff out poisonous fumes from a hideous face on the other side of their head. This description is well-known in China. In the Kingdom of the Great he satirizes the greed of landlords and nobles, and uses the medicine beast to make fun of quack doctors. In a dialogue in White Land he inveighs against the evils of the examination system, and to represent the rapacity of government officials he creates a mythical bird, which will not part with one single feather.

It is significant that Li Ruzhen, though an intellectual himself, did not try to gloss over the weaknesses of the literati of that period. Because he knew his own kind so well and disliked them so thoroughly, he pilloried them in this book. He describes how all in the Land of Virtuous Scholars wear scholar's caps, but all their food is sour; and when Lin Zhiyang tries to sell his goods they haggle interminably over the price. When the travellers go to a tavern for a drink, they find the waiter in scholar's dress and spectacles, talking like a pedant. An old man they meet is a sour, miserly scholar. When he leaves some wine in the tavern, he threatens to fine the waiter if any of it disappears. He takes home the remains of the food, and even pockets a toothpick someone has used. The behaviour of these "virtuous scholars" gives a true picture of the mean and embittered intellectuals in feudal society, especially at the end of the feudal period.

On the one hand Li Ruzhen expresses his ideals, on the other he satirizes existing abuses. Sometimes ideals and satire are intermingled, as in the episode in the Land of Courtesy. Here the author seems somewhat confused. Disgusted by the dishonesty of so many business transactions, he creates this fictitious land where buying and selling are done in quite a different way— the salesman asks a low price and the customer offers a high one. In this sense he is for the Land of Courtesy. He hopes for new human relationships, governed by self-sacrifice and consideration for others, and holds up to scorn the craftiness and deceit of his own society.

One characteristic of Li Ruzhen's novel is the absence of long descriptive passages and the constant change of scene. As he uses so much material from ancient myths and allegories, his moral is often not clear. The fact is that he tried to attack so many evils and present so many of his ideals that the novel as a whole is rather disjointed. He took much of his material from books — especially ancient mythology — partly because he was a scholar, and partly because of the government censorship. Many scholars of the Qing Dynasty were persecuted for their views. During the reign of Qian Long (1736-1795), exception was taken to all writing which contained the least criticism of the Manchu rule, and the authors were punished with death. Thus Li Ruzhen could only state his ideas in a veiled way, making use of myths or setting his story in imaginary lands abroad.

All these factors contributed towards his distinctive style. As a novelist he had certain defects already mentioned. As a thinker, of course, he had his limitations too. He is often pedantic and not daring enough. For instance, though he attacked men's oppression of women and believed that both sexes should be equal, the only way out that he could suggest was that women should also take the civil service examinations. He was against superstition, claimed that men were masters of their fate, and denied the doctrine of transmigration and the idea of retribution in another life; yet here and there he reveals the belief that men will be rewarded or punished by Heaven in the end. In general, however, his thinking was ahead of his time in his criticism of feudal society. *Flowers in the Mirror* therefore marks a new development in the Chinese novel in the early 19th century, and this is one reason why it holds an eminent place in the history of Chinese literature.

三部古典小说节选

熊 猫 丛 书

*

《中国文学》杂志社出版

（中国北京百万庄路24号）

中国国际图书贸易总公司发行

（中国国际书店）

外文印刷厂印刷

1981年第1版

1984年第2次印刷

编号：（英）2—916—04

00190

10—E—1571P